100%
recycled paper

Other *Leisure* books by Lewis B. Patten:

RIDE THE RED TRAIL
THE WOMAN AT OX-YOKE
DEATH RIDES THE DENVER STAGE
TRAIL TO VICKSBURG
TINCUP IN THE STORM COUNTRY
LYNCHING AT BROKEN BUTTE/ SUNBLADE
THE RUTHLESS RANGE/DEATH RIDES A BLACK HORSE
THE LAW IN COTTONWOOD/PRODIGAL GUNFIGHTER
THE KILLINGS AT COYOTE SPRINGS/ THE TRAIL OF THE APACHE KID
RIFLES OF REVENGE/RED RUNS THE RIVER
THE TRAP

LEWIS B. PATTEN

BLOOD ON THE GRASS

LEISURE BOOKS  NEW YORK CITY

A LEISURE BOOK®

July 2003

Published by special arrangement with Golden West Literary Agency.

Dorchester Publishing Co., Inc.
276 Fifth Avenue
New York, NY 10001

ISBN 0-8439-5211-3

Printed in the United States of America.

Table of Contents

Sharpshod

I

As he had known it would be, his mind was eased by a long day atop towering Black Mesa. It was a different land up here. The air was cooler and thinner. Back a half mile from the rim it was easy to forget that yawning cañons lay to either side of you, for they were invisible. All you saw was an endless expanse of rolling prairie that reached on and on to infinity.

The sun turned orange as it dropped toward the horizon. Will Counselman rode out of the cool shadows of a quaky pocket, crossed a bare expanse of low brush and high grass, and came to the narrow trail that picked its way gingerly down the sheer and crumbling expanse of rimrock and zigzagged across the steep slide below before it entered the secret fastnesses of the cedar benches. Before him, slung across the saddle and held in place by the saddle horn, lay the freshly skinned carcass of a deer.

Once he paused at a switchback to gaze down into the yawning void. A full two thousand feet below lay the ranch, a haphazard collection of buildings appearing like scattered toys from such a height. Briefly bitterness marred Will's smooth and dark-skinned face, bitterness mixed with obscure puzzlement. Never had he been able to understand Laird McFetridge's abrupt rages, the strange and unaccountable expressions of pure hate McFetridge regularly showed him.

Laird's abuse of him at such times was like the flick of a quirt on a raw and open sore.

He puzzled over Laird's actions of this morning as he continued his slow and careful way down the trail. Will had been mending harness, squatted comfortably in the shade before the blacksmith shop, his face knit with concentration. McFetridge had come around the corner of the building, whistling, but something he had seen in Will, some thought, had instantly darkened his face, turned his blue eyes harsh and cold.

"I thought I told you to run the horses in. Damn you, can't you do a single thing . . . ?"

"They're in. If you'd use your eyes. . . ."

Even now, Will could remember the rage that always rose in him when Laird turned this way. Flushing and turning hot, he thought: *Someday I'll kill him for sinking his damned spurs in me!*

Laird had screamed—"Shut up! Shut up! Shut up!"—and Will had come to his feet, fists instinctively clenching, face paling with rage. McFetridge was not a tall man, but he was broad. His shoulders were tremendous, his chest deep and hairy. His legs appeared too spindly to carry the huge weight of his torso, and he wore his grizzled hair long, so that only the lobes of his ears showed beneath it.

Will's pallor, his clenched fists, had seemed to infuriate Laird further. With no warning whatever, the maul of his right fist smashed out, catching Will on the side of jaw and neck, throwing him furiously back against the log wall of the blacksmith shop.

Stunned, Will had lain there for a moment before he groggily fought to his feet. He'd said: "Laird, you'll do that once too often. You'll make me forget that you raised me up and gave me a home. You'll make me kill you yet!"

Laird had come in again, frenzied, but Hugh Leabo, the only one on the ranch who could handle him, had closed from behind and pinned his arms. "Boss, you're crazy! What'd he do? What'd he say?"

Only then had come the bitter shame into Laird McFetridge's mustached face, only then had come the abject grief. "Boy," he'd said, "I'm sorry," and turned and shambled away.

Today, Will Counselman had at last made up his mind. Tonight he would catch up a pack horse, his own, and would ride out for the last time. He was twenty years old and was fast reaching a point where McFetridge's abuse would stir an uncontrollable, murderous anger in him. Today had not been the first time McFetridge had struck him for no good reason, neither had it been the worst he had taken from Laird.

The words were the worst. Laird's words could be biting and bitter and cruel, most savage when he seemed most quiet. "Your pa was a thief, did you know that, Will? A sneaking, cowardly thief. Your mother wasn't even married to him." These were the words that rankled and festered in Will and not even Laird's periodic remorse and apology could erase them. "You've got the worst of them both in you, Will. You'd like to kill me, wouldn't you? But you know you haven't got the guts. You'll wait and you'll wait and finally someday you'll let me have it in the back, won't you, Will?"

What kept him at Arrow, then? Laura. He admitted that Laura McFetridge was all that had held him there, and even that was no good. Laura thought of him as a brother and would never feel any other way.

Depression and hopelessness beat at Will. He came out of the rimrock, crossed the slide, and entered the shadow of gnarled and twisted cedars. A bunch of does bounded down the trail before him, becoming lost finally in the twilight. On a knob above the ranch, Will Counselman halted again and was surprised to see a buggy tied before the house and the clustering of horses beside it.

Company, he thought glumly and nudged his horse forward.

Here, where nestled the heart of the gigantic Arrow Ranch, the valley was a full three miles wide. For almost this full width, and for as far as the eye could see in both directions, the valley floor was the deep, rich green of waving alfalfa. Haystacks, like fat brown loaves of bread, dotted the pole-fenced stack yards. At dusk, the deer came from the cedar benches in great herds to feed in the fields, making clusters of velvet brown dots in the half light.

Will Counselman opened the gate without leaving his horse, a tall and long-muscled man, his face cast in the sharp, flat planes of taciturnity, but showing, too, the deep-seated insecurity which was the inevitable result of Laird's bullying. His eyes were brown, surprisingly soft at times, yet possessing the ability to turn as cold and hard as pieces of flint. He was badgered between abuse and loyalty, feeling the need to revolt against Laird's injustice, yet troubled by a strange and boyish affection for McFetridge when the older man was in his gentler moments.

Why have I stayed this long? he wondered now. He had often been accused of wanting a slice of Arrow when McFetridge was gone. "But you won't get it, damn you," Laird had gloated. "I raised you, but I didn't adopt you. Arrow will go to Laura, every damned inch of it."

A dog ran out, barking, and Will impatiently cursed him into sullen silence. The door of the rambling log house opened, and Laura was silhouetted against the light inside. Will felt the pull of her, and his thoughts flooded with bitterness.

From the shadows beside the house a voice asked: "That you, Will?"

"Uhn-huh."

"Get down. Come here a minute."

"What for? Where's Laird?"

"Why, Will, I guess you know where Laird is. Get down." These were the deceptive soft tones of big Hugh Leabo, foreman of Arrow.

Will shrugged and slipped to the ground. An odd uneasiness stirred in him as Leabo moved ahead of him, murmuring: "This way, Will. Come on."

He sensed, rather than heard, other movement in the dark shadows and growled: "What the hell? What's this all about?"

Abruptly a door opened, and light laid its yellow square on the ground before him. He saw Hugh's monstrous form against it. He saw, too, that men were closing in on him from all sides, felt their clawing hands, felt the swift withdrawal of the gun at his side.

"Got it, Hugh," said a voice, and Will lunged back, trying to turn.

Another of Laird's brutal traps. Will set his jaw, snarling: "Oh, no! I've taken all I'll take from Laird." He flung himself against the wall of the house, and his long arms reached out, his fisted hands making solid thumps into soft flesh and against hard skull.

Hugh's voice was different, viciously hopeful, as he shouted—"All right, I hoped he'd want it this way!"—and waded in, shoving aside the other hands, throwing his own out in long and murderous arcs.

One of them caught Will atop the head, and for an instant blackness whirled before him. Another caught him high on the cheek bone; another crushed his mouth. He swung wildly, knowing he could never match Hugh Leabo's enormous power.

Another voice, oddly familiar, grunted: "Let it go, Hugh. I want him able to talk."

The terrible pounding stopped.

Will leaned back against the logs, sucking great gasping breaths of air. The faces before him whirled and soared and finally settled.

He saw the face of Hugh Leabo, massive and accusing; he saw the face of the sheriff of McFetridge County, Carl Gwinn. Gwinn said softly: "Come in the kitchen, Will. I guess nobody blames you much, but did you have to do it that way?"

"What way? Do what? What in hell are you talking about, Carl?"

Carl said patiently: "Where you been all day, Will?"

"Up on top. Why?"

"Anybody see you? You go by the Arrow cabin up there?"

"Sure. I always do."

"You see Silas?"

"No. He was out. Fixing fence or packing salt." Silas was Arrow's rider on Black Mesa, a lank, red-haired, solitary man, cheerful when entirely alone, grumpy and sour in the presence of others.

"What'd you do all day?"

Suddenly Will balked. Increasing uneasiness and resentment brought him across the room, made him take a fistful of the sheriff's shirt in his left hand. The sheriff's eyes widened momentarily, and his hand slid downward toward his thigh.

Will said softly: "Go ahead. Use it. Get it out and put a bullet in my belly. But if you don't tell me what this is all about, I'll smash your nose clear to the back of your head."

Leabo growled. "Quit beating the brush, Carl. He knows

as well as the rest of us, but he won't quit putting on until you tell him."

Gwinn said: "Laird's dead."

"You're a liar!" Amazement brought this from Will, even as realization that the sheriff spoke the truth brought an abrupt and delicious looseness to all his body. Laird McFetridge had been a constant, unpredictable threat hanging over him. Now the threat was gone.

His hand relaxed and let go the sheriff's shirt. The sheriff, red-faced and angry, shoved his shirt tail inside his pants and backed away. "You killed him, Will."

"Oh, no. No you don't. I was up on top all day."

"You threatened to kill him. This morning. You wanted him dead bad enough. Everyone knew that, and most of them didn't blame you. So you came back down. You watched. You saw Laura drive toward town in the buckboard. You saw Hugh take the crew up the creek to start cutting hay at noon. You knew the Chinese cook always took a nap in the shade after dinner. You knew Laird was alone. So you came back."

II

Panic stretched Will's lips tightly against his white teeth. He said, his trapped feeling growing: "Carl, you've known me a long time. You saw how surprised I was. . . ." He stopped, knowing how thin this was, yet knowing no other protest.

"You acted surprised. That don't prove nothing."

Will Counselman shrugged wearily. "All right. Where is he? How did I kill him?"

Gwinn's face showed his distaste. "You smashed his head with a singletree, only that didn't satisfy you. You had to beat him to a pulp after he was dead. Everyone knew you hated him, Will. I guess we didn't know how bad you hated him."

"Who found him?" Even in the face of his fear, Will could think of Laura, could hope it had not been she who first had to see the bloody sight.

"Hugh found him. A mower horse went lame, and Hugh came back to catch another. What's that on your pants, Will?"

Will looked down. On the knee of his Levi's was a dark stain. Spattered over both sleeves were the same kind of stains. He said: "Blood. I killed a deer. It's out on my saddle."

Leabo murmured—"Smart."—with dawning respect in his eyes. "You got Laird's blood all over you. So you killed a deer to cover up. You're a cool one, kid. I got to give you credit for that."

Ignoring Hugh, Will asked: "What you going to do, Carl?"

"You come with me, Will. I doubt there's a jury in the whole country will hang you. Most everybody's wondered why you didn't do this a long time ago. You'll get maybe ten, twenty years in the pen."

So this was to be the end. Laird McFetridge had won. For an instant, Will's eyes darted from the sheriff, hand on gun grips, to Hugh Leabo, rock-solid and gigantic against the door. "I want to see Laird. After that, I want to see Laura . . . alone. Then you can take me."

The sheriff threw a puzzled look at Leabo, and the foreman nodded slightly. His face was calm, almost placid. Everything about this man was massive, from the hands that could break an axe handle like a match, to the facial features which resembled something carved from granite. Hugh said: "Hell, Carl, suppose he does make a break? Where would he go?"

Gwinn grunted: "All right. Come on, Will, and no funny

stuff. Laird's down at the bunkhouse. Laura hasn't seen him, and Hugh doesn't want her to."

He watched Will step forward and followed ten feet behind, gun drawn. Crickets chirped in the high weeds at the edge of the yard. A horse nickered in the corral. A couple of dogs circled Will's horse warily, smelling blood and growling. Another sniffed Will's trousers, and then licked his hand. Up on the benches, a coyote yipped, and the pack took up the cry until their yammering was a solid sound that hung eerily across the valley.

All the buildings on Arrow were built of logs, chinked with adobe mud. The bunkhouse was forty feet long, twenty wide. Laird lay inside, near the door, a canvas under him, a blanket over him. He lay on Will Counselman's bunk.

Will stopped five feet away. Gwinn hesitated. But Hugh Leabo stepped between Will and the bunk and yanked back the blanket. There was an odd look of pleasure upon his massive face as he watched Will.

The body on Counselman's bunk was beaten almost beyond recognition. Will knew it was Laird, but not because he recognized the features. No beating could disfigure that broad, thick torso, or the spindly legs. No amount of blood could make that gray mane of hair any but Laird's. Involuntarily Will shuddered.

Gwinn was very pale. "Now that the mad's gone, it ain't pretty, is it, boy? You think he's paid for what he done to you?"

"Who did it, Carl? Who hated him that much?"

Only for a split second did Gwinn's thin face show doubt. Then he said wearily, with a shrug: "Give it up, son. Nobody hated him but you. Nobody wanted him dead but you."

Will went out the door, shoulders hanging. They were all so damned sure. A new fear struck him, a worse fear than he had ever felt before. What would Laura think? Would she believe what the others believed? If she did, then Will Counselman was lost, for there would be nothing left at all.

Back in the kitchen, Gwinn tossed his head toward the closed door that separated the kitchen from the rest of the house. "All right. She's in there."

Will hesitated, his hand on the knob, and heard Gwinn's curt instructions: "Hugh, take some of your crew and scatter them around the house. You watch the front door. I'll stay here. If he does break out, I want him alive, you hear?"

This was fantastic, like a bad dream. Yet it was real enough. Out of a clear blue sky Hugh, Gwinn, the members of the crew—all were convinced of his guilt. Laura must feel the same. He turned back to Gwinn, his look beseeching.

Gwinn's voice had an oddly gentle tone. "Kid, go on in. You've got to know, don't you?"

"Yes. I've got to know." He turned the knob and opened the door.

He stood in the dining room that was lighted only by the glow from lamps in the big front room. To his left, a door opened to Laird's ranch office. As he passed it, he glanced inside, saw the jumble of untidy papers on the roll-top desk, the black iron safe, the litter of chaps, spurs, jackets, and hats. Laird's revolver lay on the papers on the desk, doing duty as a paperweight.

Will straightened, fought off the beaten and hopeless feeling that obsessed him. Laura had her back to him. She was seated on the enormous, leather-covered sofa before the fire. Only the top of her head was visible, and her hair shone like pure gold in the lamplight.

Will said—"Laura. . . ."—and came around the end of the sofa, watching her face closely as she turned.

The redness that tears had caused was in her eyes, but now

the tears were gone, and nothing was left but dryness and burning intensity. Her face showed him no expression whatever, being still, overly calm, without life or interest.

"They wouldn't even let me see him."

"You wouldn't want to. It's pretty bad."

"Why did he hate you, Will?"

Will shrugged, not knowing the answer to this, and countered with a question of his own: "Why should he? I never did anything to him. Why did he take me to raise if he hated me? Or, if the hate came later, why didn't he kick me out?"

An expression of pain crossed Laura's face. She was a small girl at eighteen, her lovely figure concealed tonight in the shapeless folds of a wool wrapper. Her eyes were the same blue as Laird's; her face delicately reflected the same harsh contours, the high cheek bones, the wide mouth. Yet the features Will had found cruel and harsh in Laird, he found lovely and interesting in Laura. Perhaps the difference was that harshness and cruelty had helped to form the original facial contours in Laird, while gentleness and understanding had tempered the same basic contours in Laura.

She appeared to be struggling with her emotions. At last, she asked: "Did you kill him, Will?"

Stubbornness stirred in Will. "I had reason enough to kill him. According to Gwinn, I had the opportunity. But I didn't do it, Laura."

She seemed surprised. She seemed about to speak, but Will broke in.

"Think about it for a while. The others made up their minds the minute they found him. I don't want you to do it that quick." His words came rapidly and had a touch of desperation. "There have got to be certain things in a man before he can strike another down from behind, before he can pound that man to a pulp even after he is dead. If you decide that I have those things in me, why, then, I guess it doesn't matter much whether I killed Laird or not. If you decide I'm capable of a killing like Laird's. . . ." He stopped, shrugged, and said: "Well, you see what I mean, don't you?"

Laura nodded, her eyes searching his face as though trying to probe behind it to see his thoughts.

Feeling that this should be known, Will said: "Laird raised you and me as brother and sister, but. . . ."

She interrupted. "Please, Will. Don't. Not now."

Exultation stirred in Will Counselman. She knew, then. She had known for some time apparently. Yet a new thought killed his excitement and brought back the deep depression. He thought: *That is another thing they will use against me. They will say that my interest in Laura was only as great as my interest in Arrow.* Suddenly he became aware that in the eyes of Arrow, in the eyes of McFetridge County, he was guilty, tried, convicted, and sentenced to hang. All that was left were the formalities of incarceration and trial.

Perhaps, as Gwinn had said, no jury would hang him. Yet to Will, hanging was infinitely more desirable than being penned behind bars, to become a wild and savage animal, like a bear on a chain, pacing, pacing. . . .

Gwinn's voice sounded from the kitchen door. "Will."

"All right. I'm coming."

Again he passed the open door of Laird McFetridge's office. Laura had not stirred from her position on the sofa. Will saw Laird's gun, so worn, so smooth, loaded as it always was. He thought fleetingly of the cut-and-dried pretense of a trial which lay ahead of him, and he halted. *I could get it before Gwinn would know what I was doing.*

Gwinn spoke again. "Will."

Suddenly Will Counselman grinned. "Come here a minute, Carl."

Caution stirred in the sheriff's eyes, and with hand on gun he approached. Will nodded toward Laird's gun. "I could have got that easy enough. But that would have been a confession, wouldn't it? Besides that, by the time I got away, I would have really been a killer. I'm not a killer, Carl."

The second doubt Will had seen appeared in the sheriff's face. But it was soon gone. Gwinn said: "Maybe you're smart. The deer . . . and now this. Come on, Will."

Out into the velvet dark of the cool September night they went, and, when they reached the sheriff's buggy, Gwinn grunted: "You drive. And be careful. Hugh's following along behind with a couple of others."

Will Counselman took up the reins, still finding all this hard to believe. Gwinn was a thick and solid shape beside him, and the gun on Gwinn's lap gave off its dull shine in the starlight. As Will drove through the gate, he found himself fully expecting to hear Laird's harsh voice call: "Where the hell you think you're going?"

Then Hugh shouted something, and a trio of horsemen cantered up close behind the buggy. Will took his last look at Arrow, sprawling and solid and brightly lighted, and slapped the buggy reins against the horse's back.

Against the light of the window he had seen Laura, still and motionless and brooding, her hair catching and reflecting the light behind her, had seen her shrug and turn away. *She's made up her mind, too,* was his bitter thought, and he felt as though the very last of life's goodness had been drained away.

III

Upon Laura, after she had returned to Arrow, had been piled shock upon shock. Immediately upon her arrival, she had been greeted by a grave-faced Hugh Leabo, who had helped her to the ground and, still holding her elbows, had said: "Laird's dead, Laura."

"That's not a very good joke, Hugh."

"It's no joke, Laura. He's dead."

Realization that Hugh was serious had filtered into Laura slowly, and, as it did, the color drained from her face, strength drained from her body. "Where is he?"

"You can't see him." Hugh had put an arm about her, steered her toward the house. Anger seemed to be growing in him. His arm trembled, and his voice had a curious tightness. "It's not pretty, Laura. He was struck from behind with a singletree. That killed him, but that wasn't enough to satisfy his killer. He was beaten after he was down, beaten until you could never recognize his face." He had shuddered.

Still tears would not come to Laura, but faintness had. She had slumped against Hugh's arm. They had mounted the steps to the verandah, and with his free hand Hugh had swung open the door. He had helped her to the sofa, and she had sat down limply. From her stunned mind a question had filtered: "Who did it, Hugh?"

"Who do you think?" he had demanded bitterly. "Who hated him? Who threatened to kill him this morning out at the blacksmith shop?"

The second shock. Nausea had beat at Laura. "No! Somebody else must have. . . ."

"I know how you feel. I feel that way, too. I taught Will to ride . . . and rope . . . and shoot a gun. I whittled toys for him when he was a kid. But nobody else had any reason." He had sat down beside her. "Go ahead, honey. Cry. It's got to come."

Laura did cry. Dry sobbing at first, followed by a racking floor of tears. Hugh's great arms were gentle, solid. After a while, he had brought her a pillow, and she had slept.

When she awoke, she was immediately oppressed by her knowledge that Laird McFetridge was dead. She went to her room, washed and fixed her hair mechanically, then changed into a dark, plain dress. Laird McFetridge had been a stern and dour man, never giving much affection, seemingly embarrassed by any show of affection on Laura's part. Being his way, he seemed perhaps less a father, less a close blood tie to Laura, than a presence, solid, dependable, changing.

Sheriff Gwinn had come in and talked to Laura sympathetically for ten or fifteen minutes. Afterward, she had determinedly eaten in solitary misery the dinner brought to her by Chang, the Chinese cook.

Later, she had shamelessly eavesdropped at the kitchen door, during Will's interrogation by the sheriff, and afterward murmured, trying to convince herself: "Will *was* surprised. He *was!* He's telling the truth. Oh, he's got to be telling the truth!"

She was crouched on the sofa, staring into the fire, silently repeating these words when Will had come in. Desperation showed in his eyes, a trapped feeling of fear. He was sweating lightly. His hair was mussed from running his hands through it. He was the Will Counselman Laura had grown up with, but with his assurance gone, with no sign of his rare and brilliant smile. He looked guilty. He looked much as he had always looked when Laird caught him, deliberately disobeying orders. Yet Laura was unwillingly impressed by his single argument. Never had she seen him show cruelty or maliciousness. Never had he exhibited the quality that would lead a man to belabor an enemy after that enemy was dead. During the time they had known each other, he had always been gentle despite Laird's meanness.

But what could Laura know of the dark forces that drive a man? Nothing—no one—had ever hounded Will as Laird had hounded him. Will had a man's pride. Laura could imagine how intolerable Laird's brutality must have become to him, particularly after Will had ceased to think of Laura as a sister.

She listened to the wheels of the buggy crunch across the graveled yard, listened as they entered the lane. Then she returned to the sofa and flung herself face downward upon it. Her eyes were dry and burning. An awful weight of depression hung over all her thoughts. Suddenly she gasped. "Silas . . . Will didn't see Silas, but maybe Silas saw Will."

Laura flung to her feet and raced toward the door. She threw it open and ran onto the verandah. Faintly came the diminishing sounds of hoofs and wheels in the lane. She cried: "Hugh! Hugh! Come back a minute!"

He was unmistakable, even in darkness, towering on his horse like a giant, almost dwarfing the animal by his ponderous size. He rode directly to the porch, reined in, and looked at her, his face very gentle, eyes very soft. "What is it, Laura?"

"Will said he didn't see Silas. That isn't hard to believe. Silas is like an Indian, and no one sees him unless he wants to be seen." Her voice grew excited. "Hugh, maybe Silas saw Will."

Hugh Leabo said patiently: "Laura, Will did it. You're torturing yourself by trying to believe he didn't."

"Hugh, I grew up with Will Counselman. I've got to help him all I can."

He shrugged. "All right, Laura. I'll ride up there in the morning. I'll leave as soon as it's light enough to see the trail.

But Laura. . . ." He stopped, then went on resolutely: "You've got to promise me that, if nothing comes of this, you'll quit fretting about it. He isn't worth it, Laura. Will isn't worth it."

"I can't promise that, Hugh."

He shrugged. "I guess you can't. All right. Good night, Laura." He rode out, following the sheriff in the buggy.

It was still dark when Hugh Leabo got up. He sat on the edge of his sagging bunk and pulled on his boots, from which the spurs were never removed. It was a thing he had not considered himself, this business of Silas's seeing Will, and he was suddenly glad that Laura had thought of it.

Already there was a restless stirring in the bunkhouse, although none of the crew save Hugh was up. Because it was but a short half hour until the first light of dawn would stain the eastern horizon, the 'punchers were stirring, a few awake. One of them murmured: "Can't sleep, Hugh?"

"Going up on top. Maybe Silas saw Will yesterday."

The 'puncher laughed. "That's a long ride for nothing, Hugh. You know where Will was yesterday. He was here, beating the hell out of Laird."

"Maybe. But I'm going to give him all the chances he's entitled to."

"You're a damned fool." The 'puncher turned over, and sighed heavily.

Hugh strapped on his gun and stepped outside, consciously averting his glance from the lumpy and covered shape of Laird McFetridge on Will's bunk. At the horse trough, he laid aside his hat and sloshed water onto his face, briefly wishing for coffee but unwilling to take the time to get it.

He roped the first horse that ran by him in the corral, saddled, and rode out toward the bare trail that led upward from the gate into the cedars. Light increased in the skies as he rode, and, by the time he had reached the bottom of the slide, the clouds that hung above the high rim were stained pink.

With vast and stolid patience, he edged upward across the slide, stopping at intervals to rest his horse. Many times he had made this ride, and the time it took was fixed at two hours. You could make it in less, you could shave that time by fifteen minutes, but only at the cost of exhausting your horse.

Hugh Leabo was huge and slow-moving. He could wait fifteen minutes or fifteen years with equal patience. Having learned the virtue of patience, he had become firmly convinced that anything comes to he who waits.

Very near the top of the trail, which was cut from solid rock, was a soft place, caused by the seepage of water from some underground spring. Here, Leabo did a strange thing. Without stopping, without dismounting, he noted the single set of tracks leading upward, the other coming off. He rode across this soft spot and, at the next switchback, turned and rode back. Then, smiling, he continued his upward course.

Once atop the mesa, where the trail leveled out, he put his horse into a slow trot, and this way came, at seven o'clock, down through the heavy pocket of aspen to the tiny sod-roofed Arrow cabin that squatted against a timbered ridge beside a blue and glistening beaver pond.

From the draw above it he hailed—"Silas! Hey Silas!"—and swung down at the pole corral and turned his horse inside.

Smoke raised lazily from the cabin's tin chimney. A hindquarter of venison hung from one of the projecting beams of the cabin's roof. A horse, saddled and ready, was tied to the long, pole hitch rack.

A man appeared at the door, coffee pot in hand, and

smiled at Leabo. He said sourly: "Come in, Hugh. Had your breakfast?"

"Not yet."

Hugh tossed his hat on a bunk and slid into place at the table. Silas set a tin cup and plate before him and from a skillet forked out two huge venison steaks. He took a pan of sourdough biscuits from the oven and set them before the foreman.

Sitting down himself, he grumbled: "Gittin' to be like a damned town up here. Fust Will, now you. What the hell you want?"

"Will was up here? What doing?"

"Ridin'. Shootin' buckskin."

"When was this?" Hugh ground a piece of steak between his powerful jaws.

"Yestiddy. You said you'd let me alone up here till roundup. I do my work. I got the whole damn' mountain salted, the water holes fixed, and the fences in shape. You tell Laird to keep his damned spies off the mountain, or I quit."

Hugh looked at him innocently. "I'm not spying on you, Silas. Neither was Will. What time was it when you saw him?"

"He rode in here at dinner time. Fixed hisself somethin' to eat. I followed him for a while. He kilt his deer about two."

Hugh Leabo gave a tremendous sigh. "Silas, that's good news to me. Laird was killed yesterday. The sheriff thinks Will did it. But he couldn't have, if you saw him."

Silas showed no surprise at the news of Laird's death. He growled: "Wouldn't have blamed him if he had. Laird was mean. I figured he'd get it sooner or later."

"Will's in jail, Silas." A deep, distant rumble of thunder interrupted him. He went on: "I know how you hate to come off the mountain, but you better ride back with me . . . at least long enough to get Will out of jail."

Thunder rumbled again. Hugh went to the door, looked westward at the gray-black clouds piled over the horizon. He smiled at Silas's ill-natured grumbling and watched the swift onslaught of dark rain clouds. Silas took down the quarter of venison and carefully wrapped it before stowing it beneath the blankets of one of the bunks.

Genuine regret showed in Hugh Leabo's massive face. He thought: *No need for that, Silas. You won't be coming back.*

IV

Halfway to the head of the trail, it began to rain. Leabo, riding in the lead, halted his horse immediately and dismounted to untie his slicker from behind the saddle, and Silas followed suit. Swathed from neck to knees in their dun-colored ponchos, they rode on. The air had chilled with the first gusts of wind that preceded the rain. The clouds overhead, gray and menacing, scudded past, driven by the maniacal fury of that high, enormous wind. Rain pelted down and, later, hail. The horses dropped their heads and laid back their ears in futile protest. Silas growled and grumbled incessantly.

In spite of his discomfort, great satisfaction stirred in Leabo. The rain was the final blessing. It would obliterate all the tracks of yesterday, all those yet to be made today. For he could see that it was not merely a shower, but more like a steady downpour that would continue all day and part of the night.

When he came to a fork in the trail, he took the lower branch that wound along at the crest of the rim and later joined the trail he had earlier used for his ascent of the mountain. Behind him he could feel Silas's hesitation, could hear his growled protest.

"Hell, do you gotta take the worst trail?"

Without turning, Hugh said: "I'm wet. This one's shorter."

There was no fear in Hugh as he threaded the precarious, slippery trail. To his right, a scant half dozen feet away, yawned a sheer, hundred-foot drop across the rimrock face to the slide. He had the conviction, given to some men, that when his time came to die, he would die, and that until his time came, he was safe, no matter what risks he took, no matter what he did. Ordinarily he would have considered the use of this trail foolhardy, except in dry weather. Yet it was characteristic of him that, since it served his purpose to use it today, he had no thought of any danger to himself.

Slipping and sliding, scrambling and sometimes half falling, the horses clawed along. Behind Leabo, his horse's head sometimes nudging the rump of Leabo's horse, rode Silas, angry and white-faced at this unnecessary foolhardiness but unwilling to admit his own fear.

Leabo saw the particular place he had been watching for a dozen yards ahead and tensed involuntarily in his saddle. Suddenly, as he passed this narrow stretch, where an outcropping of rock edged the trail on the uphill side, he yanked his reins around and at the same time sunk his spurs.

The horse half reared with surprise and whirled around. Again the spurs were raked viciously across his streaming sides. The rain, which had been coming from the rear, now pelted into Hugh Leabo's face, blurring Silas's face and the details of what followed his action.

Leabo reined his horse so that the animal must plunge between Silas and the rock outcropping, but this would not have been necessary, for the horse's own sense of self-preservation would have dictated such a course. Hugh felt the shock of the impact, felt Silas's horse give before it. Silas howled—"What the hell you doin', you damned fool?"—and from then on had no time for word or thought. His horse left the trail, sliding, and strove mightily to swing himself, to get his head uphill.

Hugh Leabo put his mighty strength to holding his frantic horse still. He succeeded and watched the inevitable, slow-sliding course of Silas's animal toward the rim. At the last moment, Silas sought to fling himself from the saddle, but he was too late, and the only effect his convulsive movement had was to hasten the catapulting of himself and his horse into empty air.

Turning lazily, end over end, the horse dropped. Silas, who had fallen from the saddle, seemed to float beside the animal. Then both were gone, and there remained only a high yell of anguish that gradually diminished into nothing. Over the howl of wind and rain, Leabo did not even hear the impact of their landing.

As he rode back up the trail, he discovered that his hands were shaking, yet his expression was calm and serene, betraying nothing of his inner turmoil.

"This is the last loose end," he murmured as his horse picked its own patient and careful way upward. He reached the fork in the trail, and this time, taking the easier, safer upper trail, came at last to the rim, and later to Arrow's big front gate.

Laura ran from the house as he rode in, her expression excited and pleading, but Leabo only shook his head at her regretfully. "He didn't see Will all day. I'm sorry, Laura. It looks like Will did it, all right." He turned and headed for the corral.

Laura watched his tremendously broad solid back as he rode away through the rain. Hope was gone from her, and she hardly noticed the pelting, cold rain that had, in minutes, soaked the back of her white shirtwaist, and now lay in glistening droplets upon her hair and upon her flaring woolen skirt.

She turned and made her way up the muddy walk to the house and entered the dark and dismal interior that even the bright fire that leaped and danced on the hearth could not make cheerful now. No longer ago than yesterday morning the house had been alive with the impatient bellow of Laird McFetridge and the slippered bustle of Chang who sought to please a master who couldn't be pleased.

The evenings had been pleasant with Will Counselman's company, and now in this extremity Laura was forced to admit that the odd tingle that had run pleasantly through her when Will was with her was not at all sisterly. She considered Will's plight at length, her mind darting back and forth from possibility to possibility, rejecting each one almost as it occurred. In the end she could admit but one thing, that Will was doomed. She found that she was less concerned with the question of Will's guilt than she was with his eventual fate.

All that afternoon she sat before the fire, frowning and somber, her emotions ranging a hundred times from despair to determination and back again. She was a small girl, delicately formed, but in the last twenty-four hours she had attained an abrupt maturity that made her size unimportant. At four, she sent Chang for Hugh Leabo, for her mind was at last firmly made up. If Will had killed Laird, so be it. His justification had been ample. If he had not killed Laird, then what she was doing was only what she ought to do.

Hugh's fist sounded like a maul against the heavy front door. He came in, streaming rain, and stood hesitantly on the threshold. "What do you want, Laura?"

Hesitation came to her and doubt. Hugh Leabo was tremendously loyal to Arrow, that she knew. But was his loyalty for Laird McFetridge, was it for the ranch, or was it for any owner of Arrow? She said: "I've got to ask you this, Hugh." Her voice dropped to a whisper, and she smiled shakily. "I guess I've got to demand it of you."

He was solid and dependable, as much a part of Arrow as its broad, rich hayfields. He shifted his weight and absently turned his broad-brimmed Stetson between his hands. His face was unreadable, calm and placid and patient. "All right, Laura. I'll do anything you want. I guess you know that."

She asked: "Will hasn't got a chance?"

"No."

"Well, get him out of jail. Give him a horse and some money and enough time to get out of the country."

Hugh dropped his glance to his boot toes and fidgeted. Rain dripped from his hat onto the bare floor. This was the only sound, save for Laura's quick and Hugh's regular breathing.

"Then what?"

"That's all. We'll never see him again, because he will be afraid to return. And Arrow is my home. I won't leave it."

Hugh Leabo sighed, and even in her agitation Laura could sense his vast relief. "All right, Laura. All right." He turned without another word, opened the door, and went out into the rain. Laura did not see his faint and satisfied smile.

She returned to the fire with her mind strangely eased because she had at last chosen a course and embarked upon it. She felt a strong sense of obligation to Hugh for the unquestioning way he had accepted the dangerous task of freeing Will. She felt a strong sense of dependence upon him, for he was all that remained. She had no way of knowing that Hugh Leabo counted heavily upon her sense of obligation and dependence, knowing that a good many frontier marriages were based on less. Laura was not yet aware that Hugh Leabo was interested in her as a wife nor was she aware that to him she was merely a stepping stone to wealth and power. Hugh Leabo wanted Arrow with a patient man's long-cherished singleness of purpose. With Arrow in sight, Hugh Leabo had become a dangerous man. In the course of the last twenty-four hours, Hugh had eliminated the two major obstacles to the realization of his dream. It was not likely that now he would let any other living thing stand in his way.

Hugh entered the bunkhouse, flung his hat to a bunk, and shook himself like a giant mastiff. The crew lounged about, most of them in their bunks, reading or sleeping, half a dozen of them engaged in a game of poker at the long table. Even the usual impatience Hugh would have felt at seeing them idle when there was hay to be put up was absent today.

He said: "Boys, we're going to break Will out of jail tonight." He caught their instant attention and held it. The fact that they did not question Hugh's intent was proof that all felt a sneaking sympathy for Will. Hugh said: "He hasn't got a chance, if he goes to trial. Laird used him pretty badly. If a man used me the way Laird used Will, I guess maybe I'd've killed him, too. Anyway, Will's part of Arrow, and he'll have his chance."

The poker game was forgotten. Men sat up in their bunks, swung feet to the floor, and pulled on their boots. Hugh took down his holstered Colt .45 and belt from a nail on the wall, saying: "A show of force is all we need. I don't want anybody killed. I don't want a shot fired. There ain't a jury in McFetridge County but what would convict Will. There ain't a jury in the county that would blame Arrow for turning him loose. Anybody that don't want to go, say so now."

A light smile hovered about his mouth as the crew excitedly readied themselves to ride. He glanced at the still body of Laird McFetridge with faint distaste, saying: "A couple of you load Laird into a buckboard. He'll be our excuse for showing up in town in force."

The rain continued, a light but steady drizzle that Hugh knew would thoroughly ruin what hay was already cut. Yet even this bothered him no more than the slight discomfort the rain caused him, for he continued to be aware that the rain was doing for him a job he could not have done himself. It was obliterating all Will's tracks, made the previous day, so that Will's story became impossible to check, even with the aid of expert Indian trackers. It was obliterating all the tracks that Hugh and Silas had made this morning. When Silas was found, it would be assumed that he had met with an accident, for everyone knew the treacherous slipperiness of the trails atop the mesa in a rainstorm.

A buckboard was brought to the bunkhouse door, and Laird McFetridge's body was carried to it and covered with canvas. Arrow's crew, all armed, mounted and rode behind it as it splashed down the road toward the town of Cedar Grove, making a grim cavalcade, an impressive escort of honor for the body of Laird McFetridge. Cedar Grove and McFetridge County would like this. When they discovered the real purpose behind it, they would like that, too. Arrow was a symbol in McFetridge County, a symbol of power, a symbol of loyalty. Honoring the murdered and releasing the murderer would please the town's sense of the dramatic, would serve notice, as well, that this affair was strictly Arrow's and that Arrow would brook no interference by outsiders.

The sheriff would make a token pursuit of Will Counselman, but Hugh Leabo knew it would be only that. The sheriff would ascertain which direction Will had taken and would then hide himself away on some entirely different trail to be gone a week and then return empty-handed and with expressions of regret. There the matter would lie. There it would die. Yet a purpose would be served by all this. Will Counselman, as surely as though he had been tried in a court of law, would be convicted of the murder of Laird McFetridge. He would be an outlaw, afraid to return, afraid even to walk openly or to use his own name. What slight claim he had on Arrow would be forfeit, and Hugh Leabo would see to it that, if he ever did have the temerity to return, he was caught and tried and sentenced. For by that time, Hugh Leabo would be Arrow, its owner and master, and Laura McFetridge would be only his wife.

Hugh smiled, big and solid and comfortable in his saddle. For as long as he could remember, he had planned this, waiting only for what he considered the proper moment, a threat from Will to Laird, an opportunity for Will, an opportunity for himself. The worst of it was past. There remained only the courtship of Laura McFetridge, and even this Hugh would approach with the same, sure patience that had characterized all he had done so far. When Laura did accept him, she would think it was her own idea entirely. She would believe she was gaining an honest and experienced hand to assume the management of Arrow's widespread and complex interests. Only when it was too late would she realize that Arrow was lost to her. Perhaps, if Hugh were careful, she would never even realize that. If she did—well, a woman could die as easily as a man.

V

It was full dark when Silas awoke. At first, half conscious, he heard with only a part of his stunned and befuddled mind the howl of wind in the high crags above him and felt in his chilled and broken body the pelt of cold, insistent rain. He stirred, and the pain of a broken leg rushed him instantly back into the black void of unconsciousness.

The second time he woke, it was past midnight, and still it rained. This time, his mind was clearer, and he instantly recalled that Hugh Leabo had deliberately forced him over the rim. Anger stirred in him, and the desire for revenge was born. He moved his right arm gently, tentatively. Pain shot clear to his shoulder, not the sharp and dizzying pain of a break, but rather the dull, throbbing pain of bruises. Carefully he put the palm of his right hand against the ground, against the sharp litter of crumbled shale on which he lay.

Slowly he put weight upon his right arm, and, as his body raised, he withdrew his left from under him, knowing instantly by the blindness that assailed him and the sweat that bathed him, that it was broken. He knew, too, when deep breathing sent sharp pain through him, that he had some broken ribs. By further cautious movement, he ascertained that his right leg and left arm were broken, although no bones protruded through his flesh, and that he had at least three broken ribs. Miraculously, his spine was intact, but he had bled from numerous deep lacerations.

Recalling the calmness with which Hugh Leabo had watched him struggle to save himself, Silas knew a sudden and desperate fear. He roused himself and crawled from the thicket of scrub oak in which he lay, dragging a useless and tortured leg, but he had gone less than ten yards when exhaustion claimed him, and he was forced to stop.

Silas thought over his situation with bleak calmness. The position of the stars told him that it was past midnight. Hugh probably thought him dead, so he would be safe, at least until daylight. He considered only briefly the slight possibility of finding a trail and working himself up through the rimrock. Next he pondered the likelihood of working himself carefully down across the slide to the shelter of the cedars below. He knew it would be possible for him to do this, yet he found himself reluctant to begin. From the cedars, there would still be more than two miles of crawling before he could reach the road. Once on the road, he would be at the mercy of whoever came along.

He did not know why Hugh had tried to kill him. He did know that someone had murdered Laird McFetridge, and he supposed that in some way the attempt on his own life had was tied up with that. If he were strong enough and lucky enough to reach the road, it was quite possible that either Hugh, or someone else mixed up in the killing of Laird, might find him and dispose of him for good. He decided that it was too big a chance to take. There were two possible courses—to stay here or to work his way along parallel to the rimrock until he found a cave or overhang of some sort.

Perhaps, upon finding him missing, Hugh would assume that he had crawled downhill, the most obvious way, and had died in the cedars. Perhaps, and this thought stirred more hope than he had yet felt, Hugh would simply be so sure that nothing could survive that fall that he would neglect to make sure. Years might pass before anyone stumbled upon the remains of Silas's horse. In the meantime, it would undoubtedly be assumed that Silas himself had become tired of his job and had saddled up and left the country.

Survival would depend upon his ability to maintain himself until the bones of his leg and arm could mend. His hand slipped down to his holster, and a sigh of relief escaped him as he felt the hard smoothness of his revolver grips. But it was too dangerous, now, to risk a shot. Knowing he must eat, he crawled back and forth across the shale until he found his horse and, when he did, stifled his repugnance and hacked a huge hunk of meat from the animal's hind quarter. He wrapped this in a piece of oilcloth which he cut from the skirt of his torn slicker, tied it with one of the bridle reins, and secured it to his waist. Then he began his slow and tortuous crawl along the foot of the rim.

The rain continued unabated, but the chill of it was overcome by the heat of Silas's exertion. A dozen times he lapsed into unconsciousness but, upon awakening, he doggedly continued. He had gone nearly a mile by the time dawn was tracing its gray finger along a jagged top of the rim. He had rounded at least one sharp turn in the contour of the rimrock, so that the scene of his fall was entirely hidden from his eyes. At last he found a shallow cave, hardly more than an overhang, where ages of weather had worked away at a soft place in the rock. Beside it, a basin, hollowed in the rock, brimmed with rain water. Here he settled himself, facing the valley, and fell into a long, merciful unconsciousness.

While Silas was struggling to make himself safe, things were happening in Cedar Grove. The town sprawled at the side of the river, a squat, ugly collection of frame buildings. A road entered Cedar Grove from the north, coming from Arrow, that followed the river and became Main Street within the town. The town jail was located on this second road a quarter mile to the west of the business district where it squatted under a yellow clay bluff. In summer, heat of the sun beat mercilessly against it and collected under the bluff while the unfortunate occupants of the jail sweltered.

It was a small building, constructed of sandstone blocks. Its walls began six feet underground, to discourage tunneling, and rose to a height of seven feet above ground. The roof was constructed of rough-sawed timbers laid side by side and covered with two feet of dirt. Rubbish and refuse had raised the level of the floor somewhat, so that when six-foot

Will Counselman stood erect, his head brushed the ceiling.

Tonight he stood at the tiny barred window of his cell and stared moodily toward the lights of the town. He thought of Laura McFetridge; he thought of Arrow; he thought of Hugh Leabo. He stared down the years at a lifetime of gray, half living and came to the conclusion that death was preferable.

He had not killed Laird McFetridge, as only he himself and the real killer knew. Yet he recognized the futility of even trying to convince anyone else. Laura, who had more reason to believe in him than anyone, thought him guilty. Others, not knowing him so well and having seen only his moodiness and the effects of Laird's abuse on his temper, would not fail to convict him.

Long before he heard the hoof beats of Arrow's riders, he had made his decision, which was to take the first opportunity to escape and, once free, to bend his efforts toward discovering Laird's real killer. There was enough realism in Will that he had no real hope of accomplishing this. Every hand would be against him. Inevitably he would be cornered, but, he promised himself grimly, he would never be caught.

The racket of horses on the road roused him. They swept into sight, led by the unmistakable figure of Hugh Leabo. Will heard the door bolt as Carl Gwinn shot it home, and then Hugh Leabo's deep bellow: "You know what we want, Carl! Open up and nobody'll be hurt!"

Gwinn came to the bars of Will's cell, saying: "Will, I don't know. I'll try to hold you if you say the word. I don't want no lynchings in my county."

Will laughed, already tasting the sharpness of freedom. "They won't lynch me, Carl. That's Arrow out there."

Gwinn, a short, stocky man with a seamed and weathered face, a close-cropped head of graying hair, shook his head. "I'm not so sure. Leabo. . . ." Again he shook his head, puzzlement plain in his blue-gray eyes.

Hugh's great bellow penetrated the thick stone walls. "Carl, we ain't got all night! I'd hate to have to tear your damned jail down. It's cut and dried for Will if he goes before a jury. Arrow don't like things that are cut and dried. Will gets his chance. We're here to see that he gets it."

Into Will Counselman's eyes came a sudden brightness. Ah, the loyalty of Arrow, the loyalty of Hugh Leabo. He said: "You see, Carl?"

Carl Gwinn shook his head. "Something wrong here."

A heavy pounding shook the barred door. Again Hugh bellowed: "Open up!"

Placidly the sheriff took a chair before his desk. Will saw the shame he was feeling. Gwinn murmured: "Damn it, I'll have my self-respect. I won't give you to them. They'll have to take you."

The blows against the door ceased, but after a short interval a heavier thudding began, and it was apparent to Will that Leabo had obtained a log somewhere and was using it as a battering ram. After a dozen blows, the door shattered in the center, and one of Leabo's huge paws came in and pulled back the bolt. Gwinn had not moved.

Arrow riders piled into the room, guns drawn, but Hugh cautioned sharply: "No shooting. Carl's going to be sensible." He paused beside Gwinn, saying: "The keys, Carl."

Gwinn jerked a thumb at a board on the wall where hung a collection of keys. He said: "You'll stand trial for this, Hugh."

Hugh laughed. "And be acquitted."

Gwinn nodded. Rising, he picked the key to Will's cell off the board and handed it to Arrow's foreman. His voice held a tired resignation. "No use going through this again. It'll cost the county ten dollars to fix that door." He paused, then went on resignedly: "I'm coming after you, Will. I figure you'll take the road down the river and head for the nearest settlement. If I don't find you there, I'll follow you over into Utah, where you'll likely hole up at some cow camp."

Hugh swung the cell door open, and Will stepped out. He felt an odd reluctance, now that things had progressed this far, and an even stranger uneasiness. He paused before the sheriff, looking down. "I didn't kill Laird. I won't rot in jail for something I didn't do. If you should find me, Carl, come at me with your gun smoking, because that's the only way you'll ever get me."

Hugh touched his arm. "Come on, kid." His grip on Will's arm was firm and relentless. Outside he said: "I ain't in the habit of interfering with the law. You're getting this chance on account of Laura."

He walked to a tall, powerful bay gelding beside which stood a mule. On the mule's back was a pack saddle, and from this was slung a pair of leather panniers, obviously heavily loaded. In a scabbard on the bay's saddle was a Winchester carbine, and over the saddle horn hung Will's Colt revolver and cartridge belt. Hugh said: "Grub and matches in the panniers. Blankets and slicker behind the saddle. Rations enough to take you five hundred miles. See that you don't stop till you get that far away from here."

Mixed with the relief he was feeling, Will also had a strange sense of resentment at being hurried, of being pushed. He swung to the saddle, gratefulness toward Hugh holding him silent, stifling this small resentment. Arrow's riders held themselves aloof from him, neither hostile nor friendly, waiting and watching the huge foreman to see which tack he would take. Will looked toward him also for a lead.

VI

Leabo rode away from the jail, leaving the road and taking a trail directly through the high brush, a trail that led roughly northwest toward Arrow. Will followed, and the Arrow riders fell in behind, oddly silent.

Now that the prospect of the pen was removed, Will found himself looking ahead at another life, only a little better, a lifetime of running, of hiding, of ever-present fear, a life that would make him jump every time a voice spoke unexpectedly behind him, every time a hand laid itself on his shoulder. Because of Laird McFetridge, Will had known the meaning of fear from the time he could walk. Now, also because of Laird McFetridge, he would learn how to run.

Stubbornness stirred in Will Counselman, and obscure anger, remote because there was nowhere to direct it. Dejected, his head lowered, he rode in silence behind the towering shape of Hugh Leabo. Once Hugh called back: "Gwinn made it plain he was going to hunt downriver for you. So I reckon you'd best go up on top and ride out toward Wyoming."

Will hardly heard him. Like a squirrel seeking escape from a cage, his mind darted back and forth, futilely seeking someone who might have hated Laird enough to kill him. Plenty of men in McFetridge County had hated Laird, for Laird rode a sharp-shod horse, taking what he wanted and to hell with any opposition. Arrow had grown steadily under Laird's direction, and each time it spread its boundaries wider, it earned another enemy. Yet to find one who might have killed Laird seemed an impossible task. Will thought desperately: *If there was a stranger on Arrow the day Laird was killed, someone must have seen him.* No one had come forth with news of a stranger, even after it became generally known that Laird had been killed. This forced another conclusion upon Will, one that had not occurred before. *Hell, maybe it wasn't a stranger, at all. Maybe it was one of the crew.* Yet, strive as he would, Will could settle upon no single man in Arrow's crew who might have hated Laird enough to kill him. Laird, in dealing with his crew, had always been extremely fair, all his cruelty and brutality apparently being saved for Will.

Will's brow furrowed. *Why me? Why did he hate me so?* A vicious circle of questions buzzed around in his head, and none of them had an answer. Yet somewhere there were answers, if only a man knew where to look. There had to be a reason for Laird McFetridge's murder. The murderer was well covered, for neither Gwinn, Leabo, nor anyone else doubted that Will was the killer.

Suddenly a cold film of sweat broke out on Will's forehead. If the motive for Laird's murder were other than hatred or revenge—material gain, for instance—then the murdering might not stop with Laird. Laura might conceivably be in danger.

He opened his mouth to say—"Hugh, I'm not going. Whoever killed Laird is still around."—but he closed it with a snap, the words unsaid. This unusual caution puzzled him. Could it be that he did not trust Hugh Leabo? Ridiculous. Hugh was as solid, as dependable as Arrow itself. His loyalty was legend—his loyalty to Arrow. Yet some strange reticence had held back the words already formed on Will's lips. He shrugged. He did not know where he would start to look; he did not know where he could hide from Arrow's crew and from the law. One thing, however, he had put from him forever. He would not run. He would not abandon Laura, knowing that a killer was loose on Arrow. He would stay and fight, even if the fight ended in his death under the guns of the sheriff's posse.

For two hours Arrow's crew continued northward through the steadily falling rain, going carefully on the sticky clay of the road. At last the lights of the ranch came into sight, seeming warm and friendly to Will who could look forward to nothing tonight but a cold camp, a soaked and sodden bed in the open. At Arrow's gate, Hugh Leabo halted, while one of the crew dismounted to open it. Hugh stuck a big paw toward Will, saying: "Well, it looks like this is it. Good luck to you, Will."

"Thanks," Will responded wryly. "I'll probably need it." He took Leabo's hand, unable to see more of the man than his bulking shape, but feeling the warmth of his kindness and friendship. He had a last urge to confide in Hugh and was about to say something when Hugh abruptly dropped his hand and wheeled his horse toward the gate. A chorus of reserved good byes came from Arrow's 'punchers, and then they became only a dark, blurred mass on the lane.

For a moment Will sat very still, feeling strongly his utter aloneness. The lights in the house seemed to beckon. He turned finally and guided his horse onto the trail that twisted upward through the cedars. The lights of Arrow fell behind, hidden by the grotesque shapes of ancient trees. The mule plodded stolidly behind. Other than the noise of the animals, there was nothing but the soft patter of rain.

Somewhere high on the rim, a wolf howled. A deer broke from the trail before Will and bounded away through the cedars, in long, stiff-legged jumps. At the crest of the first knoll, Will turned left off the trail, wound along a ridge for a while, and again turned toward the east up a long draw. The country grew rougher, the walls of the draw higher and steeper.

At length, Will came to the head of the draw, where it widened into a small clearing. A grove of willows made a dark patch in the center of the clearing, and here a small spring seeped out of the rock, clear and cold, running but a scant twenty yards before it disappeared into the dry and thirsty gravel of the draw. As a boy, Will had often come here. Except in winter, when cattle roamed the bottoms, no animal or man had ever penetrated this far into these rough and barren cedar hills. Since this clearing was plainly visible from the trail above, Will would conceal his camp in the grove of willows and keep his horse tied there during the daylight hours. The mule, once it was unpacked, he would lead up the steep trail to the mesa top and release it.

He set about unpacking at once, and hung the leather panniers high in one of the willows, out of reach of prowling animals. He tied the horse and mule and finally, thoroughly miserable and thoroughly alone, lay down to sleep.

For an hour he tossed and turned. His blankets were soon sodden from the rain and moisture from the ground. Midnight passed, and the air turned ever colder. Wrapped in his wet blankets, Will Counselman began to shiver. And suddenly there began to grow within him a vast and terrible anger.

He had been pushed and bullied and beaten without cause for as long as he could remember. It had grown to be a habit with him, taking Laird McFetridge's abuse until he thought no more of rebelling against Laird than he would have thought of rebelling against the weather. Laird McFetridge was dead, but even in death Laird still hounded him, still could make his life intolerable.

Suddenly he flung himself to his feet. His lean face was set in a rigid mold of fury. Yet even through his anger he felt a helplessness, a need for help. Help could be found in only one quarter—Laura. All his life there had been a bond between them, first that of brother and sister, later—in Will at least—of something else. There had been times, he could remember, when Laura's anger at some injustice of Laird's had exceeded Will's own.

Swiftly he flung his saddle onto the bay, untied the reins, and mounted. Running the horse, unmindful of the treacherous footing, he retraced his previous path and came within fifteen minutes to Arrow's broad gate. He left his horse there and went in afoot.

The ranch was entirely dark. Softly, staying on the carpet of grass, he went down the lane, quieting the startled and growling dog with a muttered curse and a pat on the head.

Circling the house, he glimpsed a light that had been hidden from him before. It came through the dining room window, yet it was soft and slight, so he guessed it was in Laird's office, and the door was partially open.

Puzzled, Will went through the back door and into the kitchen, making no sound at all, for this was something he had done many times before. He avoided the squeaking board at the entrance to the dining room, and stepped carefully to the office door to peer inside.

He did now know exactly what he had expected. Certainly not this. Laura sat at Laird's desk, a pile of yellowed paper before her. She was crying as she had never cried before. Will stepped inside, and her head came instantly around, her eyes wide with fright.

Tenderness for this small girl welled up within Will. He asked: "Crying for Laird?"

"Oh, no! Oh, no, Will!" She was on her feet, then running toward him, and all at once she was in his arms, weeping brokenly, her face streaming. He held her against his shoulder. Her voice became almost incoherent. "Will, oh, Will, I'm so glad you didn't go. If you had, you would never have known." She pulled away, drew him toward the desk.

Will grew more puzzled. On Laird's desk lay a bundle of

old letters, a couple of yellowed daguerreotypes. Laura murmured: "It's right there . . . in those two pictures. Can't you see it, Will? Can't you see it at all?"

She lifted one of the pictures, showing a young woman, softly smiling. Laura cried: "Will, this is your mother." She lifted the other, a picture of a young and handsome man, a familiar-looking man. "You are like him, Will, because he is your father."

Will stared. He could see the resemblance, all right, when he looked for it. There was no doubt at all.

"You look just like him. And the story is here in these letters. I understand so many things now that I didn't before. Your mother was Laird's first wife, but she ran away from him . . . ran away with your father who had been Laird's friend. You were born, and your father deserted her. But your mother would not come back to Laird even though he begged her. I think she was too proud. But finally she became ill and sent for Laird because she knew she was going to die. She was dead when he arrived."

VII

Laura began to cry anew, touched by the pathos of the story she was telling. "Oh, it's a terrible story! He buried her, and out of a feeling of obligation, I guess, took you to raise. Yet, as you grew up, you took on the resemblance to your father. Laird was used to you probably and didn't always see it. There were times, though, when the resemblance was so plain that all the hate he had felt for your father was transferred to you. Those were the times he was so cruel. When he realized what he was doing, he would always be terribly sorry, remember?"

She seemed to notice Will's frown for the first time. She put her hand gently on his arm. "Oh, I know that didn't help you. You didn't deserve his cruelty and you couldn't understand it. His being so remorseful after only confused you. It was awful, Will. But you know his reason now . . . you know why he did the things he did. Doesn't that help you any, Will?"

He picked up the picture of his father and stared at it. He said: "He quit her when she needed him. I think I could hate him myself for that." He flung the picture onto the desk. His face was bitter and cold.

Laura moved closer to him, put her hand on his shoulders. She said: "Will, I know you didn't kill Laird. I have been thinking . . . I have never seen you do a cruel thing, and the way Laird was killed was terribly cruel."

He yanked himself out of the past with a visible effort. "Who did, then?" She was close to him, her warmth and fragrance rising to his nostrils. Suddenly he cared nothing for Laird, for the two daguerreotypes, for anything but Laura, so close, so soft. His arms went out, drew her roughly and hungrily toward him.

Her response was not at all sisterly, was as hungry as his own. "Oh, Will. Will. What are we going to do?"

The fury that had built to such a dangerous point in him at his camp now returned. He pushed her away. "Find the killer," he said. "You don't kill a man without a reason. Find a reason for killing Laird, and you'll find a killer."

"But the sheriff's after you. You've got to go."

"I'm not going. I decided that about an hour ago."

He caught Laura's arms, drawing her toward him, devouring with his eyes every small detail of her features—the dark eyes, the high cheek bones, the full beautiful mouth. Her face mirrored at once her fear for his safety, her hunger for him, her love.

He said: "All that has kept me at Arrow since I was seventeen was you. Do you think I stayed because I wanted to? I hated Laird for the way he treated me. He made it plain enough that I could expect no part of Arrow, and I didn't give a damn for that, anyway. It was you, Laura. It was always you. I love you."

Pressed tightly against him, her voice was muffled. "I knew that. I felt it, too. But I kept thinking of you as a brother, and it didn't seem right. Tonight all that changed. As soon as I read those letters, as soon as I saw those pictures. . . ." Her arms tightened about him. She said: "Will, take me away. The whole country thinks you killed him. You can't stay hidden. The country is big, but not big enough for that."

"No." There was no compromise in him. "Alive, Laird couldn't make me run. I'll not run from him now."

Laura seemed to have expected this and made no protest. Will murmured thoughtfully: "The killer, whoever he is, wants me to run. With me either convicted or a fugitive, the search for the killer stops. Let Hugh know that I am still around. Through him it will get to the crew. Whoever killed Laird will begin to get nervous. Watch what happens here. Watch for anything . . . anything at all."

"All right, Will. When will I see you again?"

"Tomorrow night . . . after dark."

He moved quietly to the door, slipped through, and closed it behind him. In total darkness, he felt his way through the kitchen and out into the night. He thought the rain was lighter, and the air seemed warmer.

A dog sniffed at his leg curiously. Will walked carefully around the house, making no sound as he crossed the wet grass, but immediately he stepped into the road, his feet made a loud, sucking noise in the mud. He crossed the muddy expanse and again stepped onto grass at the side of the road.

He headed toward the gate, where he had left his horse. His thoughts were a confused tangle, alternately wildly happy, as he thought of Laura, and sourly depressed as he thought of the apparent impossibility of the task he had set for himself.

A faint gray light began to show itself above the rim to eastward. His summary of the situation sounded amazingly simple. Find a motive, and you find a killer. Yet the task was far more difficult than that, for there might be a half dozen men on Arrow with some motive for killing Laird, or there might be none.

He reached the gate and eased through. He noticed the way his horse was fidgeting, the way the animal eyed a tall clump of nearby sagebrush, but in his preoccupied state he disregarded it. Then he heard Hugh Leabo's soft voice. "Damn you, I thought I told you to get out of the country!"

Will started violently and swung around to face Leabo. His hand dropped without prompting to the smooth butt of the Colt, but fell away immediately at Hugh's harsh warning. "Pull that, damn you, and I'll blow out your guts!"

Will shrugged. For an instant he considered a swift fling at the saddle and a thundering escape. This he discarded, for there was no fear in him of Hugh. Hugh came toward him, only a huge outline in the fading darkness.

Will said: "I got to thinking. If I run, I'll spend my whole life running. I won't do that."

He expected Hugh's anger, for Hugh had broken him out of jail, thus laying himself open to a charge of jail breaking. He did not expect the terrible sledge-hammer blow of Hugh's fist that drove him half across the road, set his head to spinning wildly, and put him down on hands and knees in the slick clay.

Through the whirling, blinding lights, the descending darkness, he heard the sliding, scrambling approach of the big man, saw the huge, spurred boots coming toward him. His senses were dulled, his mind nearly blank from the terrific force of that blow that had landed just below his ear. Hugh reached down, collared him, and yanked him to his feet. Will's helplessness before Hugh's tremendous size and strength appalled him. Holding Will up, with his toes barely touching the ground, Hugh drew back a fist for a second blow.

Suddenly, to Will, this was the same old story, only now the brutality came not from Laird but from Laird's foreman. It was the same, but Will felt no obligation to take it from Hugh. He squirmed, throwing himself spasmodically to one side. Hugh's fist grazed the side of his jaw, tearing the skin but having no stunning force. The force of the effort threw Hugh off balance, and Will took full advantage of it, twisting again, feeling himself falling.

He was in the mud again, with the awful weight of Hugh crashing down on him. From the big man's throat rumbled an animal growl that conveyed only blind fury. Will knew that in this uneven encounter all that could save him would be luck. His fists could not match the smashing impact of Hugh's. He would break them against Hugh's massive jaw bone.

Had he known Hugh's intent, he might have kept away, might have worn down the big man's strength by evasion. But even that was impossible, for the stunning effect of Hugh's first blow remained, making Will feel that his head was floating entirely independent of his body. Hugh lay across his body, at the hips, striving to turn himself, clawing at mud that gave no purchase for his strength. For an instant, Hugh's great body raised as he half came to his knees, thus relieving the pressure of his weight on Will. Frantically taking this slight opportunity, Will dug his boots into the sliding mud, clawed with his hands, and felt himself surge forward. Yet even as he did, Hugh turned on his knees, catching Will's driving legs and straightening them.

Will rolled, a terrible fear turning in his stomach. He was a tall, well-muscled man, hardened by long days in the saddle, toughened by heavy work and exposure to the elements. Yet in Hugh's great hands he was clay, helpless and weak.

Hugh took one of Will's booted feet in one hand, holding it as a vise would hold it, and with the other grasped Will's leg just below the knee. He gave it a sudden wrench, and Will's ankle cracked, sounding as though it were broken. Excruciating, blinding pain ran up his leg.

Hugh gritted—"You won't be able to walk. But . . . damn it, you'll ride."—and put a fresh effort into bringing Will's leg across his chest for leverage.

Will's attempt to kick loose might just as well have never been made for all the good it did. Pain rose in dizzying waves to his brain, clouding thought, threatening his consciousness. Frantically he groped toward his waist and at last felt the hard walnut of the revolver grips. He yanked the gun out and, drawing himself up, raised his arm and smashed the gun barrel brutally against Hugh Leabo's skull.

Hugh grunted, but did not relax his grip on Will's leg. Will again smashed the gun downward in a vicious arc, and still Hugh did not give. Will's voice came wildly from his throat. "Are you a man, damn you? Or are you something else?" He reversed the gun, holding it by the barrel, and brought the butt down on Hugh's upturned, furrowed forehead.

At last, the pressure on Will's leg was relaxed as Hugh rolled aside, shaking his shaggy head dumbly. Will crawled away and rose shakily to his feet, almost blind from the pain of the twisted ankle. He was trembling so violently that he could not have killed Hugh had he so desired. His breath came in jagged, tortured gasps. Hugh came to his hands and knees, head rolling from side to side. He was groggy but still dangerous.

Will's breathing quieted, and he said softly: "Hugh, you'll never get closer than bullet range to me again. You'll never get those hands on me, I can promise you. You're tough, but a Forty-Five slug is tougher. Don't forget that."

He shoved his gun into its muddy holster and wiped his palms on his pants legs. He hobbled toward the horse, which had wandered away from the fight in terror and now stood trembling fifty feet away. Forcing soothing words from his throat, he mounted and rode back to look down at Hugh.

At last he said: "Stay on Arrow, Hugh. If I see you in the cedars, I'll kill you like I would a wolf."

VIII

It was seven o'clock when Laura sent Chang to the bunkhouse for Hugh. By this time, as she well knew, the crew would be finished with breakfast and would be at the table, smoking, getting their orders for the day from the foreman. Hugh did not come immediately, and Laura went out onto the verandah to wait. The rain had finally stopped, and, although the sun had not yet poked its way through, thinning clouds announced that its coming would not be long delayed.

Laura's glance went to the cedar hills across the road, and her expression softened. Will Counselman was up there, perhaps sleeping now, for he had been up all night. She hoped he would remain well hidden. Laura heard the bunkhouse door slam and Arrow's score of 'punchers filed out, halting momentarily before separating to their various tasks. Hugh towered over them as he exchanged a few words over one of them. Then he made his deliberate way toward her.

He halted at the steps and removed his hat. " 'Morning, Laura."

"Hello, Hugh." An angry bruise on his forehead caught her attention, but his abrupt scowl made her withhold comment. Instead she said: "Hugh, Will is not leaving the country as you told him to do. He is camping in the cedars."

It was obvious that Hugh's surprise was false, Laura thought. *He knows! But how?*

Hugh rumbled: "For God's sake, why? He knows Gwinn is after him."

"He didn't kill Laird, Hugh! I'm convinced of that."

"Well, I'm not! Nobody else had a reason. Nobody else had an opportunity."

Perversity and faint anger made Laura say: "Except you. You came back here to replace a lame horse and could have done it then. Hugh, be fair! Just because you hate someone does not mean that you have to kill him. Will is twenty. If he had been the type to kill, wouldn't he have done it long ago?"

Hugh's face turned white. His eyes flared at her, then dropped hastily.

Laura asked suddenly, seriously: "Hugh, do you hate Will?"

He seemed to recover. "No. Of course, I don't hate him. Why should I hate him?"

Laura shook her head. "I don't know. I don't know why I feel that you do." She was puzzled and vaguely unhappy. She had never seen Hugh as he was this morning. Although she was not looking at him, she felt that he was staring at her with speculation, and interest. Uneasiness stirred in her, causing new puzzlement. She told herself firmly: *This is Hugh. He is as much a part of Arrow as the house.* But when she looked at him again, it was not the same. Hugh was not the same. Big and awkward, he scuffed the toe of a boot in the soft ground. His eyes, when he raised them, held something that had never been in them before. It was not a man's desire for a woman. It was neither longing nor love. And because it was none of these things, his words were all the more shocking. "Laura, I've watched you grow up. I'm ten years older than you are. That doesn't matter. I love you. I want to marry you."

The wild urge to laugh was almost irresistible in Laura, but instinct told her that to laugh now might be deadly. In a few seconds, she turned from a girl to a mature woman. Although her face and mouth gave him a serene and pleased smile, her eyes were wildly troubled with fear and puzzlement. She said: "Why, Hugh, that's nice. You surprised me. I don't know what to say." She realized suddenly that her hands were trembling and brought them together, clasping them tightly.

Hugh smiled at her reply, and some of the tension within the girl eased. The bad moment seemed to have passed when he murmured: "Don't say anything. Think about it. I'm a damned big bruiser for a little thing like you. But I'd be good to you, Laura. I promise you that."

She forced herself to return his smile. Her mind said: *It will never get that far. I would as soon marry a grizzly bear.* She thought of Will with terrified, wild longing. She had the urge to say: *It will never be you, Hugh, because I love Will.* But she said nothing at all, her newfound maturity sending its warning through all her being. *Whatever you say may be dangerous. So be still, for once.*

Now Hugh turned brisk, Arrow's foreman again. He said: "We'll turn the hay that is already cut this afternoon. The rain ought to be over for a while. Laird's funeral is set for eleven. I'll put one of the boys to shining up the buggy for you, but it won't do much good what with all the mud on the road."

Laura murmured: "Thank you, Hugh." He turned away and tramped across the steaming yard toward the bunkhouse. The question foremost in Laura's mind had never been asked, but it was there, silently demanding an answer. *What are you going to do about Will, Hugh?*

While she was talking with Hugh, she had sensed that there was more to him than the good-natured amiability that appeared on the surface. She sensed, too, that her unasked question had extreme importance, and she began to feel afraid. As always, when her mind was troubled, she lifted her glance to the serene and patient bulk of the mountain, at the rim, streaked with rain, at the slide, steaming in the sunlight below it. No matter how the face of it changed with the seasons, the core and shape of it were always the same.

An odd phenomenon below the rim caught her eye. The whole slide steamed in the sunlight, wisps of the steam rising, opaque and all of one color. Yet where slide met rim another small plume rose, bluer than the mist and suddenly Laura knew, that it was smoke. She murmured: "A cedar struck by lightning and set afire. I had better watch that. It might get worse. . . ."

At ten forty-five, Laura drove the buggy into Cedar Grove. Behind her rode Hugh Leabo, and behind him Arrow's crew, all scrubbed until they shone, and wearing their best, which in some cases was shiny black broadcloth, in others merely clean work clothes.

Laura wore a black brocade gown, its severity unrelieved by any ornament or decoration. Even the lace at her throat was black. She alighted before the small white church, Hugh's great arm steadying her. Leaving her there, he stepped up into the buggy and drove it around to the side of the church.

The people of Cedar Grove came along the shaded walks, stepping carefully to avoid puddles, and nodded or spoke in sympathetic tones to Laura. She was very white, feeling terribly alone, yet she wished to get into the church before Hugh Leabo returned and went in with her. Therefore, when Sheriff Gwinn, whom she liked and trusted, came along the walk, escorting his tiny and aging wife, Laura gratefully attached herself to them.

The old church organ sighed out its mournful tones. Before the altar, on a stand hidden by flowers, was Laird McFetridge's casket, closed and sealed. Suddenly Laura shuddered, the reason for its being closed coming with a shock to her mind. Laird's face had been battered beyond recognition.

Mrs. Gwinn, in the pew beside her, laid a soft hand on her arm. "You poor dear," she murmured, and Laura smiled at her shakily.

Arrow's crew made a stir at the rear of the church, and Laura took advantage of the turned heads and whispered comments to lean close to Gwinn and say: "I have got to talk to you."

"All right. Come to dinner after the services. There will be no one there but you and I and Amy."

Laura was suddenly struck by the expression on his face, seamed and leathery and terribly serious. The thought came to her, almost with violence: *Why I believe you know it, too. You know there is a killer loose on Arrow. And you know it isn't Will. . . .*

Although he had slept but two hours, Silas awoke when the first shaft of sunlight slid down over the rim. Habit, ever strong in Silas, had not for thirty years allowed him to sleep past the coming of daylight. Only the shock, both to body and mind, which he had sustained, had held him in sleep this morning.

Pain reminded him instantly that he was badly hurt, and with a shudder he recalled his fall from the rim. With characteristic self-reliance and independence he set his mind immediately to seeking a way out of his predicament. Food and water were first. Accordingly he crawled from beneath the overhang and drank deeply from the pool of rain water in the wind-scoured rock basin.

He returned to the overhang, collecting a fistful of twigs as he went. Depositing them there, he crawled painfully around until he had collected enough for a small fire. Fortune smiled on him now, for directly in his path, as he returned, he found two dead spruce branches, hardened and cured by sun and weather. The smaller one would make a suitable splint for his arm. The other appeared to be just right for his leg.

Back beneath the overhang, able to use but one hand, he smoothed these two limbs with his knife, carefully collecting the dry shavings. He felt himself tiring, but continued doggedly until he had a fair-size pile of shavings. Upon these he heaped the smallest and driest of the twigs, then added larger ones until he judged he would get a fire in spite of the dampness of the wood.

With considerable difficulty he got a box of matches from his pocket and found one that was dry. He struck this twice against the side of the box before it lighted, and then held it under the pile of twigs. The flame caught at once, and Silas blew upon it gently, keeping it going until the damp twig caught. Smoke raised its thin plume into the air, and the warmth of the fire crept in welcome comfort through Silas's upper body. Satisfied at last, he brought himself up to a sitting position and fumbled one-handed for the slicker-wrapped meat secured to his waist.

All this had taken a terrible toll of strength and will. It would have been so much easier simply to lie back and surrender, die. This would have been the animal way, and there was a good bit of the animal in Silas. Yet, in his solitary nature, there was a spark that would permit no surrender, at least until every resource had been tried. He cut a chunk from the meat, carefully re-wrapped the balance, and laid it behind him. He spitted the horsemeat on one of the sticks and held it into the blaze. Flame licked up around it; smoke blackened it. The smell of it rose, turning Silas ravenous. Without removing it from the stick, he tore at it savagely with his teeth. Afterward, with the fire a pile of pearl gray ashes, he lay back and again dropped off to sleep.

The second time he awoke, he felt immediately stronger. He slid painfully out of his chaps, split them into long strips with his knife, and set about splinting his leg. It took a long time, and his efforts sent pain soaring through his head, turning him almost blind. His entire body was soaked with sweat. Weakness all but overwhelmed him. The splint would do only if he were extremely careful.

Yet he felt a growing satisfaction. He would defeat Leabo yet. He would rest again now, would eat and drink when he awoke. In the afternoon, he would splint the arm as he had splinted the leg. The ribs would have to take care of themselves, but would not be dangerous so long as no violent exertions forced them into the vital organs of his body.

Yet in spite of Silas's optimism, time and lack of proper care were working in favor of Hugh Leabo. Besides his broken bones, Silas was still battling shock and loss of blood. Although he was unaware of this, each time he slept, there was a fifty-fifty chance that he would never awake.

IX

At the close of the funeral service, the mourners filed through the wide double doors of the church. Some of them returned to their homes, while others prepared for the short ride to Cedar Grove's small cemetery. Hugh Leabo drove Arrow's gleaming buggy around to the front to pick up Laura and arrived just in time to see her helped into Gwinn's buckboard by the sheriff.

The sight gave him a feeling of frustration, although he did not know exactly why it should. Perhaps it was the talk he'd had with Laura this morning and the unsatisfying way in which it had ended. Perhaps it was coming off second best with Will Counselman the evening before or his knowledge that Will had no intention of quitting the country. He pulled aside to make way for the buckboard which was to carry Laird's casket to the cemetery and watched while six husky Arrow 'punchers carried the casket from the church and placed it in the back of the buckboard. He fell in behind as it drove away, with the same feeling of irritation increasing in him.

Somehow, he knew, he had to get rid of Will Counselman. The longer Will was around, the more precarious would become Hugh's position. He suspected that something had passed between Will and Laura last night, but this, like all the other vague things that were turning him uneasy, was only surmise. Had Hugh not broken Will out of jail, it might have been easier. But how could you justify a hunt for a killer you yourself had freed? For Hugh to capture or kill Will now would only have the effect of making folks suspicious at his sudden reversal.

The procession wound slowly along Main Street to the narrow stage road that ran across a low knoll and took its twisting, upward course through the cedars. After a mile of this, a small clearing appeared, a clearing dotted with weathered wooden crosses and rude stone head markers. Near the center of this plot yawned a fresh grave, and to this the buckboard was backed. Hugh Leabo drove close and got out, standing at the horse's head and holding the bridle.

Laura stood across the grave from him between Sheriff Gwinn and his wife. Her eyes were downcast and filled with tears, as the black-garbed minister intoned his short service and motioned for the casket to be lowered. Afterward, Arrow's 'punchers rode soberly upcreek, and Hugh Leabo followed Sheriff Gwinn's buggy to the sheriff's house.

His voice went out to Laura as she reached the steps. "I'll wait for you, Laura."

"That won't be necessary, Hugh. Tie this buggy there and go back to Arrow with the crew. You have your haying to do."

Leabo scowled and started to protest but found Gwinn's cold stare upon him. Angrily he tied the buggy horse to the hitching post. He had the odd and ominous feeling that opposition to him was building in Laura, was increasing in Sheriff Gwinn. Perhaps the sheriff was incensed only because Hugh had broken into the jail, yet it could be the beginning of suspicion—of Hugh himself.

Today, quite obviously, Laura would attempt to convince Gwinn that Will was not guilty, would try to persuade him to drop the charge of murder against Will and in this way give Will the opportunity of trying to track down Laird's killer. That she would be entirely successful was doubtful. Yet she might plant a seed of doubt in Gwinn's mind, so that Gwinn would question his immediate and easy indictment of Will. Once he did this, his mind would reach out, searching for other suspects.

Hugh's long strides brought him to the church in a few

minutes, and with nervous hands he untied his horse. He tired to imagine what Laura and Sheriff Gwinn were talking about, he tried to construct their discussion in his mind. Uneasiness returned and grew, and he searched determinedly through his mind for loose ends. Will's protestation of innocence had no basis that Will could prove without Silas to back him up.

Silas! There was a loose end that a careful man could not afford to leave loose. Hugh did not believe that a man could live after a fall from the rim. Yet Silas might have lived long enough to scrawl something in the dirt or on the rotten sandstone of the cliff. With Will Counselman prowling the cedars, it was possible that Will might find Silas's body and whatever Silas might have written.

Hugh's spurs instinctively raked the horse's ribs, and the animal sprang forward. For the first time since he had smashed the singletree against the back of Laird's unsuspecting head, big Hugh Leabo felt the cold finger of fear. Damn it, why couldn't things work out the way a man planned them? He went back over all the things he had done in the last three days, from killing Laird to breaking Will Counselman out of jail. He was forced to admit that he had made no mistakes with the possible exception of assuming that Silas was dead. *All right, damn it,* he thought. *I'll go and make sure of Silas. Then I can quit worrying.* Having settled on a course of action seemed to ease his mind, for he let his horse ease into a trot.

He reached Arrow's gate just behind the crew, and he halted them with a shout. Riding up, he said: "Get your dinner. Then go on up and turn the hay that's already cut. After that, you can knock off for the day."

He watched them ride down the lane, then turned and took the trail that led through the cedars. He could not help recalling Will Counselman's threat. *Stay on Arrow, Hugh. If I see you on the cedars, I'll kill you like I would a wolf.* His head dropped nervously to his gun grips and came foolishly away. Yet his eyes kept swiveling back and forth, and half a dozen times in the next thirty minutes he yanked his gun, only to slide it back again with increasing self-consciousness.

The sky had cleared during the morning. Early afternoon sun beat down upon Hugh's neck and turned the humid air muggy with its heat. The smell of the cedars, of their heated resins, was strong and pleasant in the air.

It was with a definite feeling of relief that Hugh came out of the timber and onto the angling trail that made its upward way across the shale slide. Now at least he could not be ambushed. Far below him he saw the crew file out of the lane with their teams and head toward the patch of hay that lay in brown, uneven windrows across the field that had been cut and raked the day of Laird's death.

He noted with satisfaction that all tracks had been obliterated from the trail by the two-day rain. All that now showed in the soft ground were the tracks of deer, made since the rain had stopped.

At four, he came to the foot of the rim. Here he halted his horse, dismounted, and tied the reins to a clump of scrub brush. Afoot, he began to walk along the base of the rim. He estimated that he had about a mile to go. He was extremely careful to stay on crumbled rock and to avoid the few spots of soft ground as he would a plague.

From a hundred yards away he saw the brown bulk of Silas's horse, and, as he came nearer, a flock of screaming magpies arose from the bloated carcass. In the horse's hip was a bloody hole, made ragged by the beaks of the voracious magpies. Had Hugh not been so nervous, had he not been so anxious to find the body of Silas, he might have noticed the peculiar shape of this hole, might have noticed that the hide was also missing. Yet to his agitated mind, a dead horse was merely a dead horse. Hugh was accustomed to seeing what carnivores did to dead range stock and paid it no heed.

In his search for Silas's body, Hugh noted the clump of scrub oak, the torn and broken branches, the blood on the ground. *Here's where he struck,* he thought. *Now where the hell did he go from here?*

To his experienced eye, disturbed leaves beneath the trees made a plain trail out of the grove, but there the trail halted, for the rain had beaten out all sign. Hugh halted, his puzzled eyes sweeping the slide below him. *He could have gone down there. He could have rolled.* He swung his glance upward, searching for a way up through the rim. Finally he shook his head, thinking: *Hell, I couldn't climb up there myself. And even if Silas wasn't killed, he was sure hurt.*

Irritation began to stir again in Hugh although it still did not occur to him that Silas might be alive. Carefully, exhaustively, he searched each square foot of ground for a ten-yard circle about the grove of scrub oak. At last, entirely satisfied that Silas had left no message, he retraced his steps toward his horse.

He's got to be somewhere down there in the cedars, he mused, *unless he worked his way along the base of the rim.*

This thought halted him. He stared long at the narrow and rocky path that wound its uneven way upcountry at the very base of the rim. *I ought to check on that,* he thought, and he started in that direction only to halt again uncertainly. *It's getting late. I'll look around in the cedars first, and if I don't find him there. . . .*

Considering all the angles of this carefully, he reached the eventual conclusion: *If he didn't write anything on the ground here, it isn't likely he did anywhere else. I've got plenty of time.*

X

Will Counselman slept until late afternoon. He awoke because of a vicious, hammering headache. The side of his head, where Hugh had struck him, was sore and tender, but it was the shocking force of Hugh's fist that had, he knew, caused the headache. He sat up, wincing at the pain in his twisted leg. At once he noticed the warmth of the air, the bright sunlight that sifted down through the screen of willows overhead. He found that he was ravenously hungry, and that, in spite of his headache and the pain in his leg, his spirits were miraculously light.

He thought of Laura and smiled, suddenly anxious for the fall of night so that could see her. He rose and stretched, ruefully rubbing the thick beard stubble on his face. Now that Hugh's antagonism was out in the open, now that he had openly warned and threatened Hugh, Will no longer feared discovery as he had at first. So he turned the mule loose and released his horse to graze, first taking the precaution of haltering the animal and tying one end of his lariat in the halter ring.

He built a small fire and put on some bacon to fry. From the spring he drew water, heated it, and made coffee. He was just downing the last of it, hot and comforting, when he chanced to glance at the slide and saw the unmistakable figure of Hugh Leabo, making his way upward along the trail.

Now where in the hell, Will wondered, *is he going?*

Quickly he kicked sand over his fire and, when this was done, caught his horse. He led the animal into the concealment of the willows and tied him, then returned to the edge of the grove to watch.

At the foot of the rim, he saw Hugh dismount and pick his way along the base of it. So unprecedented was this action that nothing could have pulled Will's eyes away from the big foreman. Like a giant fly in the distance, Hugh's figure moved along until it was directly above Will's camp. Suddenly a screaming cloud of magpies rose, scattering against the sun-washed ocher of the rimrock. Will's brow furrowed. *Something's dead up there. But why is Hugh so damned interested?*

For nearly an hour Hugh poked about, hardly moving from the spot where the magpies had been. Then he retraced his steps to his horse, immediately mounting and taking the downward trail toward the cedars. Will said to himself: *That is something I'm going to have to look at. But first I want to see where Hugh goes.*

He saddled his horse and rode out, avoiding the trails and staying close to the fringe of cedars against the bottom of the slide. He had gone but a short half mile when some instinct brought him off his horse. He hobbled to a break in the timber.

Noiselessly he crouched beneath a twisted deadfall, straining his ears for sound, wondering why Hugh had dismounted here. At that moment he heard the crack of a twig, followed by the sound of a small dislodged rock rolling down the slide. He wondered: *Is he hunting for me or for something else?* Had it not been for the magpies he had seen up by the rim, he would have assumed that he was the object of Leabo's search. Now he was thoroughly puzzled.

He saw Hugh Leabo above him and to his right, slowly and carefully stamping along a path that would lead him within a few short feet of where Will was crouched. Yet even in the face of Hugh's extreme care, there was surprising speed to his movement.

He looked directly at the deadfall and at Will, a brief and fleeting glance. Remembering the strength in Hugh's powerful arms, Will could not help dropping a hand to his gun. It seemed impossible, but apparently Hugh had not seen him, for the foreman moved on with no change of expression.

As he disappeared from sight, Will stood up carefully and stepped into the trail behind him. Leabo was out of sight around a bend of this narrow game trail, and after waiting perhaps a minute Will followed. Coming to the same bend around which Leabo had gone, he crept ahead more cautiously. If Hugh *had* seen him, he might now be waiting in that thick clump of sarvus, waiting to bushwhack him. Will hoped he was not, for he was not yet ready to kill Hugh, even in the face of his growing conviction that Hugh Leabo was Laird's murderer. He had no proof, had discovered no motive, and all that he based his belief upon was Hugh's strange actions and his desire that Will leave the country.

The sun by this time had dropped below the western horizon, and the air had taken on a rather pleasant coolness. Distantly from the valley came the sounds of riders, their shouts and laughter, the jangle of harness on led teams. A breath of wind from below brought the rich smell of freshly turned hay.

Hand on gun, he stepped openly around the bend in the trail, half expecting Hugh's great shout, his lunge from concealment. His nerves let down abruptly, for Hugh was a quarter mile ahead, angling directly toward Will Counselman's camp.

Unready as yet to brace Hugh, or even to let Hugh know he was watching, Will moved along the path as best he could, although with exercise his ankle was definitely better. Where Hugh had dropped lower into the cedars, Will kept to the upper course, finally coming out, a few minutes later, at a knoll that overlooked his camp. Here he crouched behind a short clump of sagebrush and settled himself to watch.

Apparently the lateness of the hour and his own desperation had persuaded Hugh to throw caution to the winds. Will could hear his quartering progress through the cedars, his crashing and panting, his continual cursing. *He's hunting something,* was Will's final conclusion. *And it isn't me.* The answer lay up at the foot of the rim, and Will resolved that, as soon as Hugh had gone, he would climb the slide and see what the answer was. If he had needed final proof that Hugh was for the moment uninterested in himself, he got it now, for Hugh came down into the deep draw, quested through Will's camp, and climbed out of the draw on the other side, where he continued his search.

Well, I'll be damned! Will reflected.

Gradually the sounds of Hugh's searching faded into the distance as the big man worked back and forth closer and closer to the road. The dinner triangle at Arrow was banged insistently, and presently Hugh returned uphill for his horse. In a few moments he was gone.

Wanting to be sure, Will climbed a way up the slide until he could see Arrow's lane far below him. He saw Hugh Leabo ride to the gate, open it, and go through. Still Will waited, knowing that until early dusk came over the land, he would be like a fly on a wall there on the slide, visible to anyone in Arrow's yard.

At last, when he judged it to be safe, he began his long and tortuous climb, testing each foothold before he reached for another. In the last deep-gray light of dusk, Will Counselman reached the narrow level space at the foot of the rim. He smelled the sweet, cloying, and unpleasant odor of the dead horse before he saw the animal, a huge and bloated shape, before him. Steeling himself, Will moved closer to stare down at the horse in the faint and fading light.

Two of the horse's legs were broken and stuck up at grotesque angles. Will mused: *Fell off the rim. Whose?* He dropped to one knee, his hands feeling across the saddle, his eyes straining in the darkness. When he did recognize the animal and the battered rigging, he gave a long, low whistle. *Silas! This was Silas's horse.*

Question followed question in his mind, and the most insistent one—*How did Hugh know he was here?*—was followed by the thought: *Hugh must have pushed him off. Then where is Silas?* It occurred to Will suddenly that the body of Silas was what Hugh had been hunting for so desperately this afternoon. It explained his questing through the cedars after his search here had failed to produce anything, for it was plain that he had figured that Silas had either rolled or crawled to the bottom of the slide. Now the question—*Why Silas?*—occurred, and the answer to that one came immediately: *Because Silas saw me in camp on the mountain at about the time Laird was killed. Hugh found that out when he came up to question Silas. He couldn't allow Silas to alibi me, so he killed him . . . or thought he did . . . by pushing him off the rim.*

To Will occurred the same thought that had earlier occurred to Hugh. It was extremely doubtful that Silas was still alive, yet he might possibly, in his last moments, have scrawled something in the dirt or on the crumbling shale walls of the rim, something that would point the finger at his killer. Will knew Silas pretty well. Silas was a dour and solitary man, long used to living alone and grown very self-sufficient from so doing. He therefore risked discovery from below, and struck a match shielding the flame with his body.

First he examined the saddle and bridle and saw that one bridle rein was gone, cut off with a knife. Excitement stirred in Will. *He was alive,* he thought. *He was alive.* Striking a fresh match, he looked the horse over, finding at once the gaping hole on the horse's hip. Stifling nausea, Will leaned close, at once interested by the odd square shape of the hole. *Magpies have been at it, but magpies don't eat hide. Somebody cut a chunk of meat out of here*. He had definitely established that Silas had not only survived the fall, but had been sufficiently alive to be interested in remaining alive. *Tied the meat to his belt with a bridle rein,* thought Will. *Must have been pretty badly banged up*.

He had gone this far, but he had not yet found Silas. Hugh Leabo apparently had given first consideration to the cedars, and, even though Hugh had searched them, there was still a fair possibility that he had missed Silas in the tangled expanse they covered. There was the other possibility, too, that Silas had not gone down the slide to the cedars, but that instead he had crawled along the base of the rimrock. Will shrugged. *I'll try that,* he mused, and began to pick his way carefully among the scattered rocks that littered the narrow strip of level ground at the head of the slide.

He had covered nearly a quarter mile when he detected a faint odor in the air. For a moment he hesitated, at last recognizing this odor for what it was, charred wood. It was pitch dark on this high promontory now, only a feeble starlight showing him the solid wall at his right, the steep drop-off of the slide on his left. He called softly: "Silas! This is Will Counselman. You there?"

He got no answer and so began again his careful, slow progress. Suddenly a voice halted him, harsh and bitter and thin. "Stand where you are. I'm used to this dark, and I can see pretty good. Take one more step and I'll kill you."

Will was silent a moment, then breathed. "Silas! How bad you hurt? Man, let me come up there. Maybe I can help you."

"Where's Leabo?"

"Down at Arrow. He was up here hunting you all afternoon. I came up to see what he was looking for." He could sense the working of Silas's suspicious mind. He asked: "Why did Hugh try to kill you? Did you see me at camp the day Laird was killed?"

"Nobody ever goes in that cabin but what I see 'em.

"What time was it, Silas?"

"Why, you damn' fool, you know what time it was. It was dinner time."

"You see me after that?"

"I followed you. I seen you kill your buck a couple hours later."

"Did you tell Hugh all that?"

"Sure. Why shouldn't I?"

"That's why he tried to kill you. Hugh was the one that killed Laird. But he wanted me blamed for it. When he found that your story would get me off, he decided to shut you up." He was silent for a long moment, then finally asked: "Silas, how bad you hurt?"

"Leg broke. Arm broke. Ribs broke. Don't worry about me. I can still pull a trigger."

"You done anything for your leg?"

The incredible courage of the man was impressed upon Will when Silas muttered: "Splinted it. The arm, too. Git outta here and leave me alone . . . leastways till Leabo's dead or behind bars. I sleep light. He ain't goin' to git me."

Will searched his mind for something he could do for Silas. Unconsciously he found himself fumbling for his sack of makings. He asked: "How long since you smoked?"

"Seems like a year. You got the makings? Mine got lost in the fall."

Will laughed softly. "Keep a light finger on that trigger. I'll roll you a half dozen or so." He moved forward, came to the dark mouth of the overhang, and saw Silas's dim, reclining form just outside it. Squatting, he swiftly rolled eight or ten cigarettes and placed them on the ground by Silas's hand. He laid his box of matches there, too.

Rising, he murmured: "I hate to leave you."

"Go on. Put that damned killer in jail . . . or put a hole in him. I'll still be here when you get back."

"All right. It won't be long." He stepped off onto the slide and carefully began his descent. Halfway down, he looked back and saw the red tip of Silas's cigarette.

Back in the cedars, he located his horse by the animal's nervous fidgeting and, mounting, set out for Arrow. The end of this was in sight now, and he moved toward it with a strong and nervous excitement.

XI

All through the noon meal at Sheriff Gwinn's, Laura's mind roiled and fretted. When at last the meal was finished, she helped Mrs. Gwinn clear away the dishes, although her help in washing them was firmly rejected. "You're tired," said Amy Gwinn, "and you want to talk with Carl. Go along with you."

So Laura returned to the parlor, settled herself on the worn horsehair sofa, and gazed for some time at the sheriff, not quite knowing how to begin or where.

"Hugh asked me to marry him this morning, Carl," she said at last.

"Fine. Fine. You could do lots worse."

She shook her head, vaguely troubled. "You don't believe in woman's intuition, I suppose?"

He chuckled, shaking his head. "Afraid not. I always figured it was a woman's way of rationalizing her opposition to something when she knew she had already lost the argument."

Laura felt a growing helplessness. She said: "Still, a woman feels things. Perhaps intuition is a poor term. A woman knows when a man wants her, for instance, and I did not feel that in Hugh this morning."

Gwinn stared at her for a moment, then burst out laughing. His glance was frankly admiring. "Be a damned fool if he didn't want you, girl. Be a damned fool. If I was younger and wasn't. . . ." He stopped and shook his head. "You're upset. Your father's death . . . then Will Counselman being accused of it." He became grimly serious. "Get Will out of your mind. Maybe he had a lot of justification for killing Laird and the court will take that into consideration when he's brought to trial. But he did it, Laura. Make no mistake about that."

She shook her head stubbornly. "I don't think he did, Carl. Suppose, for just a minute, that I'm right. Suppose Will is innocent. That means that whoever is guilty is still at Arrow, doesn't it? If it had been a stranger, someone would have seen him. But no strangers were seen."

"What about a motive, Laura? Folks just don't kill without a motive."

Now Laura's own thought frightened her. Her logical mind had been puzzling all day over this. She said: "When Hugh asked me to marry him, Carl, I had the feeling that he would have acted much the same way if he were asking someone to sell him a bunch of cattle. He was cold, business-like." She laughed shakily. "It was no proposal. It was a business proposition."

Gwinn's face again became serious, and his eyes narrowed. "What are you getting at, Laura?"

"I hate to say it. I may be being terribly unfair. But I have thought it, and you are the law, the one who should hear it."

"Get on with it, Laura!" Urgency came into his voice, and rising impatience.

"Suppose Hugh wanted Arrow. Suppose there is more to Hugh than we have suspected. Suppose he has always wanted Arrow. The day Father was killed, Will threatened him. Hugh knew he could never have Arrow with Father alive, so he killed him, well knowing that Will would be blamed for it. Grant that I'm right, Carl, what better way of removing both obstacles to his ownership of Arrow with one easy stroke than by killing Father and seeing to it that Will Counselman was blamed for it?"

"That doesn't give Arrow to Hugh, Laura."

"No, but with both Will and Father gone, Hugh realizes that I will grow to depend on him more and more. I own Arrow now, Carl, and this morning Hugh asked me to marry him. He showed no sentiment at all. I had the notion that he felt none. He acted just as a man would act if he wanted to marry me for Arrow instead of for myself."

Gwinn stood up, walked to the window, and stared moodily out. Laura watched him expectantly. After a long while, he turned. "Damn it, Laura, you're imagining things. Hugh has been at Arrow over ten years. Laird trusted him." He shook his head ponderously. "It's too farfetched."

Laura shrugged wearily. "No, it isn't too farfetched. It isn't farfetched at all."

She had a sudden, bleak feeling that she was utterly alone, and fright stirred in her. Gwinn came toward her, and she stood up tiredly, knowing that she had lost, that she had failed even to plant doubt in the sheriff's mind.

He put an arm across her drooping shoulders, saying: "You ought to go over to Denver for a while. Let Hugh run things. Stay a month or two. I'll bet that when you come back, you'll see things differently."

For an instant she debated telling the sheriff that Will Counselman thought, as she did, that someone on Arrow was the killer, although even Will had not yet settled on Hugh. She hesitated, finally deciding against this, for while Gwinn was a friend, he was also the sheriff of McFetridge County and, if he knew that Will was still in the country, would feel obliged to get out a posse after him.

Laura said: "Get my hat, Carl. I have to be getting back."

Gwinn gave her a quizzical look. "Mad at me, Laura?"

Laura's smile was wan. "No. Perhaps you are right, Carl. Perhaps I am imagining things."

She settled her hat on her head. Amy Gwinn came from the kitchen, asking with a reproachful glance at Carl: "What has he been telling you? You poor dear, he's got you all upset!"

Gwinn flushed. "I only. . . ."

Laura said: "It's nothing, Missus Gwinn. Thank you so much for the dinner. It was lovely." She took the frail hand of the sheriff's wife, trying to down the frantic uneasiness that stirred in her at the thought of leaving this safe and restful haven, of going back to Arrow and to Hugh, so big, so impersonal and strange. She thought, too, of Laird, who was gone now, whom she would never see again, and at last she thought of Will, harassed and falsely accused, yet so courageous in the face of his troubles.

Gwinn and his wife walked with her to the street, and the sheriff handed her up to the buggy seat and untied the horse. Laura waved and turned the horse, then drove out of town along the road to Arrow.

Late afternoon sun made a brassy, hot light against the land, yet long before she reached the gate at Arrow, it had sunk behind the rim of the plateau. Always Laura's favorite time of day had been this short while between sunset and dark, but tonight there was enjoyment in nothing for her. She feared to face Hugh Leabo; she dreaded returning to the big and empty house. She dreaded it until she thought of Will Counselman, of his promise to return tonight. Yet even this lift of excitement was killed as she thought: *If I am right about Hugh, then Will is in terrible danger, and I have no way of warning him, for I don't now where he is.*

XII

In the cedars, half a mile above the house at Arrow, Will Counselman tied his horse. In utter darkness, he made his way to the road, thence through the fence into the high green alfalfa. It came nearly to his chest, and the blooms of it were pleasantly fragrant, but the thickness of it caught at his feet. A dozen times he stumbled and nearly fell. Nearing the house, he slowed, silently stalking closer.

Since leaving Silas, Will had puzzled to find the motive Hugh must have had for killing Laird, and battering him afterward so that the finger of suspicion would point directly at Will. He concluded that either Laird had secured some knowledge of Hugh's past and confronted him with it, or, worse, that Hugh wanted Arrow and expected to get it by killing Laird and making Will a fugitive. Either way, Hugh was as dangerous as a coiled rattler. Having committed one murder and attempted a second, he would hesitate not at all over a third. Most likely, tonight he would post guards about the yard at Arrow, hoping to trap Will if he came again to see Laura.

As Will drew closer to the house, a light came on in the big front window. It cast its glow on the long verandah, and Will saw Hugh's huge figure squatted on the steps. He breathed: *I was right. He's waiting for me.*

Cautiously questing back and forth, he discovered two more guards, placed their positions unforgettably in his mind. One of them stood at the fence, just around the corner of the house and out of sight of Hugh Leabo. The other stood motionless at the rear wall of the house. Will thought irritably: *Damn it, I wonder where the dogs are. All it'd take would be one bark, or even a growl, and they'd all be after me.*

For a long while he hesitated here, remembering the dogs and the added hazard they presented. Then finally, shrugging fatalistically, he dropped down in the alfalfa and began to creep toward the rear corner of the house. Ten feet from the house, he raised his head as the bored guard grumbled sourly: "Hell, what damn' difference does it make whether Will sees Laura or not?" Will recognized the voice of Chip Morris, a lanky, slouching 'puncher who had been at Arrow less than a year. Chip had always been friendly toward Will, yet Will knew the man would cry out if he spoke to him.

So he waited until Chip's back was turned, and then came out of the alfalfa in a rush, gun lifted. Too late, Chip whirled. He opened his mouth to cry out, but at that exact instant the barrel of Will's gun descended, making an audible crack as it collided with Chip's skull. The man slumped in the weeds, even this making its plain and easily recognizable noise.

The other guard called softly: "Chip! What the hell you doing?"

Will realized instantly that failure to answer would invite a certain investigation. He feigned a yawn, put a hand over his mouth, and answered softly: "Hell, I'm asleep. Can't a man sit down?"

The other, seemingly unsuspicious, murmured—"Just don't let Hugh catch you."—and Will released a pent-up breath. He glanced about, trying to penetrate the darkness with his eyes. A man, he realized, could be seen in this blackness at a distance of six feet, no more. He briefly considered a bold and open approach to the back door of the house. In all likelihood there were two guards at the back door, and, even if there were not, the door never opened without a loud squeak.

Yet to Will this house and its immediate environs were vastly more familiar than they were to Hugh or to any of the 'punchers guarding it. This familiarity gave Will a slight advantage. Creeping cautiously forward, he came to the kitchen window and, remembering previous occasions when he had forced it open, could not help a wry, reminiscent smile. Directly before this window on the inside stood a table, and upon this table the cook always placed pies to cool. Will had learned at the age of twelve how to open the window from the outside by using a nail as a pry, had learned how to hold it tightly against one side of the casing to keep it from squeaking as it raised.

He fumbled anxiously between two logs at the side of the window where the chinking had fallen out, breathing with relief as he found the nail. It was rusty and bent, but it was the same nail he had used for this purpose years ago. His actions now had all the old remembered familiarity. The nail went into a hole between the bottom of the window and the casing, and a very slight pressure opened a crack there. A new grip with the nail widened this enough for Will to insert the tips of his fingers. A moment later, the window was open.

Will stooped and took off his boots and placed them carefully inside on the table top. Then, finding easy holds on the logs with his toes, he climbed in. The table creaked under his weight, but in a moment he had his feet on the floor and was putting on his boots.

Time began to bother him. Chip might conceivably groan or come to at any moment. Will knew he would have to hurry.

He stepped softly across the kitchen and pushed open the door enough to peer inside. A lighted lamp stood on a table directly before the window. A low fire glowed in the fireplace, casting far more light into the room than did the lamp. Laura's head was visible above the back of the sofa.

Will opened the door, put his full weight upon the squeaking board at the entrance to the dining room. This brought Laura's head around as he had known it would, yet the terror in her eyes before she recognized him there came as a tremendous surprise to Will. Immediately she turned back to the fire. She raised her arms, stretched, and got slowly to her feet. For a moment she peered into the flames, then she turned and came indolently toward the kitchen.

Will moved back, yet he left the door open enough for her to come through. A sound from outside froze him. He listened intently for a moment but heard nothing further.

Then Laura came through the door and into his arms with a soft flurry of sound and a softly whispered: "Will! Will darling, I've been so frightened. How did you get in? Hugh has guards all around the house."

"I know. I slugged one of them."

Allowing himself the luxury of one kiss, he then held her away, saying swiftly: "Laura, Hugh is the killer. When he came back to replace that lame horse, he killed Laird. Something got him to worrying about Silas, so he went up on top to question him. Silas saw me, Laura. He saw me in camp at noon, and he saw me kill the deer at about two. Hugh must have told Silas he was needed down here to clear me, but when he got Silas to the rim, he pushed him off."

"Is Silas dead?" Horror was in her voice, in the tight clutch of her hands.

"Not yet. He crawled along the foot of the rim until he found a sort of cave. He needs help, but he ought to live. He's got a broken arm and leg and some broken ribs. He's been living on horse meat."

"What are you going to do? Will, don't tackle Hugh alone. Please don't!"

"No. I won't do that. The whole crew would be against me, and Hugh would tag me with a bullet before I got a chance to explain. I'm going to Cedar Grove for Gwinn. Be careful, Laura. Hugh's dangerous, even for you. I think he wants Arrow, that's why he's done all this."

"Oh, Will, I know it is. Hugh asked me to marry him this morning, but it was so impersonal, it frightened me." She was briefly silent, then asked: "What will Hugh do now?"

"Nothing if I am lucky enough to get away. He failed to find Silas by daylight. It isn't likely he'll try at night." He squeezed her shoulders. "Stay here. Go to bed. I'll be back as soon as I can."

Again he heard a faint noise from the direction of the open window. Releasing Laura, he stepped that way, making but little sound on the smooth floor. Carefully lifting the table to one side, he put his head outside.

Utter darkness met his eyes. Nothing moved. Not a sound broke the silence. Feeling Laura's presence beside him, he whispered: "Where're the dogs?"

"Hugh locked them up in the bunkhouse. They were barking at his guards, and I guess he was afraid all that commotion would scare you off."

Will gave her a light kiss. "This will be over tomorrow." He eased himself through the window, silently lowered himself, and dropped to the ground. For a moment he stood still, listening, letting the feel of the night and the place seep into him, awaiting that nerve warning that would tell him his presence was known.

Satisfied at last, he raised his glance to the window. He

saw the blur of Laura's white face, and then he was moving carefully along the wall of the house. Once his holstered gun brushed the logs, and however slight it sounded like a racket in the surrounding quiet.

Reaching the corner of the house, where he had jumped Chip Morris, he stepped carefully, for he knew Chip must soon be stirring and that the touch of his foot against Chip's body might well be enough to bring the lanky 'puncher to his feet, shouting, ready to fight. Without encountering Chip, he passed the corner of the house and went beyond. Suddenly a chill of warning stiffened the hair on the back of his neck and traveled eerily down his spine. Chip was gone!

For an instant, Will Counselman stood frozen to the spot. Then panic struck him with its urge to run, to shout, to draw his gun and blaze away at the first thing that moved. He fought it down and began to consider the implications of Chip's disappearance. He recalled the two slight noises he had heard when he was in the kitchen. One of them must have been Chip coming to. The other . . . ?

Yet Will realized that if another of the guards had found Chip, Hugh Leabo would surely have been notified and would by now have seized him or killed him. He breathed a slow sigh of relief, thinking: *Hell, Chip came to and got up. He staggered a few feet and collapsed again. He's probably lying around here somewhere, but I haven't got the time to look for him now.*

Thinking thus, he eased himself into the alfalfa field, forcing himself to be cautious when his every inclination was to run, for time was getting short. Slowly creeping, he covered the first fifty yards, then stood up to look around. The glow of the lamp in the window still shone on the ground before the house, but the hulking shape of Hugh Leabo was gone from the steps. So was the shape of the other guard gone from the corner of the house. *Probably got tired and sat down. Hugh's likely prowling up and down the lane between the house and the road.*

Knowing that time was precious, Will managed to put his uneasiness from his mind and began to walk briskly through the hayfield. At the road, he climbed through the fence and began to run. Reaching his horse, he swung to the saddle, circled through the cedars until he had left Arrow's gate behind, then dropped down to the road, and put his horse into a gallop.

Considering all that had happened, all that might yet happen, he became aware of how precarious his situation still was. In Cedar Grove, he would have to convince the sheriff that Silas could clear him. He had to convince Gwinn that Hugh, big, dependable Hugh Leabo, was a scheming, dangerous killer. The hour would be late, and Gwinn reluctant to roust the townsmen out of their beds to form a posse. Yet tomorrow might be too late. Silas was seriously hurt, and, while he probably would not die, it was within the realm of possibility.

Riding hard, Will realized that he still walked a thin, tight rope, for tonight any of a dozen small things could ruin him entirely. Try as he would, he could not rid himself of the depression that dragged his spirits, nor could he banish a strong feeling of foreboding, a semi-awareness that he had missed some vital link to the chain of circumstances that he hoped would clear his name before morning.

XIII

After Will's tall form faded into the dark at the rear of the house, Laura peered intently after him. She could see nothing further, nor could she hear the slightest sound. For ten minutes she waited tensely, then with a sigh of relief returned to the softly lighted living room. She had heard no scuffle, no shout, no shots, and so she assumed Will had got clear.

Now her thoughts went back over the past few days and inevitably came to Silas who, next to Laird, had suffered most from what had happened since Laird's death. She thought of him lying up under the rim, cold, racked with pain, eating raw and rancid horse meat. She knew Silas's dour, solitary nature well, yet she recalled many times when he had been kind and gentle to her, recalled the obvious liking he had shown her, especially when she had been a child. It took her but a few short moments to decide what she must do. Silas was Will's only hope, his one chance of proving that he was innocent of Laird McFetridge's murder. Through no fault of his own he was now suffering and untended.

Laura made her decision impetuously, out of pity for Silas, although she realized, too, that by helping Silas she might well be helping herself and Will. She would get Silas's story straight from his own lips. Then, if the man should die, she could pass his story on to Gwinn. Swiftly she went to the kitchen, assembled biscuits, cold meat, canned peaches. These she wrapped hastily in a flour sack and, snatching her jacket, stepped out the back door.

On the stoop, she paused. Hearing nothing, seeing nothing, she stepped away from the house, followed a path she knew well, even in darkness, to the corral, to the huge barn beside it. She was puzzled, troubled, because the guards apparently had been withdrawn from the house, and Hugh Leabo was nowhere to be seen. From the bunkhouse windows the soft glow of lamplight showed, and from an open bunkhouse window came a murmur of talk and an occasional ribald shout.

Why should Hugh have withdrawn his guards unless he knew that Will had come and gone? If Hugh had found out that Will was in the house with Laura, why had he not seized him when he had left? There seemed to be no explaining Hugh's abrupt about-face.

Laura got her saddle from the barn, caught her horse from the corral, saddled him, then tied her bundle of food on behind. Mounting easily, she rode out of the yard, careful to make no unnecessary noise, and a few minutes later began to climb through the cedars toward the rim. Not overly familiar with the trail, she allowed the horse to choose his own way, confident that he would not get lost.

About her, the gnarled and twisted trunks of the cedars made grotesque and arresting patterns in the faint starlight. Thinking of Hugh, Laura realized that a man, a score of men, could conceal themselves a dozen feet from the trail and be unseen by her as she rode by. She wondered where Hugh was, why he had disappeared so suddenly and completely from Arrow. A disquieting thought occurred to her. *He might have seen Will come in! He might have listened at the window! He might be up there stalking Silas right now!*

As if to give point to the thought, suddenly from above, from the rimrock, came a single shot. Back and forth from rim to rim it echoed until its sharpness diminished, and was finally lost in the thick blanket of night's silence. Laura shuddered, but she did not turn back. Instead, she drummed her small heels against the horse's side, forcing him into a trot.

There was not much hope in Laura that the shot she had heard had not killed Silas. Yet if it had not, she knew what she had to do. She would find Silas, and Hugh, sure that in her presence Hugh would fear to commit a murder. She did not stop to consider that nothing on earth is quite so dangerous as a trapped murderer. She did not stop to think that the penalty for three murders is the same as the penalty for two. She could only think that, if Silas died, then Will was lost.

A faint shout, blurred and indistinct, rolled down the slide toward her, and yet another shot sounded, different in timbre from the first. Impatiently her heels drummed a frantic tattoo on the horse's ribs, and he plunged in great long jumps up the steep trail.

Not two miles from Arrow, Will Counselman heard the faint report and instantly yanked his horse to a halt. He held himself utterly still for a long moment, fretting at his horse's nervous movement, trying to place the exact location of the shot. In this country, a single shot, coming unexpectedly and echoing from all quarters, was difficult to place. It could come from the yard at Arrow; it could have come from the top of the plateau. Will realized, too, that it might not have been a shot at all but some other sharp noise which distance and his own uneasiness had made to sound like the report of a gun.

He was just easing up on the reins preparatory to riding ahead, when a second shot shattered the silence. This time, with his ear attuned to the silence, it was unmistakable as was its location. Instinct made him yank the horse around and dig his spurs into the horse's side. With a frightened leap, the wary horse plunged back toward Arrow.

Will turned bitter with self-condemnation. *Hugh found Chip and dragged him out of the way,* he told himself. *Then he came and listened at the kitchen window. He heard me tell Laura about Silas. He pulled off his guards and hightailed it alone for the rimrock. He's up there now, and Silas is probably dead.*

He considered this for a moment, his face taut from strain, his eyes narrowed and hard. He had to accept the likelihood of Silas's death, yet he realized that, if he could catch Hugh Leabo coming off the mountain trail, he might still have some chance of convincing the sheriff that Hugh had killed Silas to silence him. On ground not yet dried from the rain of yesterday, Hugh's tracks would be plain, proof enough that he had killed Silas. Even the sheriff would have to admit that Hugh would have killed Silas for but one reason—to silence him, to keep Will's alibi from being heard.

Accordingly Will forced his horse the more until he reached the foot of the trail where it led upward into the cedars. Here he paused, giving the horse time for a brief blow, while he himself dismounted to check what he already knew. In the light of a match he found the tracks made by Hugh in ascending the descending the trail earlier today. Overlaying these he found tracks of the same horse, much fresher, looking as though the horse had been pushed onto the trail at a run. Another set of tracks, overlaying Hugh's latest, and smaller, puzzled him for a moment, until he recognized the small shoes which Laird had purchased for Laura's undersize horse.

Rising, he stepped swiftly into his saddle. Cold dread made his hands tremble, and his thoughts cried out: *Laura! Damn it, why didn't you stay at Arrow? Hugh would think no more of killing you than he would of killing Silas. I wish to God I had a fresh horse.*

He alternately spurred and rested his horse. Nothing but silence from above greeted Will's straining ears. As he traveled, a huge rage was building in him and a carefulness that would admit of no mistakes this time. Hugh might have killed Silas. He might have killed Laird. But he would never kill again. Will Counselman would see to that.

No further sound had come from above. Will reached the bottom of the slide and paused, searching the light gray of this bare expanse for the darker blob which would be Hugh descending. Absently he drew his gun and checked its loads.

Afterward, he seated it loosely in the holster and started his horse upward across the slide.

The farther he traveled, hope began to build in him. Perhaps Hugh had been unsuccessful in his attempt to kill Silas, for with Silas dead, with Laura removed, there would be nothing further to hold Hugh up here. He would get off the trail, return to Arrow in the shortest possible time, would send for Gwinn and undoubtedly claim that Will Counselman had done the killing. He might even round up a posse of Arrow riders and come after Will himself. Turned wildly anxious by this new hope, Will crowded the worn-out horse, even while calculating carefully the animal's ability to make the top of the trail before he dropped.

A great silence now lay over this weird land of monstrous high rim, of deeply yawning cañon. The scrambling sounds of Will's horse and the animal's labored breathing were the only sounds, and even the breeze was stilled. There was no light save that of the stars, which made a dim, cold glow, showing nothing distinctly, revealing only slight contrasts of color and shape.

He came to the top of the slide, to the place where the trail snaked across the flat face of rimrock, and halted, becoming instantly aware that there were other horses here. He swung down at once and went forward afoot. His eyes picked out the dark shape of Leabo's horse and, beside it, the smaller lighter shape of Laura's. Giving the animals no more thought, he moved cautiously along the foot of the rim toward Silas's shallow cave.

It was impossible to walk in this crumbled shale without making noise, yet he knew that, if he removed his boots, his feet would be cut to ribbons. His eyes began to ache from the strain of trying to see in this darkness, and he grew ever more nervous, more jumpy.

Behind each jutting, uneven face in the rim he could imagine the hulking shape of Leabo, waiting, gun drawn. *Oh, God! Where's Laura? Where is she?* He forced from himself an increasing caution as he proceeded, for now all depended on him alone.

This was a blind alley of progression, and at its end lay the showdown with Hugh. There was no escape, not up the face of the rim or down the slide, for its lighter color would instantly show anything that crossed it.

Abruptly, its conversational tone making it even more startling, came Hugh Leabo's deep voice. "Stop right there, Counselman. I've got Laura here, and I'm waiting for Silas to poke his head out of that hole."

XIV

Will halted, eased himself flat against the rimrock, back to it, gun pointing in the direction of Hugh's voice. He was certain that his voice would bring Hugh's fire, yet he had to ask: "Are you all right, Laura?"

Not waiting for her answer, he dropped prone on the ground. As he had expected, flame laced from the darkness ahead, and a bullet, striking rock, whined off into the darkness like an angry bee. In the flash, Will had seen Hugh, towering and implacable, had seen the slight form of Laura held against him by the grip of his great left arm. She cried—"Go back!"—and Hugh laughed deeply.

He seemed to be enjoying himself and his mastery over the situation immensely. He said: "I've got her right up against me, Will, and it's too dark for accurate shooting. So all I've got to do is wait, isn't it? I can shoot at you, but you can't shoot back. Silas discovered the same thing, and he's trying to figure a way around it." He laughed again. "There ain't no way around it."

Will thought: *The hell there isn't!* Aloud he asked: "You killed Laird, didn't you, Hugh?"

His words brought another shot from Hugh, closer this time, for Hugh must have guessed that Will would be down on the ground. The slug showered Will's face with rock splinters, and he could feel blood oozing down his face. Inwardly he counted: *Two.*

Hugh chuckled: "Sure I killed him."

Will sensed, from the scuffling sounds, the struggle Laura was putting up against the iron of Hugh's encircling arm. Her heels must have stung the big man's shins, for he growled irritably—"Hold still, damn you!"—and cuffed her, apparently with the heel of the hand that held the gun, for the sound was flat and dull. Hugh rumbled on: "I killed him, and I shoved Silas off the rim. But the damned fool didn't die, so now . . . I'll have to shoot him."

Will backed silently off, then stepped to the very outside of the narrow level space that extended to the rim. Risky this, but it was the only way. He said: "You'll have to shoot me, too, and Laura. How will you alibi that?"

Utterly still he waited. From Hugh's gun blossomed bright orange like the darting tongue of a snake. The first bullet plowed a furrow at Will's feet, but the second hit his shoulder and spun him half around. Will's gun dropped from his nerveless fingers. Nausea welled up in him, making him groggy and weak. He swayed, yet he was able to count: *Three, four.*

Laura screamed frantically: "Will! Will, stop it! Stop it! Be still!"

Will thought: *One more.* He could feel a wetness—blood—on his right arm. And the cool stickiness of it. The shoulder itself was numb, giving him no particular pain but turning him weak and sick. Carefully he stooped and retrieved his gun with his left hand. *Can't shoot so good with the left,* he mused, *but I won't be shooting, anyway.*

He made a couple of imaginary passes in the air with the gun barrel, not entirely satisfied with this. Finally, recalling how ineffective the gun barrel had been before on Hugh's thick skull, he reversed the gun so that he was holding it with the heavy butt foremost.

Silas must have perceived Will's strategy, for he took up the load himself. He called from the mouth of the overhang: "Turn around, Hugh. I've got you skylined."

Will tensed, gathered his muscles. He could hear the faint flurry of motion as Hugh whirled, could hear the frantic struggling of Laura as she sought to throw the foreman's aim off.

The racket of Hugh's and Silas's shots nearly blended, and, before the sound had died away, Will was moving, praying as he did that neither some obstacle nor his increasing weakness would bring him down.

His strategy had been simple. It had occurred to him that with Laura in one arm and his gun in the other hand, Hugh would think it extremely difficult, if not impossible, to reload. He had, therefore, deliberately drawn the foreman's fire, had counted the shots, and knew now that Hugh's gun was empty. Yet, feeling his increasing weakness, he became aware that it might be too late. Hugh, powerful as a wild stallion, unscrupulous as a weasel, was dangerous, vicious, not easily overcome.

Apparently realizing how he had been tricked, Hugh suddenly whirled, saw Will's body coming toward him. With a savage heave, Hugh tossed Laura from him, and she fell heavily against the rock wall of the rim. Not only did this further enrage Will, but it left Hugh without the protection from gunfire that Laura's body had afforded him.

With the intent firmly in his mind to batter Hugh with the gun butt, Will, dazed from the shoulder wound, was slow to grasp the changed situation. He should have reversed the gun then and shot Hugh. He realized this too late, even as he brought the weapon down, clumsily, left handedly, against the foreman's skull. Leabo's huge hands closed over him like savage vises. Will's gun struck only a glancing blow, for Hugh had moved his head.

Dimly he heard Laura's scream, tortured and hurt. Dimly he heard Silas shout—"Mebbe I'll git you, too, Will, but if I don't, he will."—and the roar of Silas's old cap-and-ball revolver. He felt Hugh shudder when the slug struck him, felt its grazing pain against his own side.

Hugh's grip relaxed for a brief instant, and Will took full advantage of it to bring a knee upward into Hugh's belly, throwing all his strength into the maneuver. He plunged backward, toward the slide, caught himself as he teetered on its edge. Hugh pulled back his arm, then brought it forward to fling his empty gun furiously at Will's head. In the thick, enveloping darkness, Will did not see it until it was right before his eyes. There was no time to duck, no time to hold up a defensive hand. Yet he did instinctively jerk his head to one side, and so did not receive the full impact of the heavy weapon.

Lights whirled before his vision. He was driven back onto the steep angle of the slide and felt himself stumble, fall, and begin to roll. Without thought, he flung out arms and legs, and after a moment came to a stop against a jutting rock.

Time. Time. Damn it, in the time it would take him to regain the top, Hugh could reload. Will was surprised to discover that he was still clinging to his gun. Reversing it, he began to crawl. The numbness had gone from his arm, and pain swept over him in waves. But finding that he could use the wounded arm, he began to claw upward frantically.

Again he heard the roar of Silas's old revolver, and then Hugh's steady cursing. Just as he reached the top, he heard Silas's gun blast again. Not for reasons of chivalry or code but because he feared for Silas's life, Will called: "Hugh!" The big man's abrupt motion gave him his target instantly, and, steadying his elbow on the ground, Will put the muzzle dead center on Hugh, and fired.

For the briefest fraction of time, Hugh stood motionless above him. Then, going like a toppled boulder, he went over the edge of the slide and rolled end over end down the rough incline.

Will murmured weakly: "You all right, Laura?"

"Oh, Will! Will!" She came to him on hands and knees and helped him up over the edge onto level ground. She felt the blood on his arm and fell silent with fear.

Silas crawled toward them, grunting with pain. He asked sourly: "Now who, amongst all these cripples, is goin' to ride for help?"

Suddenly, from the trail below, he heard a shout and, glancing that way, saw the flickering, dancing light of a lantern. Arrow's crew, a dozen strong, drawn by the shooting, filed up the tortuous trail, halted their horses, and dismounted. They came along the foot of the rim, their shouts raising weird echoes.

Pride brought Will weakly to his feet, and he drew Laura close against him, even now stirred by her warmth and softness. He drew Laura's head around, looked down into the pale, gentle blur of her face for a moment, then lowered his mouth hungrily.

Blood on the Grass

I

One minute you were out on the grass, lulled by the strange hypnosis of its waving infinity. The next you were in Arapahoe, and the train was slowing through the untidy collection of shacks on the outskirts. There was the bustle of nervous activity as the passengers readied themselves for this short and welcome stop. A child with a dirty face and wet bottom began crying at being awakened.

Barton Pruitt stood up, tall and still-faced with his own unsettled nervousness at homecoming, and hefted his sacked saddle and war bag from the seat behind him. As the train ground to a halt, he made his lurching way down the narrow aisle.

On the platform, shaded by cottonwoods, were half a dozen people, a freckle-faced kid, and a dog that scratched with vicious concentration at a spot behind one ear. Bart tossed the war bag down and, holding on with one hand, swung down himself, dropping the saddle then atop the dirty canvas war bag. He saw Felix Chavalas, leg-spraddled and idle beside the station door, and thought: *Let's get this over with, then there will be time for other things.*

Felix had seen Bart. His glance held no surprise, but it showed the man's hostility. Felix was a small man, with the skin-smoothness characteristic of his race, and deeply tanned. His hair, eyebrows, and mustache were snowy white in sharp contrast to the darkness of his skin. He was nearing sixty, but looked no more than forty. He was the law in Arapahoe, and he needed no badge. The low-slung, walnut-handled Colt and his reputation were enough, here on the grass. Bart Pruitt had wondered if Felix would connect the green, scared fifteen-year-old kid of eight years before with the man, hardened by fist and spur and gun, who stood before him now.

Felix said: "Eight years. A man's hate cools in eight years unless he keeps it alive. Get back on the train, Pruitt." His bright, dark eyes flicked like a whip over Bart's solid shape, from wide-brimmed hat to scuffed and dusty boots. They lingered on the holstered gun, the worn and polished grips, the stiff, oiled, quick-draw holster.

Bart smiled lazily, staring unflinchingly at Felix Chavalas. "I've got a ranch out on the grass, Felix. I'm here to stay. And that's in spite of anyone or anything."

Weary resignation touched the sheriff's face, a sort of disgusted acceptance of an unpleasant fact. His bony shoulders lifted as he pushed away from the station wall. "The Spur is too big for you to fight. It was too big for your pa, and it's too big for you."

Bart smiled again, with steady certainty. "I'll break the Spur, Felix. When I'm done, they'll have their forty quarter-sections along the Platte and nothing else. They're through controlling a hundred square miles of grass because they control the water. For five years I've been buying claims. I own twenty sections of the grass the Spur is using. I mean to have it, and I mean to use it."

Worthless claims, known by every sane man in the country to be worthless. Barton Pruitt had bought them for five or ten cents an acre from owners pleased to realize anything at all from them. Buying them had been a gesture, simple defiance of the Spur, the huge ranch that had killed his father and driven his mother and himself off the grass. He had not known until a month ago of the thing that would make those acres profitable. Now he held knowledge that would make him rich, and break the Spur.

A trainman picked up the step and mounted to the coach. Hanging from its side, he waved a slow arm, and the train whistled. Felix Chavalas shifted, saying again patiently: "Get on the train, Pruitt."

There was sleepy somnolence in this mid-afternoon scene. The child who had cried in the coach pressed his nose against the windowpane as the coach began to move, and his hands, sticky with candy, made smudges on the glass.

Bart shook his head. "No. I'm here to stay."

Half faced away from Felix Chavalas, he caught the blur of the man's movement only from the corner of his eye. He swung around, recalling that Felix Chavalas did not always stand on the letter of the law in its enforcement. The smooth, fast gun came out of the sheriff's holster, and raised and descended against Bart's skull with the effectiveness of a cleaver. Felix caught him as he fell, slammed him against the station wall, and held him there.

His voice scarcely raised as he called: "Alvie! Chuck! Give me a hand here."

Two loungers detached themselves from the wall, their deliberate slowness of movement asserting their independence of this man's orders. Between them they carried Bart across the platform and tossed him, like a sack of grain, onto the steps of the slowly moving coach.

Felix threw up the war bag and saddle. He stepped back then and watched the train gain speed and roll toward the distant, ragged mist of mountains. But as he turned away, inside him was the uneasy feeling that he had only postponed trouble. Barton Pruitt would come back and be killed by a Spur bullet just as his father had been. But he would stir up one hell of a lot of trouble before he was. . . .

Night, on the grass, changed the land, softening the cruel endlessness of its distances, bringing to man and beast a privacy they did not enjoy under the glaring sun. Night was a bowl of star-studded blackness. The small creatures on the plain came out, and Barton Pruitt could hear their stirrings and chirpings as he rode across the grass toward Arapahoe. His head was a bursting, swelling ache, and every plodding step of his horse put dazzling, flashing lights before his eyes. Common sense told him to bed on the grass for tonight and go into Arapahoe in the morning with the freshness he would need. Stubbornness forced him on, a desire to be in Arapahoe at the crack of dawn when Felix Chavalas made his first patrol along the Platte.

Bart held no particular resentment against Felix. Felix was the Spur's sheriff, beholden to the big outfit for the votes that kept him in office. Yet Felix was an honest sheriff, and a good sheriff within the limitations placed upon him by the Spur. He would accede to the Spur in small things, for he was a man with sense and judgment. In the larger, important things, Felix Chavalas was his own man, tough and able and without fear.

Before dawn Bart reached the place where Henry Pruitt had brought his wife and boy ten years before. Time had played havoc with the house. There was little left of it, and it had been nothing much to begin with. Only a home. Only the promise of a future when the small success of a man with the land would make living easier and more secure. There were things here that a man could dredge from his memories as a boy—impressions mostly. He could remember the feel of the sun in his face and the grass at his back, the summer's rain and winter's bitter wind. He could recall the men tall in the saddle who rode occasionally past on the Spur's wide-spread business. He could recall the school in Arapahoe, marbles on the school grounds, and the first time he had looked at a girl and thought she was pretty. Even thought of the rolling, squalling, gouging fights with other boys brought a reminiscent smile to his somber lips.

Hate had come later. Hate had replaced bewilderment when he had come upon his mother weeping for Henry Pruitt, whose death had stilled the laughter in her as quickly as a breath of air will still the leaping flame of a candle. Hate fed the boy until he was eighteen. With Molly Pruitt in her grave a year it began to diminish. Now Barton Pruitt had cast off corrosive hatred, but Felix Chavalas was remembering only the boyish, bitter, and sob-wracked threat of eight years before: "I'll kill him! I'll kill Jess Spurlock for killing Pa! I ain't big enough now, but I'll get big enough! I'll get big enough!"

Shrugging gently, Bart twitched his reins, and the horse moved out, away from this scene of gray ruin in the direction of town. To Bart, revenge was a destructive desire, and could hurt the man who sought it more than the one upon whom it was visited. Retaliation expressed more closely Bart's need, for retaliation was the striking back of a live and active man when he had been injured.

Yet even retaliation became unimportant before the larger purpose that was deeply ingrained in this boy grown up. The grass was important, and the people who sought to settle and use it. Barton Pruitt meant to prove it had its use entirely independent of the river that the Spur controlled.

Dawn on the plain began with the faintest of deep gray

hovering like smoke above the eastern horizon. Gradually this would widen and spread, until it showed the endlessness of the rolling, waving grass. Pink came to the clouds, coloring the land with delicate pastel warmth.

As Bart put his horse into the long slope toward the Platte, a bunched group of antelope on a nearby knoll watched him intently. He came into Platte Street as Felix Chavalas stepped from his door and started his leisurely morning inspection walk.

That walk was a habit, the liking of a man who sees much of life's seaminess for the clean freshness of early morning. In this sudden understanding of Chavalas there came to Bart an unwelcome feeling of kinship that he fought, because it would weaken him in his approaching showdown with the man.

Like a wary gamecock, Felix Chavalas came down the street. Bart approached and turned his horse to present his gun hand to the sheriff. He murmured: "My head aches, Felix. Did you have to hit quite so hard?" Felix shrugged, and relaxation came to him, but it did not fool Bart who said: "Don't try it, Sheriff. If you ship me out of Arapahoe again, it will be in a box. You have had your eye on my gun and you think you can beat me, but you're not sure. Is it important enough to try?"

The faintest of smiles touched the sheriff's lips, and Bart knew logic had won. Felix said: "Come over to the restaurant. It's time for breakfast."

Bart smiled. "An uneasy truce, is that it?"

"Maybe. Maybe I'm puzzled because you don't look fool enough to come back here and try what you say you'll try."

Bart led his horse to the nearest tie rail. Even the empty street was pleasing to him, the progression of false-fronted, sand-blasted store buildings, the sagging boardwalks, the green of trees above the stores like good frames for a bad picture.

He entered the restaurant behind the sheriff. The girl behind the long counter, in freshly starched red-checked apron, seemed vaguely familiar. Her skin was a soft olive, and her hair was shining black, drawn demurely away from her oval face.

Felix said: "You were gone before I woke, Mary. This is Bart Pruitt. You went to school with him, and should remember him."

She smiled, and Bart could see immediate recognition. He straddled a stool and sat down, noting the flush his steady attention had drawn into her face. Mary Chavalas. The girl whose lively beauty had drawn the first notice of fifteen-year-old Bart Pruitt for such things. He smiled, the quiet and steady smile of a pleasantly relaxed man. Yet even with the smile to soften his face, there was harshness in him, the same implacability of Felix Chavalas. His body and his nerves held the unreleased power of coiled spring steel, and perhaps this was what put the frown on Mary Chavalas's smooth brow.

II

Not every day did Mary Chavalas arrive at the restaurant as early as this. But today was Saturday, and a Spur pay day as well. Today the town would fill to overflowing. The restaurant would grow hot and steamy, and would be filled from early morning until late evening. Even with the help of Rosa Merino, who came in on Saturdays, Mary knew that night would find her bone-weary after the long day of parrying the exuberant passes of the Spur's lonely 'punchers. Yet now there was a stir of excitement in her, roused by Bart Pruitt's lively interest. Humming, she ladled pancakes onto the griddle and laid out strips of bacon to fry.

The kitchen looked like a cavalry commissary. Vegetables were piled high on the table, waiting for Rosa. Two huge hams and a hindquarter of beef lay there beside them.

Mary thought of Bart Pruitt again, with that odd warmth, but also with uneasiness, for her sharp eyes had not missed the tense by-play between Pruitt and her father on the street. When she returned out front with a pot of coffee, Pruitt's face was somber, without the softening that a smile brings. Its harshness surprised her, and her eyes questioned him: *What have you come back here for? What can there be for you here but bitter memories and hate?*

That he understood the question her eyes asked was plain, yet he did not respond in that gallant, Spanish way and say: "I remember you." Instead, there was such a withdrawal from her that she felt rebuked. But he said: "I still hold title to my father's homestead, and I have bought others, Mary. I came back to ranch."

"Without water?"

Felix Chavalas broke in dryly: "Pruitt is going to break the Spur. He said so. Then he'll have plenty of water."

There were undercurrents of hostility here that Mary could not understand. She remembered the boyish threat because she herself had been outraged and entirely in sympathy with the boy who was so helpless. Now he had come back to kill—to exact revenge—and what she had seen in him had been only a false façade that had promised a strong man's gentleness, a capacity for love and for laughter, for behind the impressive façade was only an embittered man who would fight the Spur and die in the fight. Her face still, Mary returned to the kitchen. Scalding tears made her eyes burn and her head ache.

From her father she heard: "I'll be watching you, Pruitt. Walk softly and carefully."

And Bart's: "What law do you enforce, Felix? The people's law, or the Spur's law? If you're Spur's man, then you would have done better to finish what you started out in the street today."

Angrily Mary Chavalas flipped the pancakes and bacon and stood watching them, tapping a foot, impatient at her own anger, which could stem only from her interest in this man. She told herself with more vehemence than conviction: *He is only another brawling, quarrelsome drifter who is good with his gun and with nothing else!*

With the pancakes in neat stacks on two plates, and with the bacon stripped neatly beside them, she went back into the restaurant. Watching him as he ate, frankly hungry, all she had so emphatically told herself became no good. There was only Bart, the feelings that stirred in her when she looked at him, and something compelling that passed between them whenever their eyes met.

At nineteen, Mary was a woman, with a woman's strength, but also with a woman's weaknesses that would show whenever love entered her heart. She would never love lightly nor more than once. She would love fiercely, with zest, and once her love was given there would be no drawing back. As he finished his meal and rose, she warmed at his smile of thanks, and gave him his change with excitement brushing her at the brief touch of their hands. Then she watched him stride upstreet, broad-backed and slim-hipped, and filled with confidence.

She asked: "Will he do it, Father?"

He shook his head with a certain regret. "No, but he'll cut a wide swath trying. It looks like your pa is going to have to earn his pay for the next coupla of weeks."

★ ★ ★ ★ ★

On the corner of Platte and Fourth stood a squat, neatly painted cream-colored building with iron bars over its windows. Over the door hung a sign lettered in gold against a black background.

ARAPAHOE BANK AND TRUST COMPANY

Before this building Barton Pruitt waited, watching each new arrival on Platte Street.

At two minutes before eight, Roy Gilbreath, stocky and iron-gray in his neat business suit, turned the corner and came toward the bank. There was about him the crackling dryness, the brusque efficiency of men who work with figures.

To the banker's desk came only the penciled notations showing numbers of cattle, acres in cultivation, dollars received from sales and those spent for machinery and homely items like: "calico for wife . . . candy for kids . . . flour . . . sidemeat . . . sugar." He could not see the sweat and back-break that went into the clearing of an acre. He could not see the pleasure a piece of calico afforded a tired woman. But he could read the faces of men. If honesty was in a man, Roy Gilbreath would see it in his face. If there was craftiness, he would see that, too.

He believed in the little man, and believed in the little man's right to live. He hated monopoly and ruthless power and entrenched interests. His hate was not violent, for nothing about him was violent. But it was steady and unending. He hated the Spur, and there was nothing personal in this; it had driven him through the years to do all a man could do to break the Spur's power. He had given time and effort to buying up for Barton Pruitt the abandoned homestead claims that adjoined the claim Henry Pruitt had filed and eventually had accumulated a bloc of land. The vague hope lurked inside him that someday a man who could whittle the Spur down to size would acquire that bloc.

He saw the tall rider waiting beside the bank, but recognition did not come until he stopped before the front door, fishing in his pants pocket for his key. Then it came, for there was much of the boy, Barton Pruitt, in the man, and there was something reminiscent of Henry Pruitt, the father, in the son.

He said: "Barton Pruitt, isn't it?"

Bart nodded, pleased at the banker's immediate recognition.

Gilbreath grunted—"Come inside."—and swung the door open on the dim and musty interior that had been a big part of his life for as long as he could remember. He put his hat in its accustomed place, and went about the morning routine of getting ready for business in exactly the same order he did every morning, while young Bart Pruitt fidgeted.

With everything in readiness for the day's business, Gilbreath held the narrow gate open for Bart. In his eyes, as Bart sat down, were polite curiosity and question.

Bart said: "First, I want to thank you for your help in buying the homesteads."

"You have a use for the land now?"

Bart nodded. For an instant his eyes were guarded, and indecision touched his features. Seeming to reach some decision, he said: "Of course, what I am going to tell you must be kept in confidence."

Gilbreath nodded, slightly puzzled.

"I'll put water on that grass," Bart went on. "It's being done in Texas, and it can be done here. In Texas they have wind-driven pumps . . . windmills . . . that draw the water from the wells in a steady stream. I've got a windmill in Denver that a telegraph message will start on its way. I can put a well down in a week and have water on my grass."

Gilbreath whistled softly, but his banker's careful mind prompted the question: "How do you know you'll strike water?"

"My father struck it at thirty feet. Most of the others struck it somewhere between fifteen and fifty. All of these old wells will have caved in by now because there was no rock to be had to fortify them. But they had water . . . plenty of it."

Again the banker's caution. "What if there is no wind?"

Bart laughed. "You have lived here for years. Have you ever seen the grass when there was no wind at all? Besides, the water would be run into a pond and a supply would build up against the time the wind would quiet for a while."

Habit brought the thoughtful—"Hmm-mm."—from the banker. Just this suddenly would come what would change the country, would throw men into bitter conflict, would throw Spur unceremoniously off the grass. A smile began to show Roy Gilbreath's satisfaction, almost joy. If Bart Pruitt could put wells and windmills on his grass, a thousand others could do the same. The Spur would be left with nothing but their throttling hold on the river, and cattle cannot live on water alone, any more than they can live on grass alone.

Again caution gripped Gilbreath—and uneasiness. "The Spur will fight."

"I expect they will. But the land is mine, and there is no law against a man sinking a well. I want thirty thousand dollars, Mister Gilbreath. I want a thousand cattle on my grass."

Gilbreath fished in his vest pocket for a cigar, unwrapped it, and bit the end off thoughtfully. This was what he had wanted, a chance to throw his own slight weight into the breaking of the Spur's stranglehold on the grass. Yet the habit of conservation was strong in a man whose whole life had been built upon it. He told himself he needed to know more of Barton Pruitt, for in a large measure the success of this plan depended upon the strength of the man behind it. He knew this for what it was, though—his own indecision and weakness. He said: "Come in at five o'clock. I'll give you my answer then. The Spur puts all of their business through this bank, and, if I lend you money, I will lose that."

"You will lose for a while," Bart said, "but you will gain in the end."

Gilbreath could see the worried frown that creased Bart's forehead and knew that Bart had counted on him and that he had let him down. He said: "Settlers will come and the town will grow . . . if there is a town here by the time that happens. Come in at five."

Bart nodded, hesitated a moment more as though searching his mind for something to say that would make Gilbreath give his assent. Then he turned and strode outside.

Gilbreath watched his tall and decisively moving shape out of his field of vision. He was frowning as the front door opened and his clerk, Storrie Taylor, came in breathlessly, ten minutes late as usual, and with the inevitable apology in his eyes.

Storrie shucked out of his coat, saying: "Good morning, sir. Was that Bart Pruitt I saw on the street just now?"

Gilbreath nodded. He did not mind Taylor's habitual tardiness, for he knew Sally Taylor and knew his lateness was not Storrie's fault, but his wife's. Sally, young and beautiful, found it hard to rise in the morning. She loved luxury, drove Storrie with her impatience for it, but would not put forth any effort to make him punctual for his work.

Storrie whistled. "What's he doing in town?"

"Come back to claim his grass."

"Whatever for? There's no water on it."

Somehow the banker forgot Bart's plea for secrecy, for

Storrie was a part of the Arapahoe Bank and Trust Company, just as he himself was. He said: "He's going to put water on it. He's bringing in a wind-driven pump . . . a windmill. Says they're using them successfully in Texas."

Again Storrie whistled. "Won't Spurlock like that, though!"

Gilbreath cautioned: "Pruitt doesn't want it known. Keep it to yourself."

"Of course."

Storrie unlocked the vault and set about his other morning tasks. He was a handsome young man of twenty-five, with black hair and an engaging smile that made him universally liked. This relieved Roy Gilbreath of many routine tasks for which he had no enthusiasm. Gilbreath had been glad to get Storrie two years before, for not many of the young men in a town the size of Arapahoe found work in a bank to their liking. Yet he sometimes thought he detected weakness in Storrie, and it was a source of occasional worry to him that Storrie was married to a woman like Sally. But liking Storrie and Storrie's work, he paid him more than the usual wage so that temptation to take anything would not be strong.

His thoughts wandering aimlessly, he stared out the window into the slowly filling street. Buckboards and wagons were arriving from the homesteads along the Platte. They would come in early, for today was a Spur pay day, and by noon the town would belong to the Spur. The settlers would purchase necessities and no more, for their land had not the fertility or the level flatness of the land controlled by the Spur. Gilbreath wondered about the perversity of nature in placing such hard clay, alkali soil beside such rich and fertile soil, and over the odd chance that had caused Arapahoe's founders to select this site at the edge of the rugged clay hills for their town.

Tom Slaughter rode past the bank atop his ancient and creaking wagon, his worn wife and his scrubbed and stunted kids beside him. No better man than Tom Slaughter ever lived, Gilbreath thought—hard-working, honest. But in the fall he had perhaps one-fourth the crop he should have had, while on the Spur's rich land, only grass grew and even it was not used to its fullest advantage. In a way that paralleled early times when nomadic tribes of plains Indians that used only a thousandth part of the land's potentiality refused to allow the whites, who would have used it fully, to settle on it. Faint anger stirred in Roy Gilbreath. Strong was the demand that he decide for Pruitt now, but then he thought: *Wait and see what the day will bring. You have until five to decide.*

III

Upon leaving the bank, Bart Pruitt angled across the dusty street to Arapahoe's single barbershop. In the back room he bathed in a wooden tub, then sat in the barber chair for a haircut and shave. The barber, a small man with an invitingly ingratiating manner, a stranger to Bart, interspersed his running comments with remarks designed to draw Bart out.

"She'll be a wild old town tonight. Spur pay day. Fifty, sixty men working there. You figuring on going to work for the Spur?"

Bart shook his head.

The barber cackled: "Homesteaders in town this morning. They'll leave at noon. Homesteaders and cowmen don't mix."

A yellow buckboard with gleaming red wheels bounced up Platte, raising its cloud from the deep dust of the street. It drew up before the bank with the horses dancing.

The barber's voice held a certain awe. "That's Jess Spurlock who owns the Spur. His daughter's with him."

Bart regarded the buckboard from the corner of his eye. He saw a yellow-haired girl in a bright, flowered dress with hat and parasol to match. He could see little of her face, for her head was turned, but in her movements were imperiousness and full consciousness that she was a Spurlock.

Spurlock was a tall, bony man, carefully dressed in black broadcloth and polished high-heeled boots. The hair at his temples was gray, as was his clipped mustache. He swung down and tied the team, then turned to assist his daughter. She alighted and went up the street toward the wide verandah of Levy's Dry Goods Store. Spurlock went into the bank.

Bart wondered if what was stirring within him was hate. He decided it was not, but only the natural nervousness of a fighter who has just had his first look at the opposition. Bart had never seen Spurlock before today. The man did not look formidable. Perhaps he was not. His money, his stranglehold on the grass, gave him his power. Strip him of these things. . . .

The barber broke into his thoughts. "Every pay day they come to town. Spurlock goes to the bank and draws out the payroll. The girl stays in town whilst he goes back to pay the crew." He toweled Bart's face and doused it with bay rum. He combed Bart's hair, then whisked the cloth away.

Bart unwound himself from the chair, got his gun belt from the nail where it hung, and strapped it on. The sight of Spurlock drove Bart's thoughts back through the years. Water had been the trap then, cattle the bait. Henry Pruitt had been the one to get caught. Patience had not been Henry Pruitt's long suit. Running a dozen head of cattle, with all of his hope for the future tied up in them, he had quickly reached the place where he could take no more of the Spur's deliberate attempts to break his patience. His cattle, and those of the other homesteaders, daily walked the mile to the river for water.

"He can't hold the river," Pruitt had argued. "He can't hold it unless he fences it, and he'll never do that because it'd fence his own cattle off the grass."

But the Spur had put line riders on the river, patrolling constantly, and, whenever cattle other than Spur cattle had been found at the river, they had been driven deep into the clay badlands, ten, fifteen miles where they'd dropped, too tired to walk back immediately. A couple of days, maybe a week, would find them again at the river, gaunted with thirst and with travel, weaker and less fit for the next drive they'd be taken on by Spur riders. To the north of town the homesteaders' fences held them away from the river. To the south, Spur riders waited. The thread holding Henry Pruitt's patience had finally broken when he had found two of his steers dead not a mile from his house, their rumps bloody from the quirt lashes they had taken, the tracks all around them showing that they had been part of another drive into the badlands.

Smoking with temper, Henry Pruitt had boiled into the Spur headquarters looking for trouble that, Bart now realized, was exactly what they had wanted him to do. They had made an example of him for the other homesteaders. The Spur foreman, Les Norell, had sent him home tied across his saddle, dead from a bullet in his chest. Molly Pruitt's demand that Felix Chavalas jail Norell for murder had been wasted breath. It was declared: "Self-defense. Pruitt drew first."

For a long time Bart's hate and thirst for revenge had centered on Norell. Gradually this had changed so that he blamed Spurlock equally for his father's death. In the end he had hated the ranch, the system.

The Saturday morning crowd flowed past Bart on the sidewalk. Children yelled and laughed and bawled lustily, and all gave Bart their close attention as they passed. Felix Chavalas came upstreet, hurrying, having seen Spurlock drive into town and still not sure of Bart's intent. He paused to watch Bart with his faintly hostile black eyes. Spurlock came out of the bank and mounted to the buckboard seat.

Bart's steady regard drew his glance momentarily. Seeing Felix Chavalas watching Bart so closely brought a puzzled frown to Spurlock's brow. Then he slapped the backs of the team with the reins and rolled on. Felix, with never a backward glance, walked with his slow and measured stride toward his office in the courthouse.

Suddenly the hostility and dislike that Felix felt toward Bart became in Bart's mind representative of what the whole town would feel once his purpose here became known. Arapahoe was dependent on the Spur for existence. The Spur bought all supplies from the merchants in Arapahoe, but there were strings attached. The town belonged to Spur on pay day, and there was not a storekeeper who was not fully aware that a word, an act against Spur, would result in immediate stoppage of patronage.

Bart Pruitt shrugged with futile bitterness, aware of his weariness because of his lack of sleep last night. He crossed to the Antlers Hotel where he got a room. Inside it, he slipped off his boots and lay down on the bed.

He slept, and he was not aware that fifteen minutes later Julia Spurlock received word that he was in town. The clerk at the Antlers, remembering both the boy and the threat, passed the word along with smug pride, believing his information would raise him a peg in Spurlock's esteem. Naturally the Spur could no longer remain in ignorance of Pruitt's presence in Arapahoe. But Julia jumped to the conclusion that Pruitt had come for only one thing—to kill! So Les Norell, waiting for Pruitt to show himself later that afternoon, was sure he was waiting for a killer.

At a quarter of five, rested and refreshed, Pruitt descended the stairs and came again into the street. Tinnily, from the saloons, came the sound of pianos. Occasionally a yell rolled upstreet and Pruitt smiled, for he could recollect pay day nights, the fights and the fun.

A lounger slipped into the barbershop and came out with three men behind him. From either wing of the hotel verandah came two sober 'punchers, as though the impulse to leave had come upon them at the same time. Behind him, Pruitt heard the door open, and an instant later a gun barrel prodded him in the small of the back. Suddenly he knew that he had been expecting this, although without consciously realizing it.

He murmured: "Norell."

"How'd you know?" The man's growl was contemptuous.

Bart, tense and immobile, felt his gun being withdrawn from holster. He heard it drop and slide across the hotel porch, as Norell threw it from him. Anger came boiling as Bart turned his head and looked into the stolid countenance of Les Norell.

He asked: "Now what?"

"A lesson in knowing what town to stay out of."

The gun barrel prodded again. Below, ringing the steps, waited the Spur 'punchers who had been chosen for this chore. Norell growled: "Down in the street. Move, damn you!"

Bart took the steps slowly, bunching his muscles for the launching attack he planned. But Norell's hand planted itself between his shoulder blades, shoving him forward—hard. He stumbled, half running as he fought to stay erect. A 'puncher beside the steps stuck out a foot, and he went face down, sliding in the warm dust.

Laughter rolled along the street, the sadistic laughter of men who have the will to maim and bruise, but who want their fun first. Bart came to his knees with rage seething in his brain. There were faces other than those of the Spur 'punchers, faces that looked at him briefly, showed the shame of men who feared to interfere, and turned away.

A fist slammed into the side of Bart's head, its force driving him sideward. He flung a hand to the ground in an effort to steady himself. A boot heel, hard and grinding, came down on the hand, bringing excruciating pain, forcing his shoulders against the man's legs.

He heard Norell's heavy voice—"All right! Get him!"—and drove his boot heels into the deep dust. The force of Bart's drive brought the man he touched tumbling against him. In one swift movement, Bart came to his feet, warily crouching, and then they were upon him, raising blows on his head, neck, and face. He swung, but the force of his blows was lost because their hard bodies were too close.

They ringed him completely, giving him no chance to get his balance, no chance to slug back. The rage in Bart burned from dull red to white heat. Before this rage all feeling in him died. No longer did pain touch him as fists landed. All he felt was their shock and force.

The instinct of a fighting animal put its savage hold upon him, the instinct of a wolf beset by the pack, giving him his one chance of survival. By instinct he found the pack's leader, Les Norell, saw the broad, almost Slavic face, the heavy, thick shoulders and deep hairy chest exposed by the man's ripped shirt. Lunging toward him, Bart felt the solid crash of bone on bone as his right found its mark on Norell's jaw, and he followed this with his left that found the big man's eye socket.

The pack worried him from behind, raining blows and

kicks upon him, blows that turned his face pulpy and started his eyes to closing, kicks that put the dull, deep pain of bruises in his muscles. He ignored the blows and tore away from clutching hands, pounding at Les Norell with a savage singleness of purpose that backed Norell to the hotel steps. Norell launched himself at Bart, bald head ramming toward Pruitt's stomach.

Bart's lips cracked suddenly in a twisted grin. He brought his knee up, and it landed squarely on Norell's mouth and nose with a sound that was dull and sodden and terrible. Held for an instant in his bent-over position by the force of Pruitt's knee, Norell plunged full length in the street.

Bart whirled on a slight, dark-haired man with yellowed, uneven teeth, and dropped him with a single left to the jaw. He singled a third man out, but he was staggering now, a haze of fog drifting across his brain, dimming even his fighting instinct. He knew they would kick and pound him after he was down, but he squinted through closing eyes, and with the last strength that was in him laid his bloody right fist against a tight-lipped, snarling mouth.

They swarmed in to overwhelm him, lusting for the kill, yelling. Then, wading in from the street with his gun barrel flashing to right and left with terrible impartiality, came Felix Chavalas, a small man physically, but big with his gun speed, his lack of fear, and his authority. There was anger in him, well-controlled and icy. There was no self-doubt, and no fear.

"Break it up! Who the hell put you up to this? I'll keep the peace in Arapahoe, and, if any man-jack of you thinks I can't, he'd better step up now."

They backed away from Pruitt and slinked toward the saloon, muttering and cursing. Four of them stayed behind, still in the dust of the street. Two Pruitt had put down, two that had fallen before the slashing barrel of Felix's gun.

Overpowering weakness claimed Pruitt, and he sat down stiffly on the hotel porch step. His chest heaved, dizziness flooded in waves over him, and he swayed from side to side even sitting.

Felix asked coldly: "Why the hell didn't you stay on that train?"

That made Bart remember why he was here. It made him remember that he was to see Roy Gilbreath at five o'clock. He fished his watch from his pocket. The hands showed six minutes before five. He said: "Don't do anything to them, Felix. Remember, they're Spur 'punchers, and the Spur is your bread and butter."

His sarcasm put a flush on Chavalas's smooth-tanned face. His bitterness made the sheriff frown. Chavalas shrugged. "I can't keep them off you forever. Get out of town while you're still able." He went back down the street, stiff-backed and angry.

A boy, thin and ragged, came down the verandah steps to stand hesitantly beside Bart. In his eyes was an excited shine of admiration. "Gee! I guess you showed them."

Bart asked: "Who're you?"

"Jimmy. Jimmy Slaughter. I'd 'a' helped you, mister, but. . . ."

"But what?"

"I was scared."

Bart laughed. He got to his feet stiffly. He said: "Everybody's scared of the Spur."

He stepped across the prone body of Norell and headed toward the bank, braced for Gilbreath's refusal and ready for it. He felt the bitterness of defeat. He had counted on the Spur's hatred and opposition, but he had not anticipated the town's fear-filled lethargy.

IV

A little proddy, Bart Pruitt entered the bank, his clothes stiff with blood and dust, his face swelling and discolored. Roy Gilbreath, taking no notice whatever, again held the narrow gate for him.

Bart asked: "You were watching?"

Gilbreath nodded.

"And?"

Gilbreath said: "Tell me one thing truthfully. Did you come back to kill Norell?"

Bart shook his head negatively.

"Spurlock?"

"No. I came to ranch. Is it such a strange ambition for a man to have?" Bart paused, then resolutely changed the subject. "I'll have one windmill on my grass in a week. It isn't enough for twenty sections of grass, but it took all the money I had. I need more windmills, and I need cattle. I need riders and lumber to start building. I need cash to operate on. You can take a mortgage on the land and the cattle both."

Gilbreath murmured: "This country has taken its orders from the Spur for a long time. Twenty sections of grass that is Spur-controlled is damned poor security."

He watched Pruitt closely, but no surly resentment appeared in Bart's face. There was a tightening of the jaw muscles, determination, and nothing else.

Gilbreath smiled unexpectedly. "For a long time I've thought Spur was the life of the country, that without it the country would die. I was wrong." He sobered abruptly. "I suppose you know that if the Spur whips you, it will finish me, too? Will you spend your energy fighting them, or do what you came here to do?"

Bart said impatiently: "I want windmills and cattle on my

grass. If I fight, it will be because they force me as they did tonight." Because pain was riding him, he said rashly, wanting this decision quickly, without further palavering: "Do I get the money?"

Gilbreath sighed. "You get it. I'll draw up the papers Monday. I make only one provision . . . that two-thirds of the money be spent for cattle."

Bart's grin was spontaneous, warmed by unexpected success. It was more a painful grimace than a grin, but his eyes crinkled and showed his pleasure. He got up, with bitterness gone. "You won't regret it."

Gilbreath, also smiling, took Bart's outstretched hand and gripped it. His smile faded as Bart winced. He said: "You will have to walk softly if you want to live to use the money. They will set all sorts of traps for you, try to goad you into a gunfight just as they goaded your father. Can you cool your temper enough to stay out of their traps?"

"I can try."

Gilbreath advised sagely: "Weigh each situation. Weigh the provocation against what you will stand to lose. If your pride forces you into a fight that will lose you everything, then where is pride in the end?"

Storrie Taylor came from the back, his records put away and his hat in hand. He let his eyes run over Bart, over the visible evidence of how much a man can take and still stay on his feet.

Gilbreath said: "Storrie, this is Mister Pruitt. The bank is financing his purchase of cattle and the development of his ranch. Pruitt, Storrie Taylor."

Storrie took the grimy and bloodied hand. "I'm pleased to meet you. I hope we'll be seeing you often."

"Thanks. I hope you will, too." Bart felt an instantaneous liking for Storrie, perhaps because Storrie was nearly his exact opposite, a type of man so new in Bart's experience that he neither detected Storrie's distaste nor sensed Storrie's inherent weakness. He had felt only the pull of Storrie's personality.

Storrie murmured—"Glad to have met you."—and went out into the street. Bart said—"See you Monday."—and followed Storrie.

Les Norell was gone, as were the other four riders, and there were only the scuff marks in the dust before the hotel to show there had been a fight. The sun hung low over the distant mountains, turned large and orange by dust in the atmosphere. It threw long shadows that climbed slowly up the faces of the buildings. Coolness crept into the air.

For a moment, Bart loitered before the hotel, savoring the coolness of the evening, the brassy blue of the sky, the waving leaves of the trees over on Prairie Street. The glances of the home-going citizens were cold and hostile, reminding him again that he must buck the Spur entirely alone.

He walked up street to Levy's, where he purchased new trousers, socks, underwear, and shirt. Carrying these, he returned to the hotel, a lonely man whose mouth was too somber and whose eyes held too much bitterness.

Thirty minutes later, washed and in clean clothes, he again emerged from the hotel and headed toward Mary Chavalas's restaurant. Gilbreath's advice troubled him, for it was not in accord with his own thinking at all. Under certain circumstances, restraint was admirable, but in dealing with the Spur, Bart believed it would only convince Norell and Spurlock that he was afraid. They would increase provocation until it became unbearable. He would be operating on Gilbreath's money, of course, but his instinct was to hit the Spur first, keep hitting them and keep them off balance. Bart Pruitt had something for which neither the Spur nor

Gilbreath gave him credit, something his father had not had, something that Felix Chavalas alone had been able to see in him—confidence in the speed of his gun.

The sun was down, yet its blazing aftermath was upon the towering piles of clouds in the west, and these put an even fire glow upon the street. Supper fires raised thin plumes of smoke from chimneys, coal smoke with its distinctive and faintly unpleasant smell, for wood was scarce on the plains. Except for the nearly solid block of saloons between Second and Third, the street was quiet now. But before these saloons horses were racked solid. Most of them bore the Spur brand. Others bore the brands of the ranches far back from the river, which had their own meager water supply. It was also pay day on these scattered ranches.

The horses drowsed, hipshot and patient, with occasional tail switchings at sticky and bothersome flies. From the saloons came the low drone of voices and an occasional shout. Heading toward the restaurant, Bart again thought of Mary, and the heady excitement of anticipation stirred in him. Unconsciously he hurried his steps.

There was serene and gentle beauty in Mary. But there were other things as well, things that could send a man's blood to racing. She looked up as he entered, a tired girl with the faint shine of perspiration on her forehead. The harried expression left her face when she saw him, and she smiled, warmth in her welcome, and he knew suddenly that she had been expecting him.

The counter was solid with cowpunchers, and two others waited beside the door for empty stools. Norell's broad back loomed at one end of the counter. The man next to him glanced at Pruitt, then whispered to Norell. Bart felt tenseness come into his body. Norell looked around, venom in his bruised and swollen eyes. He had been drinking, and there also was a recklessness in his smoldering eyes.

Three stools emptied, and Bart sat down, the two others who had been waiting sitting beside him. Mary came to stand before them, never looking directly at Bart, but with a pink flush in her smooth cheeks. She took their orders, then glanced at Bart.

He said: "Roast beef and fried spuds. Coffee. Is every day as hard as this one has been?"

"No."

"How late will you work?"

"Another hour."

She moved away toward the kitchen. Bart, without turning his head, caught movement at the end of the counter. There was the scuffling of feet, and two men moved in behind him. Norell was one of them. Something sharp prodded Pruitt in the back, the muzzle of Norell's gun again, and suddenly rage soared through Bart's brain.

Norell said tightly: "I thought I told you to get out of town."

Bart growled: "And I thought I made it plain I had no such intention. Get that gun out of my back, or shoot it, because I came to eat, and that is what I intend to do."

Mary turned, and her eyes widened with fear as she saw the strained look in Bart's face, the baffled rage of the Spur foreman.

Norell hesitated, and Bart felt the pressure of the gun muzzle lessen, then heard the rustle of movement as Norell holstered the gun.

Smoothly Bart came to his feet, towering two inches over the blocky Norell. He murmured in a low and vicious voice: "I'm tired of feeling that thing in my back. The next time you pull it, do it when my face is turned to you or I'll take it away from you and beat your brains out with it." He stared at

Norell, hard, for the anger of the persecuted was strong in him.

Norell growled: "I'll do that . . . soon. You're too damned big for your britches."

He swung heavily and went through the door, hating with doubled intensity, Bart knew, because he'd been humbled before his crew. But Bart was well aware of the man's stubbornness, knew Norell could neither alter his course once he had embarked upon it nor even modify it in the slightest degree.

The man beside Bart murmured: "You remind me of a man prodding a rattler with a short stick. You're either a fool or a lot tougher than Norell."

Bart asked: "You a Spur rider?"

"Nuh-uh. Singletree. Ten miles back from the river. Even that far away folks take the Spur's orders. Pleasures me to see a man that won't."

Bart looked at him closely. He was a small man with a cheerfully grinning face that was horribly scarred by some old burn. Bart asked: "Would you like to make a business of not taking the Spur's orders? Forty a month and beans?"

"Thirty is the Spur's price. Twenty-five where I'm at. Is forty gun wages?"

Bart shook his head. "I can't tell you that because I don't know. Do you think Norell will let me stay without a fight?"

The man grinned, showing yellowed and fight-broken teeth. He shoved his hat back on his bald head. His neck was scrawny and seamed with weather like that of a turkey gobbler. He said: "When do I start, boss?"

"Tomorrow morning, if you're able. And be able. What's your name?"

"Shortgrass Riley. Shorty, or Riley, either one."

"Can you hire another half dozen men?"

Riley shrugged. "I can try."

Mary Chavalas approached with food, and Bart attacked his meal. Mary moved down the counter, lighting lamps against the creeping dusk. Her movements had an unconscious grace, although her shoulders drooped with weariness. The curve of her cheek and the line of her throat had a smooth beauty, but there was a faint frown upon her brow.

Riley gulped the last of his coffee and got up. "See you in the morning. At the hotel?"

Bart nodded.

Riley went out.

Almost as though at a signal, half a dozen men rose, paid for their meals, and went out, each with a speculative stare at Bart.

Bart said: "Suppertime is over, Mary. Close up and let me take you home."

She turned to face him, her lips curving with pleasure, but with refusal in her eyes. "I do not need an escort on the streets of Arapahoe. Not even on pay day."

Bart grinned. "Because of Felix? Maybe I do. Don't say no. It is only a few short blocks."

Mary hesitated, but finally nodded with an odd, little-girl look in her face. "All right. Rosa will finish up. I *am* tired tonight."

She went back into the kitchen and shortly came back, a shawl thrown across her shoulders. They went out into the soft dark, heavy with the smell of midsummer and growing things, loud with the sounds of pianos and laughter and drunken shouting.

Slowly Bart and Mary walked along, silently at first but with a companionable feeling that was comforting, almost tangible. Felix Chavalas materialized from the shadows, saying nothing, but as they passed him, Mary murmured softly: "Good night, Father."

Bart smiled. Felix's deliberate presence was a warning, as plain as if spoken.

Mary asked Bart suddenly: "Why won't you go away? Norell will never be satisfied until you are dead or driven away. Is a dry ranch worth being killed over?"

Pruitt exulted in her concern, but when he answered, his voice was sober. "You probably wouldn't believe me if I told you I am not staying for myself alone. My father was killed because he tried to hold what was rightfully his. Others have been driven away because they believed no grass was worth being killed over. Yet, if all men feel this way, then the Spurlocks and the Norells will own the land, and the people will become clods under their feet."

They passed the bank, Levy's, and crossed the intersection to the Chavalas house. Mary opened the white picket gate, and they went slowly up the walk to the porch. Flowering vines climbed over the porch, and their fragrance was heavy and sweet in the still air. Mary looked small and soft and white-faced in the darkness.

Bart never knew whether he took her in his arms, or whether she came to them. But he knew her face was raised, her body warm and eager with expectancy. He kissed her, gently and lightly at first, but with an increasing savage urgency. For just an instant she responded, all yielding. Then she pulled away.

"Good night. Will you be careful?"

His voice had an unaccustomed hoarseness. "I'll be careful."

He went down the walk, conscious of her in the shadows. When darkness had swallowed house and porch and picket fence, he walked toward the hotel with the old wariness, but with something new—a full awareness that today had brought him something priceless, the pure gold that was Mary Chavalas. . . .

V

The house in which Storrie and Sally Taylor lived squatted a vacant lot's distance from the courthouse, facing on Prairie. White paint failed to hide its sagging porch, the unloveliness of its small size and perfectly square shape. It was a source of never-ending dissatisfaction to Sally, as was the fact that across the alley lay Arapahoe's sprawling shack town. Storrie's gardening made its yard as pretty as any in town, yet Sally would rather have had a house on Fifth with no yard at all.

Storrie mounted the porch steps, a little puzzled at the impression Bart Pruitt had made upon him, one of calm and quiet strength, of a man slow to anger, terrible when he succumbed. Storrie had felt distaste at the violence that had bloodied Pruitt, yet had realized the irresistible pull of the man's personality and a desire to ally himself with Pruitt, with the vague conviction that by so doing part of Pruitt's strength might be transferred to himself. He scoffed, in his mind, calling Pruitt—*Drifter . . . saddlebum . . . brawler.*—yet he knew that Roy Gilbreath's judgment of men was sound, that Gilbreath believed in Pruitt sufficiently to loan him thirty thousand dollars more or less on personal security.

He opened the door and went into the small, shabby parlor. Sally sat on the sofa, feet curled under her, reading a book. She looked beautiful, perhaps more ornamental than useful, but beautiful all the same. She wore her honey hair in a bun low on her neck. The room was untidy. More than likely Sally had spent most of the day where she now was. She smiled, asked abruptly: "Storrie, why can't we live in Denver? I've been reading. . . ."

Storrie felt a stir of angry impatience. He snatched the book, flung it to the other end of the sofa. "Denver is no different than Arapahoe . . . just bigger. Why can't you be satisfied? Spurlock had his lean years here and so did Gilbreath. These are my lean years. I'll get you all the money you want, but you've got to give me time."

Sally pouted, pursing her full lips in the way that always rendered Storrie's arguments impotent. "But I don't want to wait, Storrie. I won't be young forever. What good is money when you're too old to enjoy it?"

She made him feel a failure. Any young man needs confidence in himself, and when a wife steals his confidence by showing her dissatisfaction. . . .

He forced himself to be patient. "I'm doing the best I can, Sal. I'm making more money than anyone my age in town." In desperation he dropped the argument. "What have you got for supper?"

She uncurled herself from the sofa and stood up, a warm and silken kitten. She said: "Eggs, I guess. They're easy to fix."

"Eggs!" Disgust turned his voice bitter. "Some morning I'll wake up cackling."

Sally laughed, stood on tiptoe, and brushed his lips with her own. He forgot everything but her desirability. He caught her to him, but she held herself stiff, murmuring: "Not now, Storrie. We've got to hurry. This is your night for chess with Frank."

He let her go, watching the sway of her hips as she went toward the kitchen. It puzzled him that she so cheerfully let him go every Saturday night, for she was a fun-loving girl who liked company and hated being alone. Shrugging, Storrie picked up the book she had been reading, thumbing at random through pages that pictured Denver as a paradise of gilt and velvet, rich food and free-flowing wine. He snorted. In Denver there was a place for the Storrie Taylors just as there was a place for the Spurlocks. Money always determined that.

He heard the sound of eggs frying, and, after a while Sally called him, and he took his place at the kitchen table.

She asked, returning to the old subject: "Why don't you ask Mister Gilbreath for more money?"

Storrie felt his patience running out. She worried him with her questions as a cat worries a mouse, taking refuge always in her feminine softness, in the desire that flamed in him whenever she willed it. He looked at the two fried eggs on his plate, swimming in grease and too well done. Suddenly nausea choked him, making him fling to his feet as the chair fell to the floor behind him.

He shouted: "Eggs! Money! Damn it, he's paying me more than I'm worth now! Quit nagging and be satisfied for a change, will you?" He hurled the napkin onto his plate of eggs. "I'm going downtown to eat! I want a meal I can sink my teeth into!"

He heard a cup smash against the kitchen door as he went into the parlor and would have grinned had not his own anger been so great. Sally's anger showed itself in fragments of china, shattered against the walls, never in raging words. When he came back later, she would soothe him with her kisses.

Yet tonight a new desperation rode him, for today he had seen Bart Pruitt, with nothing more than his own strength and a few sections of dry grass to offer, easily obtain the kind of money for which Storrie Taylor would sell his soul. The thought became a canker in his mind, eating unhealthily until all was blotted out but the determination to obtain swiftly what most men worked a lifetime for—money! Big money.

All through his meal Storrie thought of the long, dull evening of chess ahead with Frank Bodine, wondering briefly how this meaningless Saturday night ritual had ever got started. Well, tonight would see the last of it. He paid for his meal and stepped out into the night, reluctant to go home, but determined not to go to Frank Bodine's for chess.

The tinkle of pianos from the saloons downstreet floated to his ears. The low murmur of voices within them suddenly became a magnet that drew Storrie, who seldom drank, through the doors of the Idle Hour.

The sweet-sour smell of liquor, the laughter, the crowd, raised an unaccustomed excitement within him as he crowded up to the bar in the huge U-shaped room. The green-topped poker tables were well patronized by the Spur's celebrating 'punchers.

Storrie downed his liquor, felt its fire, and fought to control a grimace. He poured another, and this time the grimace was not so hard to control. Sipping his fifth, he vaguely and without interest heard Les Norell, the Spur foreman standing near him, say to the 'puncher drinking with him: "I've got a couple of errands. I'll see you later."

The cowhand nodded, but, when Norell had turned his back, the fellow's lips curled in a knowing grin. Outside, Norell moved up along Platte Street, and at the corner of Fourth turned toward the river and Arapahoe's shack town. It suited him, these pay nights, to head for shack town, for anyone seeing him would naturally assume he was headed for one of the bagnios. He walked openly, but tense with anticipation. Even the pain of the bruises Pruitt had inflicted was lessened by his excitement.

For ten minutes he wandered in the dark alleys of shack town, watching always to see that he was unobserved, pausing frequently in the shadows to wait. Finally satisfied, he made his way out of shack town and came at last to Storrie Taylor's sagging back gate. Knowing how it squeaked, he put a leg over it, stepping into the yard. He waited a full five minutes, hearing no sound but the distant dim noise of merrymaking.

Avoiding the boardwalk, he walked along its edge to the back porch and said softly: "Sal?"

"Here." Her voice was a whisper in the fragrant night. "Come on in. He's not here."

"I know."

The screen door squeaked faintly as he opened it. Then the blockiness of his powerful body was lost in the shadows on the porch. He could feel her nearness, but for a moment her fragrance and her softness were elusive. Then she came to his arms, a woman fierce and savage with the demand of her passion.

She whispered: "Come inside. The blinds are drawn. He won't be home for two hours. I want to look at you."

His voice was husky, barely audible. "I'm not pretty. Had a run-in with a saddlebum and came off second best."

But he followed her into the house, a short and powerful man, full of desire, but filled eternally with something else—blind loyalty to the Spur and the Spur's owner.

In the lighted kitchen, Sally's delicate hand gently touched the bruised face, and even in this gesture was intentional provocation. Sympathy made her eyes glisten. "You poor boy! Who did it?"

Norell was gruff and embarrassed, but could not hide his pleasure in her concern. "A saddlebum, I told you. Forget him. I see you for only a couple of hours once or twice a month."

His hands reached for her, but laughingly she eluded him.

"Storrie's taking me to Denver."

For a moment he was still, his powerful desire arrested while he digested this startling news. "The hell! How can I travel clear to Denver to see you?"

"You can't. You won't." She pouted. "You don't really love me."

"Damn you, I'll show you!" He advanced toward her, as though he could hold her here, make her unsay the words that would separate her from him.

She let him catch her, backed against the wall, her hands against his thick chest, pushing, but gradually losing their force, moving then across his chest, up the sides of his neck and behind his head. Her hands became alive and strong, drawing his head down, pressing his bruised lips hard against her own.

Her voice was a whisper. "Darling! Don't let Storrie take me away! Take me yourself! Oh, we could be happy. No more slipping in back doors. No more hiding. Les, Les!" Her body arched against him, and there was no other thought in him than the urgency of this moment.

But still there was reservation in Sally that set Norell's brain ablaze. He whispered: "Forget it for now. We'll talk about it later."

"Not later. Now."

"I haven't any money. I'm a part of the Spur. I can't leave, Sal." He could feel stiffness come to her body. He capitulated. "All right! All right! But you'll have to be satisfied with a shack until I can get started again."

"No, Les. You have given your life to the Spur . . . since you were fourteen. Let the Spur give it back."

"What the hell are you talking about?" Uneasiness began to stir in Norell.

Excitement brightened her eyes. "Cattle, Les! You have the authority to sell the Spur's cattle. What if you were to sell a thousand head? We could go some place where no one would even find us."

His big, powerful hands closed on her shoulders, the thick fingers biting deeply and cruelly. She gave him no time for thought. She threw herself against him in a frenzy of passion.

"Les, I love you so, I love you so!"

He would have flung her from him, but now he could not. She had stopped his first reaction of disgust. Now her suggestion would have time to work. . . .

When Norell left at nine, Sally murmured tearfully: "Oh, I don't want you to go! I want to be with you always. Will you come next Saturday?"

"I'll try."

In his voice was such an unaccustomed reserve that Sally wondered if she had crowded him too hard tonight. He might not come back! She watched him fade into nothingness against the black of night, reflecting: *If he don't, then I'll make Storrie take me!*

She was smiling as she closed the kitchen door. Either man could, if properly managed, provide the money Sally desired. Norell could get it from Spur cattle, but Storrie could get it as easily. Storrie worked in the bank

VI

Young Storrie Taylor was rather surprised at the effect liquor had upon him tonight. He had always been a moderate drinker, and before now the invariable effect had been to create drowsiness. Yet tonight the activity of his brain amazed him, as did the feeling of recklessness and sense of well-being. He had the heady assurance that tonight anything would be possible for Storrie Taylor.

He left the bar and walked deliberately to the largest of the poker tables. "Open to all comers?" he asked.

"Sure. Sit down."

Storrie still had all of his month's pay in his pocket. He took out a handful of gold and silver coins and bought chips. Two Spur 'punchers sat across from Storrie. The houseman indicated them with a wave of his hand. "Sam and Ramón. I'm Jake. This one"—indicating the player on Storrie's left—"is Hawkins. Sam's dealing." He cut the cards expertly and shoved the deck toward Sam. "Run 'em."

Storrie knew the 'punchers only by sight. The gamblers were strange to him, but he knew Felix Chavalas would allow no sharpers in Arapahoe, particularly on the nights the Spur was in town.

With strange new confidence Storrie glanced at his first hand. It did not surprise him that he held two aces, nor did it surprise him that he drew the third and a pair of sevens to go with them. The hand played out, Storrie laid his cards down, face up, and raked in the pot.

Ramón dealt, and Storrie won again. It was bad, this early winning, for it stimulated the false confidence created by the liquor. He won, and he lost. By ten, he had a single yellow chip left before him. At ten-thirty, he brought Baldy Rurbank from behind the bar to vouch for him, and began signing I.O.U.s.

Midnight found him sober, sick, and with three hundred dollars' worth of I.O.U.s out. He ordered a drink and tossed it down, as though to combat the desperate depression that had crept inexorably over him. But the drink rose in his throat, and Storrie ran for the door, his hand clutching his mouth. When finally he crept home, he was relieved that the house was dark.

If Sally heard him come in, if she felt the careful easing of his body onto the bed, she gave no sign. But Storrie did not sleep. His mind was filled with the horror of what he had done. His month's salary was gone. The I.O.U.s amounted to a hundred dollars more than his savings. Yet unwittingly he had furthered Sally's plans. For once the initial step into embezzlement is taken, the second is easy.

Morning was gray and gloomy. Sunday, and Storrie had all the day to think. Maybe before night he would have thought of a way out. . . .

When Bart Pruitt awoke, he found the gray Sunday morning to his liking. Rainy days always brought memories of his boyhood, when rain had meant staying indoors while the house filled with the delicious odors of baking cookies, munching them later while his mother read to him. He lay still, thoughts returning to the present, to grass and Roy Gilbreath, to Mary Chavalas, and finally to Les Norell. How much he had to do!

Cattle were easily enough bought, but a man had to look for them, haggle for them. Windmills must come from Denver. Men to dig wells could undoubtedly be found on the hardscrabble homesteads. Yet all of these things took time. And until all the materials were at hand, Bart wished to keep his windmills secret, for until the Spur recognized the deadliness of his plan to themselves, they would remain inactive. He would be no definite and immediate danger to them.

He got up, stretching long, flat muscles full of resiliency and power. He scrubbed his face in cold water, combed his hair, and then dressed, glad that the fracas last night had not entirely closed either of his eyes, but a little reluctant to parade his beaten features in Arapahoe of a Sunday morning.

Knuckles rapped sharply at his door, and he opened it. Shortgrass Riley was standing there, hat in hand, eyes blurry and red.

Pruitt grinned. "Worse for wear, but on your feet. How many men were you able to hire?"

"I got three, and they're all flat broke. They're waitin' downstairs, hoping their new boss's got enough *dinero* in his jeans to buy them breakfast."

"How about you?"

"Me, too. Three, four drinks always gives me the notion that I'm hell with the pasteboards, but I never am."

Bart started for the door, but Riley stopped him.

"Ain't you forgetting something?" He unhooked Bart's belt and gun from the head of the bed. "Sunday don't mean no more than another day to the Spur. Hook this around you."

As Bart buckled on the belt, a church bell pealed. When the two reached the street, it had begun to rain, a fine mist pleasant and clean.

From the walk where they had been sitting, three dejected 'punchers got up. Riley said: "This here's our new boss, boys, and he'll stand your breakfast, provided you want to eat it instead of drinking it. Boss, the tall, hungry one is Slim Taney, the lady-killer is Dude Ahlberg, and the dried-up old feller is Cooky. I feel kind of sorry for the Singletree, because you've hired their whole crew."

Warmth ran suddenly in Pruitt's veins. He was not, then, entirely alone. He said, smiling: "All right. We'll eat, and then get busy."

Mary Chavalas's restaurant was closed on Sunday, so the five headed for the Arapahoe House Saloon and Restaurant. Bart sized up his crew as they sat around, waiting for breakfast.

Slim Taney stood a full inch taller than Bart, was lean and stringy, and stoop-shouldered. A stained mustache drooped past the corners of his mouth, and he was missing two front teeth. But in his eyes was steadiness and a certain speculative coldness. Bart did not underestimate Taney, although the man's gun was old and rust-specked.

Riley said: "He carries that thing for looks. Slim's a rifle man."

Bart shifted his attention to Cooky. His white shirt was soiled and limp, his pants wrinkled. He needed a shave badly, and his whiskers showed just a faint touch of gray. His eyes were blue and faded, and about him was an air of vague distraction. He caught Bart's eyes, flushed, and grumbled something unintelligible.

Dude Ahlberg, hardly taller than Cooky, was broad and muscular. He was probably only a few years older then Bart. Riley had called him "lady killer." He possessed a certain handsomeness of which he was fully conscious, and an air of recklessness that could not but attract women. Pruitt decided: *I will not send him to Denver. Too many distractions there.* He said to Slim Taney: "I want you to catch the afternoon train for Denver. Go to the Queen City Machinery Company tomorrow morning and pick up what they've got for me. Hire a wagon and team in Denver. Cover the load with canvas and bring it out to my dad's old homestead. I'll meet you there." He pulled a buckskin bag from his pocket and shook out a small handful of gold coins, giving some to Taney. "Answer no questions, don't let anyone look under the canvas, and stay away from liquor. Can you do that?"

"I can."

Bart turned to Cooky. "You go circulate around the homesteads. Hire me half a dozen men who are good with picks and shovels. Tell them to be out at the Pruitt homestead

Monday morning. Pay is a dollar and beans, and they can work all summer if they want to. If there's a carpenter or two among them, so much the better."

Ahlberg was staring at him, one eyebrow raised, his lips curved in a questioning and faintly amused grin.

Pruitt said to him: "Tomorrow morning you and Riley and I will ride out looking for cattle. You boys know the country. You likely know who might want to sell."

The waiter brought them a huge platter heaped with flapjacks, another loaded with country sausage. A swamper behind him carried a steaming pot of coffee.

Riley asked: "How many cattle you want? How much grass you got, and where is it? This is Spur country around here."

"I want a thousand head before I'm through. A hundred will do to start. I've got twenty sections of grass smack dab in the middle of Spur range."

"No water?"

"I'll put water on that grass. I'll show the Spur that there's water to be had without going to the river for it."

Riley whistled, a long, low sound, half amazement, half consideration of what such a move would mean. He said: "That forty you're paying us is gun wages all right, if you do that."

Bart said: "Maybe. Maybe not. But if any of you want to back out, do it now, and no hard feelings." When no one said anything, he smiled and rose. "See you all later, then." He paid for the meal and turned out into the misting rain.

Dark gray clouds hovered over the land. The air was cool. Bart walked uptown, and, as he reached the white frame church, the doors opened and the Sunday morning crowd drifted out, milling on the walk for a moment before heading homeward.

A buckboard rolled toward Bart with a woman at the

reins, and headed along the road toward the homesteads. She was young, dressed in black, with white ruffles of lace at throat and wrists. A plain woman, growing plump, yet in her expression was serene contentment. Briefly and unaccountably Bart compared her quiet mien with Julia Spurlock's haughty arrogance and her discontent with material comforts without happiness. He remembered his mother and thought: *It don't take money or land to make a woman happy. To be happy is either in you or it's not, and what you have has little to do with it.*

Mary Chavalas came from the church with her father, and the two walked toward Bart, with Felix scowling and Mary smiling. Bart knew now why he had walked out of his way to pass the church, when his plain intent had been to get his horse from the livery and ride over the grass. Mary Chavalas was so firmly in his heart and thoughts that already he wanted each day to begin with the sight of her.

She murmured: "Church would have done you no harm this morning."

His face clouded, for instinctively he was certain that at some time during the service the minister had quoted: "Vengeance is mine, saith the Lord." He said patiently: "Mary, Felix is sure I've come back here for revenge. But Felix is wrong. Please give me a chance to show you how wrong he is."

She nodded, and allowed Felix to turn her away toward home. There was stiffness in the sheriff's straight back, plain dislike in his manner. Such outward evidences of displeasure put a smile on Bart's wide mouth, for they told him that Mary's interest in him had been evident to her disapproving father.

He walked downstreet toward the livery, and, as he neared it, he saw Storrie Taylor mount and ride out along the road that led toward the Spur's sprawling home ranch. He got his horse and took the same road, but headed toward his own grass, toward the house his father had built so long ago.

VII

As he left the river, the long rolling ridges of land leveled off into the vast plain resembling the sea's ground swells. The grassland teemed with wild mice, ground squirrels, prairie dogs, antelope, coyotes, wolves, and occasionally a deer. Birds were everywhere. In the fall, ducks and geese came winging overhead. Spring saw this grassland in blossom, but now, in midsummer, it was yellow and dry. Cattle made dark red spots upon it, Spur cattle, fat and sleek with an abundance of food and water.

Without conscious thought, Bart Pruitt headed his horse unerringly at the old homestead, and came to it in the late morning. This house must serve for a while as headquarters. Today he wanted to see what repairs were needed. He wanted to lie full-length in the grass and stare at the sky, recalling boyhood days that had ended in such bitterness and defeat. And he wanted to savor his coming triumph.

As he topped a low ridge and looked down into the bowl where the Pruitt homestead squatted, he saw a horse and rider. The other rider glimpsed him, also. For an instant he thought she would gallop away, but instead Julia Spurlock reined around and approached him as he dismounted before the house.

She asked: "What are you doing here? This is Spur range."

He corrected: "It's my range . . . my house." Catching her frown of annoyance, he said deliberately: "You'll have to arrange another meeting place, now that I'm here."

A flush stained her cheeks, and she asked sharply: "Who are you?"

"Bart Pruitt." He felt a touch of shame because of his elation at being able to fluster this Spur heiress.

"But Norell. . . ."

He nodded. "Yeah, somebody told him to run me out of town, but it didn't stick."

"What do you want?"

He let his eyes rove over her, from ankles revealed by her riding skirt, to open-throated blouse, to the full swell of her breasts. Her insolence annoyed him, so he was deliberately insolent in return. "Nothing from you. Nothing from the Spur. I want this grass which belongs to me, and I'm going to take it."

"And water your cattle in the river?"

He shrugged. "My father tried that. I may have a better idea."

She flushed with anger. "What is it about a big thing someone has built that makes men like you want to tear it down? You never succeed, but you are always trying."

His own anger at her manner began to ruffle him. "What is Spur built upon . . . honesty and hard work, or deceit and fraud? The intent of the Homestead Law is to give each man his own parcel of ground, not for one man to stake phony claims along a river, preventing other men from filing because of his stranglehold on the water."

Another rider had approached, but neither noticed him until he spoke.

"My point exactly, Julia, and well phrased."

Startled, Bart whirled, and saw a tall spare young man whose hair, the straw yellow of the grass, was long and curled slightly over his neck. He wore gray broadcloth, hardly the garb for riding on the grass, but perhaps suitable for meeting

Julia Spurlock on a Sunday afternoon.

Kneeing his horse closer, he stuck his hand down to Bart. "Frank Killen. I get out the Arapahoe *Clarion* and starve to death in the process. I have hopes that some day Julia will marry me, and I will no longer have to starve."

"Frank!"

"It's true." Self-mockery was in Killen's narrow face. "This is a day and age when a man's brain alone certainly will not make a living for him."

As he swung from saddle, Bart saw that one leg was perhaps an inch shorter than the other, and this gave him a bobbing motion as he walked. He had the high forehead of the intellectual, and his body was thin and without much strength. Julia's face turned oddly soft as she looked at him.

He said: "Arapahoe is the Spur's town, and the *Clarion* is the Spur's paper. I find myself in sympathy with what you hope to do, yet I cannot express that sympathy or I will alienate Julia, which I cannot afford to do."

Frank Killen, Bart realized, was a man embittered by failure, whose refuge was in public ridicule of his own failure, a man still sure of his own capabilities but who had found no place for himself on the frontier. Bart also found his first estimate of Julia Spurlock's character in need of revision, for apparently she had such a deep understanding of Killen's inner torment that she could pass over his bitter, sarcastic comments lightly.

Killen said: "The Spur will whip you out of the country with your tail between your legs. But I admire your guts and wish you luck."

Bart said dryly: "Thanks."

Killen turned suddenly diffident. He said, a little hesitantly: "I wonder if you would grant me a favor . . . like forgetting you saw Julia and me together. Jess Spurlock is well aware I have my eye on a place at the Spur's dinner table. He would rather I didn't get it, and would discourage Julia from seeing me if he knew she was."

Suddenly Bart laughed, his frank liking for Killen plain in his face. "I've already forgotten."

Killen smiled. With the smile all bitterness was gone. It made him younger, and Bart could understand Julia's strong attraction to him.

Killen murmured: "Of course, we will have to find another meeting place now that you are here."

He climbed into his saddle. Arrogance gone, Julia followed him meekly from the yard.

The overcast had gradually cleared away, and the sun had poked through in spots, laying a dappled pattern of sunlight across the land. Rain had stopped during Bart's ride here, and already the grass was dry. Bart off-saddled and lay down, pillowing his head on the hard saddle and staring at the ever-changing aspect of cloud and sky. There was peace to be found in the limitless infinity above. Bart found peace and, later, sleep.

In the living room of the Spur ranch house, Jess Spurlock stood before the big fireplace, tapping his pipe lightly and impatiently against the mantel. Storrie Taylor sat on the edge of a chair, turning his hat around and around in his nervous hands.

Spurlock asked: "What makes you think you have information that would be valuable to me?"

"If I tell you what it is, will you pay me what it's worth?"

"What if it's worth nothing at all?"

Storrie shrugged, realizing that he could scarcely haggle over price before Spurlock knew what he had to sell, but also that, once the information was out, Spurlock could refuse payment and order him off the ranch.

Storrie said: "I guess I'll have to take the chance. The information I have may save your ranch. I need four hundred dollars today. If you decide it is worth it, you can pay me more later."

Spurlock growled. He said impatiently: "Well, what is it?"

"Pruitt's bought up twenty sections of the grass you're using and is bringing in windmills to pump water for his cattle."

"Hell, he can't pump enough water for cattle!"

"It's working in Texas." Suddenly Storrie saw failure in Spurlock's disbelief. He went on frantically: "Can't you see what it will mean if he succeeds? It will not be only Pruitt. Every quarter section of your grass except what Pruitt holds is open to homesteading. There'll be a land rush that'll take every damned blade of grass you've got. You'll have your patented land along the river and nothing else. You won't even have this house, unless you can get somebody to homestead it for you."

Spurlock rammed his pipe into his pocket, walked to the window with his swift strides, presenting his broad back to Storrie. He was silent for minutes. Finally he turned, his expression shrewd. "You've been helping yourself to Gilbreath's money, and now you've got to put it back, is that it?"

Storrie leaped to his feet. "No!"

Spurlock said nastily: "Get your stinking carcass out of here, so I can air the place out. You'll get no money from me. If you don't like that, I'll let Gilbreath know what his boy's been up to."

An angry retort died on Storrie's lips. Even if he was guiltless of defalcation at the bank, such a charge by Spurlock could result only in an examination of the bank's records and the revelation of his gambling losses. Gilbreath, who frowned upon gambling by a bank employee, would discharge Storrie. But even as he stood there, a new plan was born in Storrie's active mind. He shrugged, saying: "All right. You win."

"Then get out!"

Storrie knew he would have to move fast now, for Spurlock, convinced he was an embezzler, wouldn't wait long before exposing him. As he rode toward town, bitterness gripped him, steadily and increasingly. He thought: *All right! All right, by hell! If that's the way it has to be, then that's the way it will be!*

Sally entered his thoughts, and suddenly he could hardly wait. With what he had in mind, within a week he could be on a train heading out of town. Let them try to find him then. Just let them try!

VIII

The Queen City Machinery Company located on the bank of Denver's Cherry Creek, near the Blake Street bridge, was a long, low frame building that housed all sorts of mining machinery. Its owner was a grizzly bear of a man named Hoffmeier, a greasy, bearded oldster a full inch taller than Slim Taney, and twice as broad.

"Windmill?" he said. "*Ja,* I got it in here." He led Slim through a maze of steel and cast iron, and eventually reached a pile of timbers, bar iron, rods, and curious metal devices. "I get telegraph message from *Herr* Pruitt. He want six more of these. Tell him I order and ship direct to Arapahoe. Tell him it take two, three weeks."

Slim nodded. "I'll tell him. Let's get this pile of junk loaded so I can get back." That this jumble of iron and lumber could ever be put together to draw water from the ground seemed impossible to him.

Hoffmeier summoned half a dozen laborers by his bellow, and the pieces of the windmill were lifted with block and tackle by a hoist that ran overhead on a steel track and carried the stuff to the front. Slim supervised the loading of the wagon, then tossed a tarp over the load and lashed it down. Hoffmeier gave him an envelope containing assembly instructions, and Slim mounted to the seat, his disgust growing.

"I should have stayed on the Singletree," he growled as he headed the wagon homeward. "This pile of scrap iron won't pump water."

The mules plodded steadily through the early morning sunlight. Slim rode slouched over, completely relaxed, the stub of a cigar dead in his teeth. Occasionally he spat disgustedly.

As he passed a saloon near the edge of town, the doors were flung open and a swamper came out, emptying two buckets into the street. The familiar sour odor of liquor assailed Slim's nostrils, and suddenly he yanked the mules to a halt and yelled: "Fetch me a quart, and be quick about it!"

The swamper went back inside and returned, carrying a brown bottle. Slim paid for it, pulled the cork, and let the fiery stuff gurgle down his throat. Then he grimaced, corked the bottle, and wedged it against his lean, bony buttocks. He cursed the mules to start them, then settled back with less disgust at the prospect of this long drive on a jolting wagon seat when, as anyone knew, a man was meant to sit a saddle. A mile from town, Slim took another drink. Two hours out, he began to sing.

Tipsy, but not drunk, at noon Slim halted the mules, watered them in the river, and tied them to a tree. He sat down with his back to a cottonwood, and, as drowsiness stole over him, he guiltily remembered Pruitt's cautioning him to stay away from liquor. Slim Taney could remember many things in his past of which he should have been ashamed, but was not. There was his desertion from the Army. There was that killing in the heat of drunken anger. There was the armed robbery of a saloon and the wounding of the owner. Yet he had had his own rigid code, and his word, once given, had always been good. And he believed that when a man no longer respected his given word, he had passed the point of no return.

Slim Taney came staggering to his feet. He stumbled to the river and soaked his head in the cool water. He harnessed the mules and hitched them to the wagon. He threw the bottle into the water and watched its bobbing course downstream. Then he mounted the seat, with his head throbbing, to continue his journey. In place of the bottle now, his smoothly oiled rifle was on the seat behind him.

Common sense told him: *Hell, Norell don't know I'm coming, and don't know what I'm bringing.* Yet an odd uneasiness led him to keep the rifle within easy reach, for reassurance.

When he reached the edge of the Spur's domain in late afternoon, the effects of the liquor had not entirely worn away. Here the road entered a thicket of cottonwoods and willows that grew on either side of the river. The sun hung brassily halfway up the sky, and its glare on the water was dazzling. Heat billowed from the grassland in shimmering, view-distorting waves. In a cottonwood a pair of black and white magpies squawked and scolded.

Premonition laid its cold hand against Taney's spine. He clutched his rifle, peering futilely ahead, but blinded by the glare. A single shot broke the silence, and Slim grunted heavily. Half a hundred magpies rose from the cottonwoods, screaming their raucous song. The mules plunged against their traces, and the wagon lumbered ahead, picking up speed. Taney hauled back the reins, dizziness floating over him and with his last strength, as he fell, yanked on the brake and set it. Then he was down in the dust of the road, but with the rifle still clutched in his bony hand.

Les Norell walked cautiously to him. He toed the still form while covering it steadily with his Colt. Satisfied, he stooped and pried Slim's rifle from his hand, walked to the river, and threw it far out into the water. Returning, he knelt and listened to Slim's heartbeat. An expression of disgust spread across his broad, thick-lipped face.

"Damn you, now I'll have to finish you off!" He raised his revolver, thumbed back the hammer, but the muzzle wavered, would not center steadily on Taney's head. Norell cursed his own weakness bitterly. He growled: "Damn you, I can't finish you off like I would a beef. But what the hell am I going to do with you?"

Uneasy hesitation laid its grip upon him. Finally, grunting with the exertion, he heaved Slim's bony body up onto the wagon bed, rolling it into a slight depression in the canvas.

He muttered: "Maybe he'll die on the way in."

From the thicket he got his saddle horse and tied its reins to the tailboard of the wagon. Then he mounted to the wagon seat, released the brake, and rolled along the road. He drove into the yard of Spur headquarters at early dusk, and, as he faced Spurlock, his heavy voice was sharp. "I got the damned windmill, but if you want that 'puncher finished off, you'll have to do it yourself."

Norell's tone put a scowl on Spurlock's narrow, thin-lipped face. He shouted across the yard, and a couple of riders squatting beside the bunkhouse came toward him.

"Take this man in the house. Tell Julia to look after him."

They rolled Taney off the wagon and carried him toward the house.

Spurlock said: "If he don't die, we'll ship him out of the country as soon as he can travel."

Something in his tone stirred doubt in Norell. He muttered: "You've got this windmill, but Pruitt can get more. You'll have to think of something better than just stealin' 'em. I'll run Pruitt out, if you want, or I'll kill him." He fingered his bruised face. "You could never go straight at anything. But you'd better go straight at Pruitt, or he'll beat you. He's tougher than you think."

Spurlock laughed, the arrogant laugh of a man sure of himself. "He's already beaten. He's on a cattle-buying trip. He'll be back some time this week, thinking he's got water for the cattle, but he won't. The cattle will be thirsty after that long drive. They'll go to the river and trespass on Spur. That will bring Felix into it." He shrugged. "It's simple."

Some vague idea stirred in Norell's brain. Something in this situation offered a solution to his own difficulties, to the tortured conflict between his love for Sally Taylor and his loyalty to the Spur. But it evaded him, and finally he said sourly: "All right. Have it your own way. I don't know what the hell you have me around for. You never listen to me." He stalked away.

All through supper Norell brooded, but later, standing in the yard, he heard the bawl of a cow far out on the grass, and the thought crystallized. *Cattle! That's it! Pruitt's cattle. Sally wants money, does she? Well, by hell, Pruitt's cattle will give it to her. . . .*

Bart Pruitt had fully intended to purchase only a hundred head, as evidence of his intent to stay on his grass. However, on one ranch whose owner had been killed in a fall from a horse only a week before, the widow was anxious to sell, so the herd was gathered for a drive to the railroad.

Pruitt, Riley, and Dude circled the mixed herd at dusk on Monday. Pruitt estimated the cow count at three hundred, and most of the cows had calves beside them. Roughly two hundred and fifty steers and heifers were yearlings. The balance was steers, perhaps five hundred, ranging in age from two to five.

Riley said: "Steers need less water and will travel farther for it. I would say that steers were your best bet."

Bart Pruitt nodded, and wheeled his horse toward the house, with Riley and Dude loping behind. He could buy a hundred or two and ask for the right to cut the herd. He would pay a premium, but would get only the best. Or he could take the entire herd of steers at a flat price which would be five to seven and a half less per head than if he took only a few.

He decided to take them all, and at dawn began the dusty, tedious task of cutting them out and bunching them preparatory to beginning the drive. The herd was held in a small, bowl-shaped depression, in the exact center of which was a muddy bog hole, a seep, undoubtedly furnishing water in spring and early summer, but now rapidly drying up. Dude and Riley, with three ranch hands, held the herd bunched, while Pruitt, Mrs. Oglethorp, and an Oglethorp rider cut out steers and drove them over the rise.

The sun came up, gilding the land with the bright freshness of early morning. Dew disappeared from the grass, and the sun rose, and still the cutting went on. The steers ran heavily, but not as swiftly as the horses, and on occasion they would buck as they ran with sheer exuberance and good spirits.

At noon, Pruitt started them toward the Platte, after shaking Mrs. Oglethorp's hand and assuring her: "The rest of the money will be waiting for you at the Arapahoe Bank. I tally four hundred and seventy-one head, and I've paid you three thousand. That leaves eighty-seven seventy-five I still owe you. We'll water in Sand Creek tonight, and ought to get home by dark tomorrow."

She went back then, and for a while the steers, not yet lined out for the drive, kept breaking back, keeping Bart at a gallop, shouting until he was hoarse. It was strange, he thought, how even steers were individuals. By the time this drive was ended, he would know each of these five hundred-odd animals individually, would know the laggards that hung back in the drag. He would know, too, the outlaws, the stubborn and ornery ones that took each opportunity to break away to the shade of a clump of brush, or to gallop wildly back in the direction from which they had come.

He grinned. He would make believers out of these before this day was over. A rope for them. If, each time they broke away, a man would follow and bust them hard onto the ground, after a couple of experiences with rope and man and hard-packed ground, they would become more agreeable.

Five miles from the Oglethorp ranch, Dude and Riley caught up, their horses sweated and blowing hard. Riley wore a frown of worry on his ugly, scarred face. "You're playing it pretty thin, ain't you, boss? Driving in five hundred thirsty steers without even a seep to water them from?"

"Maybe. But when the Spur knows what I'm up to, they'll move fast, and I've got to be set before they find out. Taney's bringing the windmill, and Cooky the help to dig a well. If we water the cattle tonight at Sand Creek, they can go a couple of days without it. By that time I'll have water on my grass for them."

"What if Norell gets wind of what you're up to?"

"He won't. The only ones who know are Gilbreath, the banker, and you boys."

Riley shrugged, but his frown remained. "I wish I could feel as sure about it as you do. I keep wondering what we'd do if something was to happen to Slim an' the windmill."

In the drag of the herd, dust rose in blinding, choking clouds. Because Bart would give no man a more unpleasant job than the one which he himself held, he sent Dude to ride one flank, and Riley the other, remaining himself in the drag.

The day wore slowly on, and the cattle quieted, plodding docilely enough with little urging and no trouble. At full dark they reached Sand Creek, a mere trickle in the middle of a wide and sandy creekbed. The cattle spread out, a thin line a quarter mile long, and the sound of their drinking was an odd and pleasant sound in the darkness.

Pruitt bunched them where the creekbanks were high, himself standing one of the first four-hour watches, while Dude stood the other. Later, Riley relieved Dude, and later still, Dude relieved Bart.

At sunup, they drove again, after a hearty breakfast of broiled antelope.

Riley voiced a thought that had plagued Bart all of yesterday. "When are you going to brand, boss? Until you do, you're a sucker for any light-fingered saddle tramp in the country."

"We'll brand when we get home. While Cooky's men are digging the well and getting the windmill set up. I could have branded back at Oglethorp's, but we'd have lost three days doing it. And three days might be all the Spur needs to put me out of business."

Weariness and fatigue colored all of Bart's thoughts. But

there was satisfaction found in the sight of the undulating backs of the cattle. He had begun something solid and enduring. It was not finished. It would never be finished. But there was joy in the building, and peace a man found in no other way.

Understanding of the men who had built the West began in Bart, and something of the everlasting thrill of conquest touched him. A home would rise on the grass because Bart Pruitt made it rise. There would be a woman, and there would be young Pruitts yelling in the yard. These were the things that endured, the rock-hard foundations upon which empires were built. . . .

IX

At seven on Wednesday morning, Cooky and his five men, one of whom was the tall, bony homesteader, Tom Slaughter, began digging Bart Pruitt's first well, twenty-five yards from the low point of ground and two hundred yards from Pruitt's house. The cattle had arrived and were being held loosely bunched on the grass, many of them lying down, the remainder grazing, contented to rest and fill their empty bellies. But restlessness would increase unless they had water—and soon. By tomorrow night it would be nearly impossible to hold them, and to hold them where they were after tomorrow night would be to invite a stampede toward the river.

For an hour now, Bart had watched the southern horizon, but no telltale dust had arisen to announce Slim Taney's coming. At last, Bart saddled and rode in the direction of the river.

He struck the road above the Spur's turn-off, closely watching the ground for a wagon's tracks. There was evidence that a bunch of horses had been driven along this road, and this was puzzling until at the edge of the Spur's domain, where the road crossed the grass, Bart found where the horses had been turned off the road, and where the wide tracks of Slim's wagon began. Nothing more than this was needed to tell Bart that the Spur had the windmill! The Spur had Slim Taney, if he wasn't dead. Someone had talked, and, because they had, the Spur had brawny hands at Bart Pruitt's throat.

Whirling his horse, he touched spurs to the animal's sides. At a hard and reckless run, he went up the road, but long before he reached the Spur's turn-off, caution and returning sanity slowed his pace and warned him that to bolt into the Spur yard with this kind of foolhardiness would be to play directly into their hands as his father would have done. Barton Pruitt was fast with his gun, fast enough, perhaps, to kill Norell. Yet what man could ride into the Spur and kill the foreman and live to ride out again?

To Bart's direct nature, indirection was entirely alien. Yet here was a situation where only indirection could avail. There was no time to obtain another windmill. There was only time to recover the one the Spur held. Unless attacked by a half hundred men, the Spur was a fortress. Only a raid under cover of night, while the Spur slept, was feasible. Heading again toward the bunched cattle and the Pruitt homestead, Bart began to plan.

Pruitt's well was down fifteen feet at dark. The diggers were working in three feet of water and bailing constantly. Timbers taken from the house shored the soft earth walls so that cave-ins would become unlikely. Bart rigged lanterns, and the digging went on, with half of the men rolling in their blankets to sleep in shifts, while the other half worked.

Unseen by either Cooky or the diggers, Bart, Dude, and

Riley mounted at nine and rode out, taking a route that would bring them to the rear of the Spur instead of the river side. A crescent moon hung low on the western horizon.

Behind a low rise half a mile from the Spur headquarters buildings, Pruitt swung to the ground, saying in a low, cautious voice: "Dude, hold the horses. Riley and I will go look things over."

He and Riley removed their spurs, stuffed them into their saddlebags, and walked swiftly westward, their legs rustling against the tall, dry grass. In Bart was the tension of prospective action.

When they came over one of the last long, rolling rises of ground, they could see the twinkling lights of the Spur beneath them. Squares of light in the windows of the ranch house showed its sprawling, baronial splendor. Built of gray, square-cut blocks of stone, it towered three stories above the ground to gables and towers and fancy scrollwork. Vines crawled up the sides, and a wrought-iron fence surrounded the green and flowering yard. Even at night, the Spur ranch house was pretentious, as startling to come upon on the plains as it would have been in a steaming jungle. It was like a gigantic octopus, controlling the throttling tentacles that spread in all directions across the plain.

Pruitt squatted in a hollow of ground and fished in his pocket for his sack of makings. Thoughtfully he rolled a smoke, shielding his match as he struck it. He said: "We've got to wait until the last light has been out for thirty minutes."

Riley's voice was tight, but held a certain eagerness. "How you going to work it?"

"Why, it should be easy enough. You and Dude locate all the horses, while I find the wagon and hitch up. When I give you the go-ahead, you take the horses out, and I'll drive the wagon out. They can't follow afoot. By the time they catch the horses, enough to follow, we'll have the start we need."

Riley sighed. "You make it sound easy, but what if they spot us before we can get rolling?"

"Act drunk, like you were a Spur 'puncher just coming in from town."

"What if you can't find the wagon?"

"I'll find it. I've *got* to find it."

There was more confidence in his tone than he could feel. There were a dozen buildings on the Spur large enough to accommodate a freight wagon. He would have to catch and harness mules, working in the midst of more than thirty men who lived in the saddle and slept with one ear open. Chances of success were slim, Bart had to admit, yet he had no alternative. Already his cattle would be smelling the river, and, when the drift started in that direction, Cooky would be helpless to hold them. Before noon tomorrow he had to have water. For the Spur would have men with rifles along the river, shooting down Pruitt cattle as they came to drink. Wryly bitter, Bart shrugged in the darkness. If he failed tonight, it would not matter, for he would be dead.

Riley said: "All the lights are out but one, boss."

"All right. Let's get the horses."

The two returned to where Dude stood with their fidgeting, impatient horses. Bart swung up and led out, and Riley briefed Dude on the plan.

The Spur lay below them, dark and sleeping. A dog barked, and from the grass a coyote taunted. With only the small squeaking of saddle and stirrup, the soft footfalls of the slowly walking horses, they rode into the stronghold that was the Spur. From the corral a horse whinnied and a mule voiced his bray. Bart smiled. He had located his mules. Now to find the wagon.

One thing he had not considered before. Both wagon and

windmill might have been destroyed. If so, this dangerous long-shot raid would be useless and foolish. Bart dismounted and tied his horse to the corral fence. Then, moving wraith-like through nearly total darkness, he groped toward the barn as the most likely place to begin his search.

Riley made his way through the horses in the corral, catching the mules. Dude rode from building to building, searching out other horses that might be stabled, finding them by their soft whinnies.

Bart started as a voice called from the bunkhouse: "Who in hell's that?"

Deliberately Bart stumbled against a metal pail, and sprawled full length on the ground, affecting a low, drunken cursing. He got to his feet and said in the same low, thick voice: "Aw, shut up! Can't a man have a drink or two and come in late without rousing the whole damned place?"

But the bunkhouse door remained open, the dim shape of a man stayed there, and, as Bart staggered toward the barn, his insistent voice called. "Wait a minute! If you're going to bed down in the barn, gimme your matches first."

Pruitt stood stupidly, swaying slightly, as the man approached. He snarled: "Go to bed . . . lemme alone," but, as the man came within reach, he sprang, his hard fist swinging.

Surprise brought—"What the hell?"—from the man before the fist slammed into his jaw. Bart bore him backward, hands at his throat and, as both fell, drove his knee hard into the man's groin. Releasing the throat, Bart drove his fist again and again into the 'puncher's face until the body turned slack.

Rolling clear, Bart waited on hands and knees for a full minute. Then he got up carefully and went on toward the barn. He fell over a wagon tongue, staggered across the floor, and came up with a bang against a pile of doubletrees. He cursed, but he had felt a wagon wheel, and his hands traced the outline of a wagon seat, of a canvas-covered load behind it. He reached under the canvas and felt the cold steel of a pump, of piled-up timbers, and the wire-tied bundle of windmill vanes.

He heard Riley approaching with the mules and threw open both wide doors, careless now of the noise he made, for haste was the essential thing. Besides, careless noise would create less curiosity then stealthy noise.

The dog ran barking across the yard toward Bart who growled a vicious: "Shut up, damn you!" Surprisingly the dog obeyed, sniffing curiously then at Bart's boots.

In the dark, harnessing was difficult, and tension built up intolerably in Bart as he heard stirrings from the bunkhouse, as he saw a light gleam from the house. A man came from the bunkhouse carrying a lantern, and Norell's voice boomed: "Douse that light, you fool! Somebody's fooling around in the barn!"

Stubbornly ignoring the commotion, Bart backed the first team of mules to the wagon and fastened the tugs. Riley backed in the second team, and Bart fastened the tugs on one side while Riley fastened them on the other.

A shot rang out in the yard as Bart sprang to the seat, reins in hand. Riley faded into darkness. Then came Bart's wild yell: "Dude! Turn 'em out!"

He heard the pound of horse's hoofs, yelling, a volley of shots. Uncoiling the long whip, he laid it full across the backs of the mules, and, lumbering into the confusion of shouting and milling men, the wagon gained speed as the whip in Bart's hand made the mules lay deeply into their harness.

Men ran from the bunkhouse in long underwear, wraith-like and ludicrous shapes in the dim light that spilled from the ranch house window. But there was nothing either wraith-like or ludicrous about the guns they carried. Bullets cut through the wagon's canvas cover and clanged loudly on the iron windmill parts.

Norell boomed: "The horses, you fools! They're running off the horses! To hell with the wagon! We can catch that later. Stop them damned horses!"

Bart's mules were running, terrified by the racket of shots and shouting. He whirled through the gate, a hair's breadth behind the last of the horse herd, and for an instant Riley rode beside the wagon.

Riley shouted—"We're clear, boss!"—with disbelief ringing in his voice. "I'll pick you up soon's we've drove these horses a ways."

The road was only a scarcely visible streak ahead of Bart. He would have cut directly across the grass but for his knowledge that time would be inevitably lost in taking the direct route. Washes and gullies cut the grass, and detouring around these would lose for him everything he would gain by shortening his traveling distance.

He had a half hour start at the least. Even if Dude had missed a horse or two, it would still take the Spur that long to round up horses and organize a pursuit. But, at best, Pruitt could only expect to bring the wagon safely home with a short half hour in which to prepare his defenses.

He kept the mules at a run, excitement pounding in his veins. The raid had come off only because of its audacity! The Spur was so big, so powerful, that no one in the outfit could have expected anyone to have the impertinence or foolhardiness to attack it.

He heard the pound of hoofs behind him and thought—*Riley and Dude.*—but there was only one horse. The floating thought ran through his head: *One of them is down!* Involuntarily he pulled the mules to a trot. He had lost Slim Taney.

Now he had lost another. He could not hesitate between windmill and ranch, and the lives of men. Whichever of the two this was could take the windmill on in, and Bart himself would go back.

The galloping figure passed the tailboard of the wagon and tried to pull up, but Bart's sudden slowing made him overshoot. This was all that saved Bart's life. Beside him, flame poured from a gun muzzle, and in the brief flare he saw a face, neither Riley's nor Dude's, twisted and grimacing. Then it was past the wagon, and horse and man made a blob of plunging action.

The horse reared, whirled on his two hind legs, and flame again shot from the rider's gun. The bullet seared Bart's thigh like the burn of a branding iron. Pruitt yanked his own gun from holster, flung it upward with lightning speed. It bucked in his hand as flame shot from its muzzle.

The horse, coming down from its rearing stance, tottered and fell sideward, but the rider did not spring clear, remaining with the horse as it fell across him. The sound of the horse's fall was solid and sickening.

Pruitt yanked the mules to a halt and sprang from the seat, setting the brake. On the grass lay the crippled and struggling horse, the rider's foot caught and twisted in one stirrup.

Bart yelled: "I'll get you out, but forget you've got a gun, my friend, or I'll kill you as fast as I'll kill the horse!"

He got no answer, and because of the need for haste he slammed his gun into holster, circled the horse to avoid the thrashing hoofs, and caught the man beneath the arms.

The man was limp. With a swift, twisting motion, Bart's hand freed the 'puncher's foot and yanked him clear, dragged him back, and let him down. Bart struck a match, cupping the flickering flame with his hands. A red stain was spreading from the man's groin.

Bart ripped the shirt away, tore open the flap of the Levi's, and, seeing the wound, shrugged resignedly and threw the match away. His bullet had coursed through the horse, missing bones that might have deflected it and had entered the rider's groin. Carefully he felt for a pulse. Finding none, he straightened and returned to the wagon. *Hell, why did he have to come after me? Why didn't he go after the horses like Norell told him?*

The damage was done, the fat in the fire. Felix Chavalas who, so far, had a hands-off, if hostile, policy would be after him, or the Spur would, and there was little choice between the two. Had there been no casualties, the Spur might possibly have chosen to let this pass, willing to lose the windmill in preference to having it known that the Spur had been successfully raided by only three men.

Pruitt shrugged bitterly, asking himself: *What did you expect? Did you think you could put up a fight for your land without hurting someone?*

Suddenly he realized that the Spur still would have to explain to Chavalas why Pruitt had raided the Spur. Perhaps Felix would not be drawn into it yet; perhaps Bart would not have to fight Mary's father—not right away. In a fight with Felix, Bart would be at a disastrous disadvantage for, if he won, he would lose Mary and would be forced to become a fugitive. If he lost, he would lose both his ranch and his life.

Bart knew suddenly an oppressed feeling, realizing that the tremendous weight of the Spur hung over him, awaiting only the right moment to crush him. It revolved in the end around Felix Chavalas. Was Felix the Spur's man, or was he his own man?

Bart let the long whip snake out across the backs of the mules. He told himself to meet each thing as it came, and turned off the main road to take the rotted old trail toward the Pruitt homestead.

X

In the yard at the Spur, Norell defiantly faced Spurlock, answering the accusation in the tall rancher's eyes. "Damn you, I was asleep! So were you! Stop looking at me that way! I'll get the damned windmill back."

Spurlock said—"Kill him."—surprised at the realization that fear had given birth to the blunt order. He growled: "That's what you've been telling me to do, isn't it? Didn't you say to go at him directly, or he'd beat me? Well, I'm going at him directly now. Kill him."

He didn't like the crafty look in his foreman's eyes as Norell said in a lowered tone: "It's time you got something straight in your mind. I'm foreman of Spur. I'm not your executioner, and I'm no hired killer."

"Scared?"

"Maybe. Maybe I'm tired of getting the hind end all the time. I killed Pruitt's pa for you, but you're siccing me onto a gunman this time. I want something more than a pay check an' a pat on the back."

"What do you want?" Behind the façade of graying gentleman, Spurlock's eyes glittered, showing the hardness that had made him a range king. "I want Pruitt's cattle. I want you to stand between me and Felix Chavalas, no matter how I kill Pruitt." He hesitated, then said: "I want Pruitt's land, and the right of water in the river, too."

Spurlock could feel his anger rising, and the impulse gripped him to send his foreman packing. Then the thought of Pruitt came back, and for the first time in his life Spurlock could envision the disintegration of the Spur, until the house was weed-grown and shabby, until only a handful of scrubby cattle grazed the patented quarter sections along the river. He could see Pruitt, instead of himself, the big man in Arapahoe, the man with the money to make the puppets dance on the ends of their strings.

He said—"The cattle, yes . . . the land, no."—and felt ashamed to be bargaining with a hired hand. Yet he had always bowed to expediency when necessary. The Spur was the important thing, his reason for living, the source of his power.

Norell was grinning, a crafty grin that told Spurlock he had something further to ask. Again anger began to build.

Norell said: "Pruitt's fast, and he's tough. I want Chavalas kept off my neck even if you have to go to the governor to do it."

Spurlock sneered. "You're afraid."

The taunt failed to ruffle Norell. "No more than you are. But I want to live to enjoy . . . well, I just want odds in this game, that's all."

Spurlock shrugged, saying resignedly—"All right."—because there was nothing else he could say.

He watched Norell's broad back disappear toward the bunkhouse, and, because he had to find some justification for wrongdoing, he told himself the Spur produced enough cattle to feed half the State of Colorado. Arapahoe lives because of the Spur. Isn't the good of the many more important than the life of one quarrelsome drifter? Spurlock had had plenty of practice in deluding himself, for in his background was poverty, hunger, and humiliation, a drunken father, and a mother who sought release in promiscuity—and social ostracism for himself because of his parents. So now he refused to acknowledge that it was not the good that came out of the Spur that interested him half so much as the importance the outfit gave him in the community. He was a big man in Arapahoe. He was getting to be a big man in Denver City. Someday, perhaps. . . .

Spurlock's early life along the St. Louis riverfront had

created in him an insatiable thirst for wealth. He had the wealth. Now he wanted power. Yet if he lost the wealth, the power would become forever unattainable. Feeling entirely justified now in any course he might take, he was returning to the house when with one part of his mind he heard Norell's shout: "Get them damn' horses! We'll get the wagon later!"

He must warn Norell and the men that no word of this raid was to leak into Arapahoe. Spurlock could not stand laughter at his expense. Of course, Arapahoe would laugh only behind his back, but laugh all the same.

In the living room Spurlock sank into a leather-covered chair before the big fireplace where last night's embers still smoldered. He bit the end off one of the expensive cigars he had shipped from Havana and lighted it thoughtfully, abandoning himself to recollections.

Coming to Denver City during the gold rush, he had early seen that beef for the gold seekers, for the thousands who would follow them, would in the end become more important than the gold itself. He had hired down-on-their-luck miners, had gotten them to stake homestead claims along the banks of the Platte. He had paid them wages while they proved up on their claims, then had bought them out. One or two who had balked at selling had stayed—underground in unmarked graves. Building the Spur had been slow. Spurlock had started with little more than an idea, a handful of scrubby cattle, and a saddle horse. His own gun had at first enforced his demands, but he had stopped that when he had come to realize that no matter how powerful a man becomes the people sicken of killing and that eventually the killer must pay for his crimes in some manner.

He had found Norell useful, not only as foreman, but as a man to take over necessary enforcement chores. Norell, loyal and proud of the vastness of the Spur, could always be relied upon to carry out orders without question. But something had happened to Norell, counteracting his loyalty to the Spur. Upstairs, he heard the wounded Slim Taney groan, and heard Julia's slippered steps as she went to him.

Norell was getting soft—or scared. A year ago he would not have given a second thought to finishing off Taney. Spurlock thought: *It is time for Norell to go. I'll let him get rid of Pruitt, then. . . .* The ruthlessness that had built a ranch from nothing was at work again, and with its return came rejuvenation to Spurlock. Once rid of Pruitt and Norell, if trouble threatened, there were the Wes Hardins and the Bill Bonneys. Money could buy anything. Anything at all.

In the bunkhouse, Norell's heavy Slavic face was somber with thought. He had no intention whatever of meeting Pruitt face to face, except as a last resort. Norell was no coward. Neither was he a fool. He had the intelligence to know fear, but he had the courage to overcome it when necessary.

Now he was puzzling over how to get rid of Pruitt without the risk of an open challenge and shoot-out. He wanted Pruitt's cattle, to obtain Sally Taylor. Dead, he could enjoy neither Sally nor the money the cattle would bring. Briefly he considered a raid or an ambush, but here he came up against danger from Felix Chavalas, who might never touch Spurlock, but would not balk at going after Norell. Norell had demanded that Spurlock stand between him and Chavalas in case of trouble, but he did not delude himself that this could guarantee his safety. The thing, then, must be done with guile, in some way get at Pruitt with no danger either to the Spur or Norell himself. Maybe Pruitt and Chavalas could be pitted against each other, Pruitt as the lawbreaker, Chavalas as the law enforcer. If Pruitt won, he would become a fugitive. If he lost, he would be dead.

When no immediate solution offered itself to Norell, he sighed and called into the night from the open door—"Chuck!"—and, once the answer came: "When Alvie comes back with the horses, corral 'em and go to bed."

"But, Les, you ain't going to let Pruitt get away with it, are you?"

"He won't get away with it."

Norell closed the door and sat down on his bunk to remove his boots. He shucked out of his shirt and dropped his pants to the floor. In thin long summer underwear, he showed biceps as thick as a man's leg, a flat belly crisscrossed with rippling muscles, a chest that breathed like a bellows. With a long sigh, he lay back on his bunk and pulled a thin blanket over him. His problem did not keep him awake. He never even heard the 'punchers come into the bunkhouse, one after another, talking in subdued voices until they fell asleep. He did not know that Chuck waited until one o'clock for Alvie, and, when the cowhand did not return, took a lantern and followed his tracks. But when he awoke, it was Chuck who woke him.

"Les, Les, he killed Alvie! Damn him, he killed Alvie!"

Norell sat up. The dim, gray light of dawn filtered through the windows. He could see the shock, the hatred in the little 'puncher's seamed and leathery face.

"Les, let me go get Pruitt now!"

"Shut up. Let me think."

Norell slipped into his clothes and went outside. As Norell gave the pump handle a few quick jerks and ducked his head under the icy water, he considered Chuck as the tool with which to kill Pruitt. But Chuck was a fool. He'd only get himself killed.

He growled: "Let Pruitt alone. He's mine."

Chuck started to protest, but the look in Norell's eyes silenced him.

Norell's anger began to stir at Alvie for disobedience of orders. His voice was a snarl. "Rouse the crew, damn you! Get out and round up some horses. Alvie got just what he had coming for going after Pruitt instead of the horses."

Chuck turned away, surly and grumbling.

Norell called: "How was Alvie killed? In the back, or the belly?"

"The belly, low where it would hurt. The bullet broke his spine." Chuck slouched away, and Norell watched the angry set of his narrow shoulders.

Abruptly, and from nowhere apparently, the plan came fully formed and perfect enough to startle the unimaginative Les Norell. Had he been told that the plan had been in his unconscious for years, he would have laughed. Yet this plan had lived in the back of his mind, of no use until change came to Les Norell himself. Sally Taylor had created in him the desperate need for sudden wealth, and Pruitt had shown him that the Spur could be taken.

Norell began to laugh at the plan's simplicity. He laughed at himself for not having thought of it before. He laughed at the dupes who would carry it out for him. Then he thought of Sally Taylor, of her beautiful white body, of her full lips and darting pink tongue. She would belong to him completely. Pruitt would be dead, Storrie Taylor out of the way, and the Spur's twenty thousand cattle would belong to Les Norell!

XI

Dawn on the grass found Bart Pruitt puzzling over the windmill drawings, tenseness only partly relieved by concentration. The well was finished, down twenty feet and holding nearly ten of water. Three diggers were posted on nearby knolls with instructions to fire their guns when the Spur's riders were spotted, then return at a gallop. Riley was with the cattle. Dude slept. Bart and the remaining diggers sorted through the wagon, and slowly the windmill tower began to rise.

At sunup Bart knocked off, and he and his crew squatted to sip Cooky's scalding black coffee, to tear at chunks of fried beef. Finished, they relieved the watchers, and Pruitt relieved Riley.

Riley met him with vast puzzlement in his eyes. "What the hell's the matter with them Spur *hombres?* They've had time to catch up with their horses. Why haven't they jumped us?"

"They'll likely get around to it before the day's over."

By mid-afternoon the windmill was finished and stood, a gaunt skeleton against the sky, its vanes turning slowly in the wind. Water, still muddy, gushed from the pipe, running in a sluggish stream into the hollow and forming a slowly enlarging pool there.

Jubilation, not entirely killed by apprehension, stirred in Bart. The Spur had not attacked. The windmill was finished, and there was water on the grass for his cattle. But his uneasiness was increasing and eventually left him no thought for anything else.

He called Riley, saying briskly: "Water the cattle and let them go. Give Dude the first watch. I'll be back before midnight. I've got to find out what's holding them back. If they're not jumping us, it's only because Norell's got something better in mind."

He swung into the saddle and trotted away. At sundown, he reached the buildings at the Spur, and dismounted to creep close, to watch the busy but normal activity in the yard.

A few horses stood in the corral, perhaps a dozen, certainly not enough to mount a raid against Pruitt. Still puzzled, Bart slipped back, mounted, and took the roundabout way that would bring him out on the Spur's lane before it met the main road. There was one more thing he had to see—the place where he had killed the pursuing rider the night before. Perhaps the sign could tell him something.

The sun was down when he reached the spot, but ample light reflected from the towering fluffy cloudbank for him to see that both horse and rider had been carried off, and to discern the marks on the ground made by willow branches brushed back and forth to eliminate sign. A frown creased Pruitt's forehead. This was not the Spur's way. Riding again toward town, his anticipation of seeing Mary was dulled by his sure knowledge that, if the Spur had not attacked him, it was only because they had some more terrible and effective weapon at hand.

Yet what could they do more terrible than killing him and destroying what he had built and bought? The answer came easily to Pruitt's mind: *Discredit me. Make the sheriff do their killing for them.* He rode into town at dark, stabled his horse, and walked slowly through the soft dark toward Mary Chavalas's restaurant.

The livery stable hostler, a gangling, red-haired kid, passed him, hurrying, his face a blob of white as he went by. Caution touched Bart, instinct telling him this boy was afraid. Half a block ahead, light from the open door of the Idle Hour washed the boy's form briefly as he went in.

Passing the word that I'm in town, mused Pruitt. Now he moved more carefully, and a warning voice within him was saying: *Don't be a fool. Turn toward the tracks and reach the restaurant from the other direction.* But his pride and stubbornness were such that he strode firmly on upstreet. Shortly Bart would know where the stalker was, for a tongue of flame would tell him.

He asked himself: *Will it end this time?* He shrugged, not knowing the answer. The feeling was strong in him that, when the time did come, he would know it, yet he had seen men die and their surprise could be accounted for only by their belief that they had been betrayed by this same feeling. A hundred yards ahead he would cross the dim beam of light from the doors of the Idle Hour. He would have only short notice then of his stalker's intention to murder. Once in that beam of light, a man in the shadows would be invisible to him until a gun blasted.

Bart paced steadily forward, his hand still and stiff at his side. There had been something vaguely familiar about that bowlegged form, just as there had been vague recognition in him as he'd bent over the man he had killed last night. Reaching the outer dim fringe of light, movement in the darkness was more a feeling to him than an actuality, but it made him leap backward. The voice and tongue of flame came simultaneously, with Bart hearing only—"Damn you, Pruitt, you. . . ."—before the blast of a .45 cut it off.

Then Bart's own gun was in his hand, hammer coming back as the weapon cleared leather. He shot toward the flash, a little high and to the right, where the man's chest should be. He heard the unmistakable sound of a bullet striking into flesh.

Men poured from the doors of the Idle Hour, and Pruitt called: "Get back inside and drop your guns before you come out! Whoever he was, he shot first, but if Felix wants me, I'll be at the restaurant."

For a moment he stood there, aware he was invisible to their light-blinded eyes, then he turned and walked toward the restaurant, never bothering to look behind him.

* * * * *

A shot on the streets of Arapahoe, while not unknown, was unusual enough to merit curiosity. Mary Chavalas came to the door of the restaurant, her full-bodied shape in sharp silhouette and strikingly pleasant to Bart's eyes. Her voice held controlled alarm. "What happened?"

"Man took a shot at me."

There was a natural fragrance about Mary that Bart found stimulating and exciting. Alarm, momentary and fleeting, widened her eyes. "You didn't . . . ?"

"Kill him? I don't know. All I could see was his gun flash. I hit him, probably in the chest."

"Who was it?"

He said: "I don't know, Mary. I told you I couldn't see him."

Many things had been reflected in these few moments in Mary Chavalas's sensitive features. These had been fear—for Bart. Doubt had followed as fear was banished. Now she was sure he was a savage, interested only in revenge. "It was a Spur rider, wasn't it?" she asked.

Bart took her arms, shaking her gently. "Mary, I stabled my horse and was on my way here for supper. The kid from the stable passed me and went into the saloon, and seconds later a man came out. He was short, and bowlegged. I could see that much before he moved into the shadows. When I came into the light, he shot."

She wanted to believe him, but could not. He stared at her, his eyes turning unfriendly and angry. Suddenly and savagely, he crushed her to him, stopping her struggles as he lowered his head. She turned her face aside. Tears in her widened dark eyes rolled down her cheeks. Bart put his hand behind her head, bringing her face around. His lips found hers and held them, full of the demand that coursed in his veins.

Her breasts rose and fell with her hastened breathing. Her body molded itself to his own, and she stood on tiptoe, reaching, hungry.

When he broke away, he buried his face in her hair, murmuring hoarsely: "Mary . . . Mary!"

A man running past put fear back into her eyes, and swiftly she drew Bart into the shadows. "Get out of town! The Spur will say you shot first or that he was unarmed! They'll say anything so that Father will have to arrest you. Please, please! Go now while there is still time."

At the stubborn tone in his voice she shrugged fatalistically, as though she had known what his response would be. "Is Arapahoe a town where a man has to be afraid to defend himself, Mary? Are there no rights here but Spur rights? If it *is* that kind of town, perhaps I'd better go."

Mary's violence surprised him. She flamed at him. "It is a good town . . . or was until you came! Now it is different. Already a man is dead because of you."

Bart thought—*Two are dead.*—but held his silence. His face made an angular, shadowed image in the dim light, and her eyes, now pleading and soft, searched it.

She said, her voice subdued: "Is there nothing you want here but land and revenge and cattle?"

Mary Chavalas was trying to bargain, shy as a woman must be with a man who has not spoken out. Blood grew hot within Pruitt's body as he said: "I want you, Mary."

"Then take me. Take me away from here . . . now . . . tonight!"

He shook his head. "No. There would always come a time when I'd look at you and remember what I ran from . . . and why."

Her shoulders slumped, and her head dropped. She said: "To a woman, love is everything. To a man. . . ."

"Mary." Pruitt felt helpless as men will always feel helpless when a woman forces a choice between herself and the man's sense of right and duty.

Her head lifted, and her eyes blazed. "All right. Have your revenge, but do not expect to have me, too!"

Weariness came to Pruitt and great discouragement. He heard the brittle steps of Felix coming down the walk, the click of Felix's high-heeled boots on the boardwalk.

Bart said: "I'm here, Felix. But do you need that Spur rider at your back?"

The sheriff whirled, his voice deadly. "Get back to the saloon, damn you! When I need deputies, I'll appoint some."

Pruitt saw the man's surly expression as he passed through the restaurant's beam of light. Following him was the doctor, a tall, thin, but paunchy man with a sour, horsy face, and with a black bag dangling from his bony hand.

Felix said: "Look the man over, Doc. Make your report here as soon as you can."

The doctor and the Spur rider passed out of sight in the darkness. Felix growled: "Get inside. I thought I told you to walk soft."

Pruitt opened the door and let Mary precede him. He said over his shoulder: "When a gun flares at you in the darkness, there is only one sensible thing to do. I did it."

"Suppose he did shoot first? Who saw him do it? Who's to say you shot in self-defense? The saloon was full of Spur riders. None of them saw it, but they'll all say they did . . . maybe say it was murder, that the Spur man was unarmed."

Pruitt remained silent, a growing sense of injustice within him. The door opened, and the doctor came in, glancing briefly at Pruitt.

He said: "As long as this man's in town, there'll be more need for an undertaker than a doctor. Through the heart in pitch darkness." He sat down at the counter. "Give me a cup of coffee, Mary." Then he turned to Chavalas. "I'll have the death certificate at your office in the morning."

Chavalas asked: "What happened to the Spur riders?"

The doctor cocked his head, listening. From the night came the pound of many hoofs, diminishing rapidly. "There's your answer."

Bart sat down, murmuring: "Is it too late for supper, Mary?"

Chavalas exploded. "Damn you, Pruitt, Norell will be in before midnight to sign a complaint. Get out of town before. . . ."

But Mary's voice broke in, soft, but without expression: "No, Bart. What do you want?"

Bart said: "A steak. And quit looking at me like that. Am I supposed to go hungry because a bushwhacker tries to kill me?" Anger put recklessness in him, yet guilt was a restraining hand upon the recklessness. He turned to the sheriff. "Be real sure of yourself when you come after me, Felix. Be dead sure you're right. Because if you come only because of the Spur's pressure, you'd better have your gun in your hand."

All that had seemed so good—Mary, the vast grassland, water gushing from the windmill pipe, now were worthless to him. With a curse he rose, and slammed the door behind him.

XII

One week dragged by. In all the country lurked a stillness, a deceptive stillness, as though even the grassland waited thirstily for blood to spill. On Saturday afternoon, Norell rode into Arapahoe, tense as a man will be when he stakes everything on one last throw of the dice. At the Idle Hour, he had three drinks of whisky in as many minutes, then walked to the hotel to sit on the verandah and take up his vigil.

The homesteaders left the stores and headed their rickety wagons out of town. As the supper hour approached, the sun sank brassily behind the western mountains. Felix Chavalas came from his office, walking with measured strides, and stopped at the corner, letting his glance run upstreet and down. His habitual watchfulness would mark each strange face on Main Street and catalogue each potential danger to the peace of his town.

He saw Norell, and Norell could imagine his puzzled thoughts. Felix would be asking himself what he had asked himself all week: *Why hasn't Norell been in to sign a complaint? What has he got up his sleeve?*

Norell smiled faintly, musing: *You'll find out soon enough, Sheriff. When I need you, I'll let you know.*

Felix moved down Platte and entered Mary's restaurant. Although seemingly relaxed, Norell saw everyone on Platte Street, and at last saw tall, slight Storrie Taylor. Storrie appeared to be full of his own thoughts and unaware that anything existed except them. Norell rose leisurely and stepped down to the walk, savoring the aroma of the imported Havana. Dusk had passed its gentle hand across the land, and full dark was only minutes away. When Norell saw Storrie go into the Idle Hour, he strolled slowly toward shack town.

He followed his well-known route, and dark had fallen when he at last came into the alley behind the Taylor house. Sally would be waiting in the secret dark of the porch, perhaps smiling gently with a beautiful woman's assurance, or perhaps tapping her foot because of impatient passion. But she would wait.

As Norell stepped over the fence, only then did it strike

him that to a large degree his plan depended on Sally's co-operation, on the strength of her desire, both for him and for luxury. What if her desire were not strong enough?

She came off the porch into his arms, and he would have pulled him down onto the damp grass but for her protest. "No. Inside is safer."

She wore only a thin dress, and her body beneath it was vibrant and alive.

Norell's voice was hoarse. "I have to talk to you. Stay away from me until I finish, or I'll forget what I wanted to say."

Sally laughed, but led him inside, her body swaying seductively. Norell took a last impatient puff at the cigar and laid it carefully on the edge of the table.

He said quickly, so she would not notice this: "How would you like to have the money from ten thousand cattle . . . twenty thousand . . . maybe even the Spur in the bargain?"

Triumph glowed in her face. Excitement brought her close, perfume heady, hair silky, fragrant and soft. "How will you do it?"

He outlined his plan, wording it carefully, but he need not have worried. He had underestimated the lust for wealth that consumed her. He had underestimated her ruthlessness.

She breathed: "It's perfect, Les! Perfect! Storrie will be out of the way, and so will Spurlock. Pruitt will no longer threaten the Spur, and you can take your time looting it. But what about Julia?"

Norell laughed. "She's sick of the Spur. She thinks no one knows it, but she's been meeting Frank Killen, who would like nothing better than to take Julia and head for the city. Julia will take a tenth of what the Spur is worth and be glad to get it, especially after rustlers start to work on the cattle."

He nodded his head toward the stub of the cigar on the table edge. "It's one of Spurlock's. He ships 'em in special from Havana. Let Storrie find this one. He'll recognize it quick enough. Put on a good act. Deny that anyone's been here. Make him browbeat it out of you. Cry when you finally admit it was Spurlock." He watched her closely. "Think you can put it over?"

Sally Taylor was smiling, the enigmatic smile of a confident woman. Anticipation was in her smile as well, and Norell felt a faint uneasiness. *Damn her, she's going to enjoy it!* was his thought, and it disturbed him. Unconsciously he was pitying Storrie Taylor, not because he liked Storrie, but because deep within him was the unrecognized awareness that someday he himself might stand where Storrie now stood.

He said: "Storrie will kill for you, Sal. I would. But remember this. If I ever have to kill a man for you, I won't stop with him. I'd kill you, too."

She came to his arms, her body against his, smilingly confident that she knew well how to make a man forget his troubled thoughts. Her breath was warm in his ear.

"I love you, Les! I love you! I want you."

Flame exploded in a searing, blinding flash in Norell's brain. His arms went about her savagely. But at that moment, steps echoed on the porch.

Norell muttered: "What the hell?"

Sally, alarmed, laid a hand over his mouth. "Run, Les . . . run! If he finds you here, everything is ruined!"

Les bounded into the kitchen and onto the porch. The slam of the back door and the closing of the front, simultaneously, were blended. Sally, flushed and wide-eyed, could see that Storrie wasn't sure he had heard the back door slam. Later he would remember, and would know he had.

Storrie at once noticed Sally's flush, her excitement, the guilty and surprised look on her face. He sniffed, thinking he caught the faint aroma of cigar smoke.

Sally murmured: "You are home early. Was Frank Bodine dull tonight?"

Storrie said thickly: "I didn't go to Frank's. I went to the saloon." Suspicion turned his voice sharp.

Sally smiled. "All right, Storrie. Are you hungry?"

He nodded, scowling. Sally went into the kitchen and began to make coffee. She reached for the eggs, hesitated, then broke two into a pan. She could hear him prowling about—froze at the sudden silence as he found the cigar stub.

His voice, calling through the door, was still and cold. "Sal?"

"What is it, darling?"

He asked: "Who's been here?"

Innocence and surprise filled her voice. "No one's been here. Why?"

"Liar!"

She came into the room, indignant. "Storrie! You have no right. . . ."

She was pleased at her sudden start of fear, at the guilty flush she felt stain her cheeks. She put her glance on her toes, and kept it there, feeling the heat and anger of his stare.

"Damn you, who was here?" His fingers dug into her arms, and he shook her fiercely. "Who was it?" His voice rose to a shout. "Who was it?"

Sally looked up at him, defiance in her eyes. "No one."

His hand made a short arc, and the sound against her cheek was sharp and flat. He put his hand on her chest and pushed. Sally went backward, crumpling into a heap on the floor.

Storrie whispered viciously—"Bitch!"—and picked up the cigar. He looked at the band, saw the word **Havana**, and suddenly he snarled: "Spurlock! Money! Selling yourself like a common. . . ."

He stalked toward her, red before his eyes, madness in his brain. Stark terror made Sally's eyes bulge, made the veins stand out on her forehead. "Storrie, please! Don't! I'll tell. . . ."

Her voice broke his spell of madness, and, as he quieted, her terror fled, the calculating smile returned.

He asked nastily: "How much did he pay you?"

She stood, facing him valiantly. "Nothing. I love him, do you hear? I love him! He. . . ."

Storrie hit her, and she went to the floor again. Storrie looked at her, his features running the gamut of emotion. He whirled to a desk, found his gun in the drawer, and stalked furiously into the dark street. Embittered as only a wife's infidelity can embitter a man, he took no notice that a man trailed him half a block behind, nor did he hear the dim beat of horse's hoofs back of him as he rode out of town.

He spent the night in a ravine and did not know that Norell, on the brow of a knoll half a mile away, waited there for dawn. And when dawn came, Storrie was ready. He had hollowed a niche in the steep bank of the arroyo, a niche that commanded a view of the lane leading from the Spur. Storrie would be looking at Spurlock's back from the time the rancher entered the arroyo until he left it. He would himself be unseen, unless Spurlock happened to turn. But Spurlock would have no chance to turn, for Storrie's bullet would smash into his spine the instant he entered the arroyo.

Les Norell's patient vigil was rewarded. Dawn light told the foreman all he needed to know. He was smiling as he slipped back to his horse, mounted, and rode to the Spur.

Spurlock was seated at the long kitchen table, eating, when Norell came through the kitchen door. The smell of frying bacon and flapjacks was pleasant.

Norell said: "Felix wants you in town. He wants you to

sign the complaint against Pruitt."

Spurlock scowled. "You sign it. I've got other business this morning."

Norell's eyes hardened. "You want me to get rid of Pruitt. You've said I can do it my own way. This is a part of getting rid of him, and I want you to sign that complaint."

Spurlock put a cold, haughty stare on Norell, then with obvious irritation he rose and shrugged as he said grudgingly: "All right. But you had better move fast. Pruitt's windmill is pumping. Time is getting short."

Norell laughed. "Don't worry. This week will wind it up."

"What's so damned funny?" Spurlock settled his wide-brimmed Stetson on his head.

Norell said: "Pruitt. Chavalas. You. Everything." And laughed again.

Snorting, Spurlock went out the door. When he rode from the yard, Norell followed, but he cut to the north and was atop his knoll when Spurlock came into sight—riding to his death. Spurlock rode erect, left hand holding the reins, right hand straight and stiff at his side. A man habitually alert, thought Norell, and felt a touch of doubt. Suppose Storrie missed? One instant's warning was all Spurlock would require. He would whirl, and his first bullet would kill.

An eternity passed. Spurlock's horse paused briefly at the rim of the arroyo, then dropped his head and went into it. Another eternity for Norell, and finally a single shot. Dust boiled from the arroyo. Norell ran to his horse and mounted.

Spurlock's horse came running from the ravine, riderless, and Norell dropped into it, gun in hand, hammer back and ready. He snarled: "Drop it, Taylor!"

Storrie's face was ghastly. His voice was scarcely audible. "He had it coming! He had it coming, I tell you! Sally. . . ." Storrie still held the gun loosely.

Norell crowded his horse against the bank clerk, and his own gun made a chopping downward motion. Storrie howled, and the gun dropped from his numbed fingers. Norell dismounted. He said—"I want the Spur."—and looked across at the crumpled, lifeless figure in the dust. "With him dead, I can have it. Get your horse and ride. It will be afternoon before I can get in to see Felix. You will have at least that much start."

Hope stirred in Storrie's eyes and a gratitude that made Les Norell feel shame. With a last look at Spurlock, Storrie pounded out of the ravine, a thoroughly terrified killer atop a speeding horse.

Les Norell looked down at Spurlock, a little surprised and a little disturbed because this had been so easy. Then he thought of Sally, of the vastness that was the Spur, of the thousands of cattle that roamed its wide acres. To his amazement he found that his feeling toward the Spur had not changed at all, and abruptly he realized that to him as to most of the people in this country the Spur was more than land and cattle. It almost possessed a personality and will of its own. Norell had thought his boundless loyalty had been to Spurlock. But now Spurlock was dead and the loyalty still existed. It must, then, have been for the ranch and not for the owner.

Norell smiled, and suddenly peace flooded through his mind. Hard this had been because he had thought he was violating his ingrained loyalty. Now he knew he had violated nothing, and he could go ahead with no more doubt to plague him. Pruitt was next, but Chavalas would take care of Pruitt. The thing was almost done.

XIII

By a circuitous route, Norell returned to the Spur. In his mind, he was guilty of Spurlock's murder, until the realization struck him with surprise: *Why, I have done nothing! The law can't touch me!*

He went to the cook house and ordered the grumbling, sour-faced cook: "Get me some breakfast."

After he had eaten, he made his rounds of blacksmith shop, corrals, even looking in distastefully at the chickens. He thought: *By hell, I'll get rid of Julia's damned squawking chickens.*

There was pleasure and deep satisfaction in picturing himself the master of the Spur. There was excitement in visualizing Sally as his every night. If there was a nagging thought that Sally might be unfaithful to him, as she had been to Storrie, he put it firmly from him, in his egotism convinced that Storrie was less of a man than he.

The Spur crew came and went throughout the morning. But there was no excited announcement that Spurlock's body had been found.

At last, toward noon, his nerves drawn tight by waiting, Norell sent a rider to Arapahoe on an errand. Lounging against the bunkhouse wall, rolling cigarette after cigarette in shaking fingers, he calculated the time it would take the man to reach the arroyo, the faster time on the return trip. He heard the pound of hoofs thundering up the lane before anyone else.

The rider tore into the yard, shouting: "Norell! Hey! Spurlock's dead . . . down in that dry wash with a bullet in him!"

Before he could throw himself from the saddle, men were running, carrying the tools they had been using—a bridle, a blacksmith hammer, a half-coiled lariat.

Norell shouted: "Pruitt, damn him!" And barked at the rider: "Shot where?"

"Right in the middle of the back! Maybe he ain't dead! Hurry!"

Norell bellowed: "Saddle up, everybody! If Felix won't take the bastard, the Spur will!"

He saddled a horse, and swung up. Already half a dozen men were lining out at a gallop. Norell overtook them and rode at their head. Dust strung out for a mile as every available rider got into saddle. At the tail end of the column came a buckboard, with Julia Spurlock driving, dry-eyed and white-faced.

A hasty glance told Norell that Spurlock had not moved, yet he quickly dismounted and dropped beside the body to listen for a heartbeat. He rose, scowling, although all he felt was relief and satisfaction. He faced the sober 'punchers and snarled: "Pruitt'll hang for this, if I have to tie the knot myself! A couple of you stay with Julia, and get him back to the house. The rest of you come with me."

There was no galloping now, only the steady and remorseless movement of a close-packed band of grim-faced men, stolid, and with unquestioning loyalty. Pruitt had long ago sworn he would kill Spurlock for killing his father; he had done it, and he would pay. Doubt that Pruitt was the killer never entered their heads. Who else would want to kill Spurlock? Who else could gain by Spurlock's death? Deviousness such as Norell's would have been incomprehensible to these honest men.

Chavalas would have his chance. But if he failed or shirked his duty, the Spur would see justice done. The weapon Norell wielded against Bart Pruitt now was a hundred-fold more terrible because of this conviction of rectitude. These were not men fighting for pay, or profit.

Yet until this last killing from behind they had held a certain admiration for Bart Pruitt. Of course, he had killed Alvie and Chuck, but both had made their plays and had been beaten fairly and openly. The risks of the game. The Spur had stolen Pruitt's windmill. Pruitt had recovered it. Alvie had taken on the fight alone, and had disobeyed Norell's orders, getting killed for his pains. Chuck had sought to avenge Alvie, and had been shot himself. But Spurlock had been given no chance. He had probably not even known his killer was near until the fatal bullet had smashed his spine. And so the anger of Spur's riders mounted as they rode.

Felix Chavalas saw them as they entered the lower end of Platte Street. Standing spraddle-legged, he waited for them to approach. His deep-tanned face, so startlingly framed by the mane of pure white hair, showed only his usual hostility, a warning that until he was dead Felix Chavalas would be the law in Arapahoe and on the grass. Townsfolk came into the street, uneasiness in their wondering eyes, in their hands that would not stay still. Mary Chavalas looked from the window of her home, then hurried toward the front door.

Norell said bluntly—"Spurlock's dead . . . shot in the back."—and gave Felix time to digest this before he said: "Will you get Pruitt, or does the Spur have to do it for you?"

A flush darkened Felix Chavalas's face. His eyes narrowed, turned hard. Norell looked away. Felix said: "Tell your riders I have never needed twenty men to tell me how or when to do my job. Pruitt knows damned well I'd give him credit for being above a back shooting. That's why he did it this way. Well, come on and sign a complaint. I'll get him for you."

Norell tried hard to stare Felix down but failed. He swung in his saddle and called to the men behind him: "Take the day off. Stay in town. But stay sober." He stepped off his horse and handed the reins to one of his riders. "All right, Felix. Let's go."

At the front of her house, Mary Chavalas hesitated. The grim-faced Spur riders were plain enough announcement that Bart Pruitt was in grave danger. Yet knowing his stubbornness, she knew that her warning would be less than useless unless she could tell him why they were hunting him. It was unlikely they were after him for the shooting on the street several nights before. Something else must have happened.

She was waiting on Third as Felix and Les Norell approached. She spoke composedly, but inside her was turmoil and terror—and premonition. "What is it, Father?"

Felix scowled at her interference. He would have made an evasive answer, but Norell said sharply: "It's Spurlock! Pruitt's killed him . . . shot him in the back!"

Sparks flashed from Mary's eyes in her instantaneous defense of Bart. But she choked off her sharp answer, seeing by Norell's attitude that Pruitt was already condemned.

Felix said impatiently: "Come on . . . come on! Let's get this over with."

He moved on toward the courthouse with his measured pacing, a coldly efficient human instrument pitted against his fellowmen, to bend them to his will or break them in the effort. The reasons for men's crimes did not concern Felix. The laws he enforced were to be interpreted in one way only, and that literally. He was not the judge of whether or not Pruitt was guilty. Norell could sign the complaint, and Felix would have to serve it. Once Pruitt was in jail, Felix would be out of the thing altogether.

But, thought Mary with quick fright, Bart would never surrender himself to the doubtful justice that the Spur's judge and the Spur's jury would dispense. And if he would not surrender to Felix, this could end only in death for Felix—or death for Bart. Her thoughts were swift as Felix and Norell walked away from her. Her decision was made before they entered the courthouse door. She ran up Platte, holding her skirts high so that they would not trip her. Reaching home, she avoided the porch and ran around to the stable.

She saddled Felix's own black gelding, smiling wryly as she considered his rage when he found the animal gone. But she could never reach Bart first if she did not take this fast and spirited horse. She lifted herself into her smooth-worn sidesaddle, and let the horse have his head as she began her circle around the town. To Felix, her action would be a betrayal, but in her own mind Mary had no other choice, for now she was forced to admit what she had never admitted before, even to herself—that she loved Bart Pruitt, that the only crime he could ever commit that would still her love would be for him to kill her father.

But someone had murdered Spurlock! Mary's frantic wish brought words tumbling from her. "Oh, I wish I knew him better! Then I'd know whether he could have done this thing or not!"

Something told her: *You cannot love him or you would not doubt.* But even this was wrong, for love and trust were different things, and each could exist without the other.

The endlessness of the grass, the waving, changelessness calmed Mary's tortured thoughts. The grass laughed at human frailties. The grass was here before men came. The grass would always be here when men had gone. Yet always the grass was the prize, the thing men fought for, or at least the tangible expression of the thing they fought for—a place that was all their own, security that only the bounty of the grass could provide. To some men, security meant a living, and to others their own individual strength was all the security they desired. To men like Spurlock, security was wealth and power, but even he could defeat his own desires because wealth created its own problems of insecurity.

She came down the long slope to Pruitt's homestead with the sleek black foam-specked and winded. She saw the lazily turning windmill and the contented cattle before she saw the man, shoulder against the doorjamb, a wheat-straw cigarette dangling from his wide, firm lips.

Some girls would have rushed to him, with words spilling out like wheat from a punctured sack. Mary did not. Seeing him, she reined the black around, approaching at a sensible pace. Only her eyes, unreadable but intent, told him that something was amiss. She saw the deepening of interest in him even before he straightened and flipped the cigarette away.

Mary Chavalas was watching closely for betrayal of nervous concern that would come to him if he were guilty. But she failed to find it, seeing only the same strong masculine awareness of her, his lively desire lightly masked by gentleness.

He touched the wide brim of his hat, raising his hand to assist her down. His puzzlement was honest, or seemed so. He murmured, smiling widely: "This is a surprise. I'm glad you came. Did you want to see how a man makes water run out of the ground, or did you come to see me?"

A flush rose to Mary's cheeks. Having carefully calculated the lead she had over Felix, she knew she had time for probing, but abruptly she had no patience for it, telling herself angrily: *You have decided you want him. Why, then, do you persist in torturing yourself with doubts?* She said: "Spurlock is dead. Shot in the back. Norell has sworn out a warrant for your arrest, and Felix is coming to serve it."

Bitterness came into his face, increasing as he saw the full scope of the Spur's trap. They had covered all the bets, so that no matter what he did, he lost. If he fled, the Spur had won. If he resisted Felix, either Felix killed him or he killed Felix, and either way was the same for the Spur. If he allowed Felix to take him, he went to jail, there to stay until perhaps months from now he came to trial. If what the Spur would give him could be called a trial. While he was in jail, the Spur would have a free hand to destroy his windmill and run off his cattle. Gilbreath would have no choice but to foreclose his loan.

With anger rising in him like the flow of inexorable tide, he asked Mary: "Why did you come to warn me? What do you want me to do?" His jaw did not soften, nor did his eyes lose their chill as he said: "I'm sorry, Mary. I made one mistake when I came into this country. I should have done what Felix accused me of wanting to do. I should have hunted down both Norell and Spurlock like I would a pair of wolves. Everyone is convinced that I came to Arapahoe to kill. If I had the name, I might just as well have had the game. I would be in no worse fix than I am now." He jerked his head to look at the western horizon. "How much time have I got?"

"Ten minutes. No more than that." He started to turn, but Mary laid her hand on the corded and bronzed forearm. "Let me have two minutes of the ten to tell you something."

She spoke timidly, for hers was not a forward nature. Yet she could not let him go without his knowing. She watched him turn, watched the warmth as it softened his eyes and expression. His neck was a column of sun-bronzed strength meeting his massive bony jaw, now covered with whiskers.

He stared at her while she groped for words, and finally he said: "You mean it's the same with you as it is with me? Is that what you want to tell me?"

Mary nodded, and raised her eyes. She said: "Only Felix

could come between us. Don't let him."

Suddenly Bart Pruitt smiled. He reached for her, but as his arms felt her softness, her womanliness, and the strength of the fire in her, his smile faded. He kissed her, and, as he stepped away, he said: "No. I won't let him."

With Mary nearly running beside him, he went to the hastily mended pole corral and took down his rope from the gate. While she watched, he saddled and swung up.

Mary asked: "What will you do?"

"I didn't kill Spurlock, Mary. I'll try to find the man who did."

Her lips formed the words—"Good luck."—but her eyes gave him a far more important message. They gave him a purpose stronger even than the one that now controlled him.

When he had gone, Mary mounted, waiting until she saw the lift of dust to westward. Then, at a hard run, she rode in the direction opposite to that Bart had taken to lead Felix away for a few miles. She could give Bart at least this much start. But she trembled as she anticipated Felix's cold and cutting anger, the things he would have to say about a woman who would betray her own father for a murdering outlaw.

XIV

For a while, Bart Pruitt drove his horse with little mercy. But eventually his helpless rage calmed, and he eased up. Dismounting, he loosened the saddle cinch so that the horse could more easily draw great gusts of air into his lungs.

Looking backward, Bart saw the lift of two dust trails against the sky, one close behind the other, and realized that Mary had added greatly to his chance for escape. He was temporarily free, but he was a fugitive and fair game. Now each killing, whether in self-defense or not, would be tallied against him.

For one brief moment despair brought to him sickness of brain and body, a weight that beat against him ruthlessly. Then his mind, with its youth and vigor, pushed aside the bleakness of despondency and began to plan. To plan was to live. To surrender was to die.

So long as he remained free, Shortgrass Riley and the others would hold together what he had. The Spur would let them, for to interfere would be to prejudice their own case against Pruitt. The problem facing him, then, was to cling to his freedom and to make no foolish move that would jeopardize it. Somewhere he must begin his search for the killer of Spurlock. His mind began to reach out for suspects, but in the end he was back where he started—considering the Spur foreman, Norell. But Norell was not a man to back-shoot and, besides, was too bound by loyalty to the Spur to betray the owner. Nor could money buy a man like Norell. That there was another coin more potent than money did not occur to Pruitt, for he knew nothing of Sally Taylor or of Norell's passion for her.

Discarding Norell reluctantly, he briefly considered Frank Killen, whose wish for the ease and luxury the Spur could provide had been so outspoken. Pruitt found it hard to believe the man could kill. But he asked himself bitterly: *How do I know what a man will do? Somebody put a bullet in Spurlock's back, and there has to be a reason for it somewhere.* Then the thought of himself in the rôle of Spurlock's avenger brought a wry smile.

He tightened the cinch and swung into saddle, heading toward the clay hills. He kept the horse at a walk, conscious now of the desperate need to conserve the animal's strength. As to where he would go and what he would do, he had no idea until he finally thought of Roy Gilbreath, whose stake in Pruitt's life was the greatest, except Mary, of any single person on the grass. *I will ride in and see him tonight,* he thought. *If he has no ideas, I will be no worse off than I am now.* Carefully keeping to the tops of the bare clay hills where wind would scour away his tracks, he rode slowly deeper into grassless and barren badlands that bordered the vast range where only Spur cattle roamed.

Night lay heavy and hot and oppressive over Arapahoe when Bart Pruitt reached the outskirts at nine. On lower Platte Street, light from saloon doors made a pattern of irregular squares on the dusty street. Up here on Fifth were the homes of the town's business people, and a few were sitting on their porches, talking in low voices behind thick-leafed, flowering vines. It was a peaceful, sleepy sound. Somewhere a guitar thrummed softly. A child cried, and a dog barked.

Bart's nerves were string-tight, but he rode openly, and erect, well knowing that furtiveness begets only suspicion, to Gilbreath's two-storied, brown frame house. Before it he halted uncertainly, because the house was dark. Finally he swung to the ground and looped his horse's reins through the iron ring on the stone hitch post.

Quiet but alert, he went up the walk, his hand never far from his gun grips. He was startled as a woman's soft voice asked: "Are you looking for Mister Gilbreath?"

"Yes, ma'am. Is he here?"

"He is ill. Could you come back tomorrow?"

"Seriously ill?"

"Why, not too serious. Perhaps worry more than anything else."

Bart had murmured doubtfully—"Well, tomorrow. . . ."—when Gilbreath's voice came through the darkness: "Come up on the porch. The yard is a poor place for talk."

Pruitt wondered at the dull apathy in Gilbreath's voice as he mounted the steps to the porch.

Gilbreath, clad in a long, white nightshirt, murmured: "Sit down, Pruitt. You are taking a big chance, coming into Arapahoe."

"You've heard, then?"

"I've heard that Chavalas is looking for you. You took my advice too lightly."

Pruitt said: "You believe I killed Spurlock?"

"No." It was as though Gilbreath had needed only this direct question to settle his doubts. "But the position you are in is as serious as if you had." He sighed and said, the apathy again in his voice: "The news I have for you will not help. Storrie Taylor is gone, and with him is gone some twenty-five thousand dollars of the bank's money." He sighed again gustily. "I must admit it's a shock. I've notified Chavalas, but I'm afraid he is more interested in catching you than Storrie."

In Bart Pruitt's mind something vaguely insisted that this was no mere coincidence. Yet he could not conceivably tie Storrie Taylor to Spurlock.

Gilbreath said quietly: "The loss of that money means that the bank will be unable to advance you anything further for at least thirty days. I regret I can't even honor your draft for the cattle you bought from Missus Oglethorp."

Anger flared in Pruitt, and the accusation sprang to his lips: "I'm in trouble with the law, so you make this an excuse to renege on your promise to me!" He was instantly contrite, however, for he realized suddenly that to a bank the size of Gilbreath's the loss of twenty-five thousand dollars was serious if not catastrophic. He said: "I'm sorry. I know how you must feel, but you leave me nothing to fight with."

"I am sorry for that. I had hoped. . . . Never mind. At least, if you are caught, I'll see that there is money to defend you if I have to supply it myself."

Bart suddenly stood up. "I won't be caught." Inflexible stubbornness turned his voice hard. Realization of how strong were the jaws of the trap that held him only served to increase his stubbornness and anger. "Where would Storrie go? Did he take his wife?"

Puzzlement edged into Gilbreath's voice. "No, he didn't take her. Perhaps he means to send for her. Watching her may lead to Storrie. He was crazy about her, Pruitt. I have no doubt he stole the money for her."

Pruitt said: "Storrie'd stick out like a sore thumb on the grass. But in Denver. . . ."

Gilbreath said sharply: "Storrie is no concern of yours. Your problem is your own hide."

Bart nodded reluctantly. "I guess you're right."

"What are your plans?"

"Someone back-shot Spurlock. Until I find whoever it was, I'm the man Felix wants. I never thought I'd be trying to catch Spurlock's killer, but it looks like that's the job I'm stuck with."

He got up, smiling wryly. With a murmured good bye, he went back down the walk. As he untied his horse, he was thinking of Mrs. Oglethorp, wondering what her thoughts would be at Gilbreath's refusal to pay her the balance due on her cattle. Also he wondered how he would pay his riders and the homesteaders who were sinking more wells on his grass. He wondered how he would pay for the other windmills he had ordered and which now were on their way to Arapahoe.

In the darkness a train whistled, eerie and forlorn, as it ran down the long, slow grade from the east. Bart turned his horse, filled with his own vaguely uneasy thoughts, trying still to fit Storrie Taylor's embezzlement into the puzzle of Spurlock's death.

Cloaked in darkness, he did not realize how plain and recognizable a shape he made against each lighted window until, just before he reached the bank, he heard a shout lift suddenly: "Pruitt! Hey, it's Pruitt!"

A feather of moving air stirred along his cheek bone, and immediately afterward came the sharp, echoing report. Instinct drove Bart's spurs against his horse's ribs. The animal lunged ahead, with Pruitt lying low along his neck, clinging like a burr. Flashes winked from both sides of Platte Street as he swung into Third, heading west, seeking to leave this town by the shortest route and reach the sanctuary of the grass.

Joshua's store stood on one corner here, and behind it a weed-grown lot littered with an accumulation of tin cans, packing boxes, and crates. Somewhere in that lot a can banged faintly, and instantly in Bart was the cold touch of perception. Too many men lined Platte Street. There were men in that lot. A trap!

He veered to the other side of the street even as the orange flames of gunfire spotted Joshua's lot.

A man howled: "He's getting away! Get him, damn it!"

Bart completed his circle, for he had seen the shapes against the grass that could only be men and, still galloping, came again into Platte Street.

Downstreet, Chavalas's voice barked: "Close the street behind him! We've got him now!"

Suddenly everything he had stood since his arrival in Arapahoe piled up in Bart's mind—Felix's gun against his skull, Norell's beating, the theft of the windmill, and both attempts to kill him. He sang out recklessly: "Not yet, Felix!"

He pulled the horse to an abrupt stop, swinging off, his fingers fumbling at the saddle cinch as he hit the ground. The saddle came off, the bridle, and the quirt that hung from the saddle horn made its vicious singing swing against the horse's rump. Covered by the noise of the horse's run, Bart looped across the street, carrying the saddle.

A buckboard stood here, empty, its tongue resting in the dust. Bart laid the saddle in the back where it would not be noticed, then, stooping low, he ran downstreet, still covered by the pound of his horse's hoofs in the direction from which Felix's voice had sounded.

He yelled as he ran—"Here! . . . down here!"—covering the fact that he was running, covering also the timbre of his voice by the panting exertion of the run.

Like a string of popping firecrackers, guns crackled as Bart's horse ran the gauntlet.

"Get the horse," bawled Felix. "An Injun trick! He's hanging under the horse's neck!"

In pitch darkness, Bart grinned and stopped, still with the tension gripping him, still with anger and excitement heating his blood. Men who had been behind him passed, their boots thundering against the boardwalk. A man tripped, fell, and rose cursing.

Abruptly the shouting stopped. A man yelled—"Did you get him, Felix?"—and another swore with mild amazement. The train whistled again, its sound ear-splitting and seemingly right in Platte Street.

With a swift look at Mary Chavalas's dark restaurant, Bart moved silently up Third, not beginning to run until he had put a half block between himself and the confusion on Platte. On Prairie he slowed to a walk. This way he came to the rear coach of the train as it stood, hissing steam, in the station.

He waited beside it, but not until the train began to move did he put foot on the step and swing aboard. Felix would think of the train when he found Bart's saddle, but by that time the train would be halfway to Denver.

For the second time in as many weeks, Bart Pruitt was riding away from Arapahoe by train. The first time, in spite of a mild concussion, he had returned, filled with youthful enthusiasm, sure that what he planned could be done. Now he doubted it. Always it was this way, when one man tried to buck entrenched interests. If they could not get him one way, they got him another, slyly using the law as a tool with which to break the law.

Bart straightened as the conductor came down the aisle.

"Ticket?"

Bart fished in his pocket, and handed the conductor a gold eagle. The conductor made change silently, his narrowed eyes reading: *Outlaw. On the jump from Chavalas. I'll telegraph back at the next stop.*

He walked on up the aisle, punching tickets. The *clackety-clack* of wheel against rail lulled Bart, and the strain of today and of the days past began to take their toll. He slept, not awakening until the train stopped, wheezing, at a whistle stop ten miles out of Denver to take on water. He saw the conductor peer in at him from the doorway, then scurry into the station, where he talked rapidly to the seated telegraph operator, who promptly began to pound his key. The conductor came out, glanced furtively at Bart's window, and swung aboard as the train began to move.

Bart clung to wakefulness now, for he well understood the trainman's actions and knew he must leave the train before it reached the station in Denver. After another hour he felt the train slowing as it entered Denver's first sordid scattering of shacks. Lights twinkled, the lamps of workmen and farmers, the early risers. Bart went into the washroom and closed the door.

Wasting neither time nor motion now, he yanked up the

window and pushed himself through. His boots struck the cinder roadbed where it began to slope away, slid momentarily, and then caught, throwing Bart end over end down the steeply sloping bank. His arms went instinctively to his head, protecting it, but even with this precaution he could feel the rake of gravel against his brow before he stopped.

He stood up, feeling for the solidness of gun and holster before he began to dust himself off. Then, recovering his hat and climbing back to the railroad tracks, he started his walk in the wake of the train.

He could not rid himself of the feeling that Storrie Taylor in some way held the key that would unravel this whole puzzle. Gilbreath had said: "Never mind Storrie, look out for yourself." Yet circumstances had forced this flight to Denver when in his mind had been the plain intent to hide out in the clay hills near Arapahoe. Now that he was here, he would make an effort to find Storrie, would satisfy once and for all this vague feeling that in Storrie lay the answer.

Finding Storrie would serve a double purpose, for in recovering the bank's money Bart would be helping himself. Again in possession of the stolen money, Gilbreath would fulfill his commitment to Bart, and at last Pruitt would have the funds with which to fight.

XV

Everywhere Bart Pruitt went, he always stood out in any crowd, so tall, so somber of face, so thick of shoulder and chest, yet with the light-stepping carriage of a man much smaller than he. In the crowd of workmen with whom he entered the city he knew he was noticeable, and could feel their stares upon him, upon the gun swung low at his thigh. He thought of the chagrin Felix Chavalas must be feeling, the pressure that Norell would be putting upon the sheriff, and a slow smile broke across his features. Then came a frown. Every law enforcement officer in Denver would by now be on the look-out for him. He could never dodge them all. Yet he must, for above all he must avoid a shoot-out. He could not afford to rack up a score against himself here.

Night would be the time for him to appear, he decided, for at night gamblers and gunmen and the saloon crowd were on the streets, and cowpunchers in town for a spree. In such a crowd he might pass unnoticed. He circled the town, found a small, inconspicuous boarding house, and took a room. In it he sailed his hat onto the bed and settled himself beside the window to watch the street as the sun poked its circle of gold above the plain to eastward, and the day began. . . .

All during the long, frantic ride that killed Storrie Taylor's horse before he had reached Denver, he viciously cursed the chance that had put Les Norell so close upon Spurlock's heels that day. Killing had left Storrie weak-kneed, drained of strength, mouth dry and trembling. Over and over he muttered: "Damn him! Damn the cheating bastard! He had it coming! He had it coming!"

When his rage against Spurlock had exhausted itself in self-justification, he turned his anger against Sally, whose lust for ease and luxury was to blame for his present awful difficulties. "I'd have made money for her!" he almost shouted. "If she could have waited a little!" It gave him satisfaction to think of Sally, her lover dead, her husband gone, but then he suddenly growled: "No, she's not hurt. The world is full of men."

When his horse fell, Storrie sailed out of the saddle, struck the ground. He got to his feet, dusted himself off, and headed on afoot. At a small ranch house a mile farther on, he purchased another horse, at an outrageous price, paying out of a sheaf of bills in the thick, string-tied envelope.

In Denver, he rented a room in an out-of-the-way boarding house. He let his whiskers grow. With Chavalas covering all trails, he felt that, for the time being at least, he would be safer here in Denver. Later, he would go to the mines in the mountains, avoiding the well-traveled routes. There were a thousand places in the West where folks accepted a man with no questions concerning his past. But he would be no mere clerk. With twenty-five thousand dollars a man could build an empire. He would become bigger than Spurlock, wealthier, more powerful. Then he would locate Sally and let her see what she had lost by her infidelity, and, when she begged to be taken back, he would laugh.

Staring moodily from his window, he saw a man come slowly down the street, glance curiously at the boarding house. Storrie fought the odd feeling of having seen this man before. The stranger was tall, dressed like a cowhand. He put his shoulder against a cottonwood across the street and rolled a wheat-straw cigarette. As he touched a match to its tip, he lifted his eyes directly to Storrie's window. Storrie ducked back instinctively before he realized that the curtains were drawn, that no one could see in. Yet in this instant, recognition had come to Storrie. The man was the one from whom he had bought the horse after he had killed his own.

Panic touched him. He recalled now that he had withdrawn enough money from the envelope to pay for the horse in front of the man, being too concerned with his own frantic haste to remember to be careful. Storrie's mind was like a rat's, seeking with cornered savagery for a way to elude this man. Then came the memory of how easy it had been to squeeze the trigger, once his sights had been centered on

Spurlock's back. A crafty smile brought cruelty to his narrow face.

Rob me, will you? he thought. *We'll see about that. Go on . . . watch the door. I'll come out soon enough. I'll let you follow me, then I'll turn and see you, and begin to run. All of a sudden I'll dodge into an alley. You won't be expecting that, will you? You've got me pegged wrong, just like Sally and Gilbreath and Pruitt and the rest of them. But you'll be surprised when a bullet tears into your belly.*

Storrie felt an anticipation he had not believed was in him when, at seven, he descended the stairs, his clothing untidy and a thick black stubble of whiskers a shadow across his jaw. His Colt revolver was jammed into the waistband of his trousers, his coat buttoned over it.

He paused on the walk, as though undecided, and was careful never to let his glance touch the man across the street. Then briskly he went toward mid-town at a rapid and purposeful walk. Near the newspaper office he crossed the creek, his steps sounding hollowly on the bridge's loose planking. He slowed imperceptibly when he hit the deep dust of the street on the other side, waiting for the thump of footsteps behind him on the bridge.

The sun was fully down, color had gone from the clouds, and only the gray of dusk remained. The street was nearly deserted. This was the supper hour. Suddenly a chill traveled down Storrie's spine. Suppose the man had a bead on his spine, was planning to drag him beneath the bridge and rob him? As Storrie dived aside, the shot roared in his ears, flat and wicked.

Panic put him into a full run before the echoes died away, weaving from side to side in a frantic effort to throw off the man's aim. Twice more shots sounded, and Storrie could hear the man's running steps on the bridge. He ran on. His breath came in ragged sobs. The sweat of exertion and terror bathed him from head to foot. Suddenly between two buildings yawned a narrow passageway, no more than two feet wide, and into this he ducked.

Stronger almost than Storrie's will was the urge to keep running after he reached its end. Had he been more familiar with the town, he probably would have run on. But uncertainty drew his steps to a reluctant halt. He crouched at the end of the passageway, his gun in one hand, the other pressed over his mouth to still his gasping, wheezing fight for breath.

The man came into the passageway, pounding through it toward Storrie. There was no caution, only haste and the plain fear that Storrie had eluded him. Yet his gun was out, held much as a man would hold a candle upon entering a darkened room. Storrie thought: *I'll let him go by and get him from behind.*

Bart Pruitt had just turned the corner onto Market Street when he heard the shot from the bridge. Almost immediately the white blur of faces appeared at the windows of the pleasure houses along this street. The second and third shots, so close upon the heels of the first, drew Bart's wide smile and he murmured: "Missed! Try again."

He put his back against a wall, waiting, his curiosity and his attention closely upon the two dim, running figures half a block down the street. The first went past, intact and full of terror, and in that instant it took him to pass Bart recognized Storrie Taylor. The fastidious and well-groomed Storrie was unshaven and unkempt! He saw Storrie duck between two buildings, and without conscious thought stepped away from the wall to intercept the pursuer. The man's gun was drawn, and his hat was gone. In his face was a peculiarly intent expression, and he did not see Bart until too late.

Bart's gun barrel came down in a slashing blow, catching the man on the cheek bone. His feet stopped running instantly, and he dived forward, to sprawl full length at Bart's feet, stunned. With scarcely a pause, Bart picked up the chase where this man had left off and went into the passageway, gun held high before him, eyes probing at the blackness ahead for trash and crates which might trip him up.

Not quite in time did he see the accumulation of rusty tin cans ahead of him just beyond the end of the passageway. His feet plowed into them, scattering them with a racket that was raucous and deafening in this enclosed space, and plunged to his knees. At that exact instant, Storrie fired. The bullet that would have found the center of Pruitt's spine only grazed his back, tearing his shirt and giving him the brief sensation of a burn. Rolling to face Storrie, he tried to center his gun on the embezzler. He failed, and Storrie had a never-to-be-repeated opportunity to kill him.

But Storrie's nerve was gone. Storrie turned to run back out of the passageway. With little liking for this, Bart put a shot down the passageway, just below the knee level and heard Storrie's scream, as Storrie went tumbling down. Before Storrie could move, Bart was upon him, wrenching away his gun and tossing it into the darkness.

He said urgently: "Storrie, the police will be here in a minute! Put your weight on me and let's get the hell out of here."

"Where did you come from?"

"Never mind! Never mind! Get moving."

With Storrie using him as a crutch, he felt his way through the scattered tin cans and trash and finally down the alley into the street. At its end, he could hear cautious stirrings back in the passageway, the telltale clatter of cans where Pruitt had fallen. The police had already arrived!

Storrie was groggy with pain, dizzy and staggering. In the swiftly falling darkness he resembled nothing so much as a drunk being helped home by a friend. The pair drew little notice from those on the street and so were able, in a matter of ten minutes or so, to put the buildings of Denver behind them. On a high point of ground to the east of town, Bart stopped. In the darkness he bound up Storrie's leg, with strips torn from the embezzling bank clerk's shirt.

While he was doing this, he asked: "What was that fellow chasing you for?"

Even through his pain and weakness evasion held Storrie silent, although he finally conceded: "He was trying to rob me."

Baiting him, Bart asked: "Why?" But Storrie would say no more. Bart murmured savagely: "You will talk, my friend. Before I am through, I'll know everything you know. Make no mistake about that."

Faintly from the town below rose the inevitable night clamor, the shouts, the screams, a woman's laugh, the bellow of a man as he moved into a fight. Twice there were shots, so closely spaced that they could not but tell their story of violence and death. Denver was an infant city, undisciplined and wild, building and orderly by day, unrestrainedly violent by night.

Here on the grass it was quiet except for these sounds that were muted by distance, and the far-away whistle of a train. Thinking, and allowing Storrie to rest, Bart lay quietly, hating the job he had to do, hating the brutality it would take to do it.

Storrie watched him with unreadable eyes and must have thought that Bart slept, for he crawled closer. At last Bart felt his hand reaching, searching for the gun at Bart's thigh.

Bart's elbow came out savagely, catching Storrie in the belly with a force that doubled the thin man over. Bart came to his feet, reaching down and yanking Storrie up.

"It's time for talking," he growled. "Where's the money?"

Storrie laughed wildly, crying out with too much haste: "Hidden! You'll never find it."

Bart's fist crashed against his mouth, and he went down, nearly disappearing in the dark that shrouded the ground. Bart reached for him, but Storrie yelled: "Here . . . here! Take the damned stuff! You'll get it, anyway."

A thick, heavy envelope struck Bart in the face, and he caught it as it bounced away. He asked harshly—"What else have you got to say?"—and began to guess, finding it easier than he had expected. Someone had to have told Spurlock about the windmill. Storrie was the likely choice. He went on from there. He growled: "You told Spurlock I was bringing in a windmill. You offered him the information for pay, but he wouldn't pay. So you killed him."

Storrie was silent, and Bart yanked him again to his feet. Again his fist smashed into Storrie's mouth, but this time he held Storrie erect and did not let him fall. When he drew back his fist for another blow, Storrie winced away, crying out thickly: "Sure I killed him, but not for that! The bastard was slipping in my back door when I went out the front! I had a right to kill him for that!" His voice rose to a howl. "Didn't I? Wouldn't you kill a man for that?"

The story, and its implications, had a sordidness that sickened Bart. He said—"I guess I would."—and knew he had the truth from this weak man.

Storrie's voice was low. "What are you going to do now?"

"Take you back. Felix wants *me* for that killing." He released his hold on Storrie's collar. "Come on. There ought to be a farm somewhere close. We'll get a couple of horses. With hard riding we'll be in Arapahoe by noon tomorrow."

So incomprehensible to Bart would have been the thought that Norell could possibly have seen Storrie kill Spurlock and done nothing about it that he did not question Storrie further, and, to Storrie, Norell had simply chanced to be riding behind Spurlock. In his pain and utter despair, he thought only of escape, and it did not occur to him to tell Pruitt something that might have saved him.

XVI

Les Norell lost no time in moving toward the completion of his plan. Spurlock was dead, and Pruitt had been blamed for the killing and was a fugitive. Storrie had a double reason for putting miles between himself and Arapahoe, being both a murderer and an embezzler. Now all that remained was to dispose of Julia Spurlock.

He had deliberately stayed away from Storrie Taylor's house and Sally, for he did not want his connection with her known until he had tied up all the loose ends of his devious planning. Yet Sally was in his thoughts every moment, and there were times when his desire to see her became nearly unbearable.

This morning he rode out to the Spur, taking the old stagecoach road. The day was hot, with rising heat waves making shimmering mirages on the plain. By mid-morning he had left the land the Spur controlled, but still rode, steadily and swiftly, his destination a certain small, hard-scrabble ranch half a dozen miles from the Spur's border. The ranch, the property of one Adolf Neese, lay close to the river, on a thirty-foot bluff, an untidy collection of buildings hastily erected from odds and ends of scrap lumber, yet its corrals were extensive. In times past, Norell had handled Neese in a roughshod way for the very thing he would now ask Neese to do, so when he rode into the yard, it was with both hands clasped in plain sight on his saddle horn.

He yelled—"Hello the house!"—and rode in at a walk, seeing the hulking, black-bearded Neese, blocking the door.

"What the hell is it this time?" Neese bellowed.

"No trouble, friend. No trouble this time."

Neese stepped onto the sagging stoop, shifted a wad of tobacco from one cheek to the other, and spat against the bare ground before the door. "Then get the hell away from here."

Today was different from the times when Norell had ridden in with a score of Spur riders behind him. He felt painfully alone, especially after Neese's hulking sons began to drift from behind the house, from the crumbling outbuildings. Silently and sullenly they surrounded him, big, young, and dangerous, waiting for the old man's nod.

Norell growled: "Listen to me! How would you like to pick up ten cars of Spur beef this week and know that Spur riders would be at the far end of the place because I sent them there? How would you like to take another four, five hundred head the following week from the other end and know the riders would be down on this end trying to find out what happened to the first bunch?"

A deep-throated growl rumbled in Neese's throat, and his eyes were bits of hard and polished obsidian that gleamed between his narrowed lids. Norell gave him time to consider, seeing suspicion slowly fade as Neese said: "Spurlock's dead, and that's all you have been waiting for, huh? What's your cut to be?"

"Half. There are twenty thousand cattle on the Spur. With me helping, you can get away with damn' near half of them before Felix Chavalas butts in. I'll even go further . . . give you a bill of sale for every steer you take. You can sell 'em easy then, and keep your skirts clean."

Norell had planned this with care. Each bill of sale would be signed awkwardly and just a little differently, so that later it would be easy to prove they were forgeries. There would be no one to say differently, either, for as soon as Julia signed over her interest in the Spur, the outfit would raid Neese's ranch, leaving neither Neese nor his sons alive. But before Norell could begin negotiations with Julia, he had to have money—big money—and wholesale cattle rustling by the Neeses would provide that.

Karl, the oldest of Neese's sons, spat out a string of obscenities. "Don't trust him, Pa!" But Adolf Neese growled: "Shut up, Karl." And to Norell: "Get down and come in. You'd better be talking straight, without no men behind you."

As Norell swung from saddle, Karl lifted his gun from its holster before Norell's feet touched the ground. Norell knew he would not get that gun back until Karl was ready to return it.

He followed Adolf into the house, and the four boys crowded in behind. This was a womanless house, filled with the rank odor of stale bedding, the reek of cooking. It was more of a wolves' den than a home, simply a place to sleep when their prowling was done.

Uneasy, Norell spoke swiftly. "You've moved Spur cattle before and left nothing to show they'd been moved. Be as careful now. Let me know the night before you hit so I can pull the riders away."

Karl said: "Pa, the son-of-a-bitch is laying a trap."

"Shut up!" Neese shoved his face close to Norell, and his breath was hot. "Karl will take the first bunch. If anything goes wrong, you're a dead man, Les. A thousand riders won't help you. I'll break you apart with my hands. Now get out of here and don't come back."

While Norell was no coward, he could feel fear. Big himself, Neese was bigger; savage and unscrupulous himself, Neese was more so. Neese was a carnivore that lived off the flanks of the herd, yet he would not hesitate to live off its heart. Feeling cold, Norell went to the door, and at this exact instant Bart Pruitt and Storrie Taylor jogged past on the road!

Uneasy already, Norell saw the disastrous collapse of his plans. Not yet could he ask help from Neese for a chore like this. He mounted, reached down a hand for the gun Karl was holding. With it holstered, he rode down the trail to the river and, sheltered by cottonwoods and the high bluff, was ahead of Pruitt and Storrie before they had gone a mile. . . .

All through the long night, Pruitt had crowded the horses. Now, in morning's blazing heat, he felt pity both for Storrie and the weary, patiently plodding animals. Storrie was pale from loss of blood, and his face was wracked with pain. He slumped forward, head hanging. One foot only did he have in a stirrup. The other leg dangled, the rough bandage Pruitt had put there soaked with blood.

Bart said: "The doc in Arapahoe will fix you up, then you can go to bed. There's no bones broken. The bullet passed through the muscles and made a clean hole."

Storrie turned a bloodless face upon him, a face twisted with hate. "Damn you! Damn you to hell!"

Pruitt shrugged. "Should I hang for a bullet you put in Spurlock's back? Should I lose everything I've got because you couldn't keep your hands out of Gilbreath's till?"

But he knew that no matter how right he was, he could

never quite justify himself either in Storrie's eyes or his own. Had it not been for Sally Taylor's infidelity and greed, Storrie might have remained a weak and personable bank clerk, rising slowly toward eventual management of the bank. A woman could make or break a man, and which she did was determined by her own character.

Pruitt's thoughts strayed from Storrie and Storrie's faithless woman to Mary Chavalas. She was nearer to him now than she had ever been before. Turning Storrie over to Felix would lift the cloud of outlawry from Pruitt's own head. With the ruthless Spurlock gone, Bart would have the chance to sink his wells, erect his windmills, and settle down to raising cattle and building a home for Mary.

The Spur would wither, but would not die, not with ten rich sections of bottom land on the river. Julia Spurlock could live comfortably, even lavishly for the remainder of her life on that. Homesteaders would settle on the grass, sink wells, and erect windmills. Land that had supported the Spurlocks and a handful of thirty-a-month cowpunchers would support hundreds of families. Ditches would spread from the river, their lacy network bringing lush new growth to the plain. Gone would be the cattle empires, yet beef would still flow to market from the grass. Better beef. Fatter beef. Beef rounded to perfection, with grain and hay.

Pruitt saw Storrie jerk as though smashed by an invisible fist, saw him tumble from saddle. The report of a rifle rolled across the grass, and ahead Bart's eyes caught the light puff of black smoke. Instinct brought him off his horse, down in the long grass.

He crawled for thirty feet, then poked his hat above the grass tips and jerked it quickly back. He drew no fire, so he poked it up again. Still nothing happened. Knowing it was foolish, but stirred by quick and unreasoning anger, he jumped to his feet and made a dash for the horses.

The rifle on the knoll opened up, bullets kicking up dust behind his sprinting heels. A hasty glance showed Storrie's throat a ghastly mass of torn flesh and blood. Suddenly the full rage of which Pruitt was capable turned his face white and bloodless. The chill of killing savagery brought the hair on his neck up, stiff and straight. Release from the accusation of murder had been only short hours away. Now all chance was gone. He leaped to the back of his horse and sunk in the spurs. Jaded and beat, the horse nevertheless bounded forward.

Insane with fury, Bart made no effort to avoid the continuing fire from the knoll. In seconds he covered half of the three hundred yard distance before the horse's utter weariness caught up with him. Yet his reckless charge, his fury had broken Norell's nerve. Winchester empty, with barely time to reload before Pruitt would be upon him, Norell chose to run.

Pruitt had closed the distance between them to a hundred yards, too great a range for his Colt, when Norell began to draw away. The temptation to blaze away, to empty his gun in a forlorn hope was gone. Pruitt's rage spent itself quickly.

He thought of Storrie, perhaps not yet dead. Whirling his horse, he rode back to where Storrie lay in a dark pool of his own blood. Storrie was dead, had been dead when he hit the ground.

There was an unaccustomed sag to Pruitt's wide shoulders as he remounted and turned his horse's head eastward. Again he was a fugitive, and this time there was nowhere to turn. He had no doubt that before the day was out he would be accused of killing Storrie for the money he carried. Both Felix and the Spur would intensify their efforts to capture or kill him, and the end was entirely sure and certain. Felix had said: "The Spur is too big for you to fight. It was too big for your pa, and it's too big for you." He had been right.

Yet, suddenly and incomprehensibly, all of the old feelings he had known as a boy, all the bitterness and hate, returned now, intensified by injustice. His voice was tight and strained as he cried aloud: "Run? That's what he wants you to do. But the old man didn't run, and neither will I."

The knowledge was sure in him, now that he had recognized Norell as Storrie's killer, that the foreman's crafty planning in some way lay behind all that had happened in Arapahoe the past week. But what was it Norell wanted? Until Bart knew that, he had nothing to go on, nothing whatever.

The urge to hunt Norell down and kill him was nearly irresistible, but even this would solve nothing, would even make matters worse, for then Norell's connection with Spurlock's death would never come to light. The humorous words of his father returned to him suddenly: "You've cut yourself a big piece of pie, Son. Let's see if you can eat it."

XVII

Ravenous hunger has a way of increasing a man's irritability. Bart Pruitt had eaten nothing last night, this morning, or at noon. He needed a fresh horse, too, for as soon as Norell could reach the Spur, he would surely mount a pursuit to pick up Pruitt's trail. Spur riders, freshly mounted, would sight their quarry before nightfall hid the man who fled across the grass.

Pruitt began to reason, asking himself: *What will Norell expect me to do? What would I expect if I were Norell?* The answer was obvious. A pursued man would surely strike away from the Spur as quickly as he could, perhaps hoping to pick up a fresh horse along the way. Pruitt smiled grimly. *I'll do the opposite, then. I'll even get my horse from the Spur.*

He held a course parallel to the river, but nearly a mile away from it, and riding slowly so he would raise no betraying dust. After an hour, he saw a pillar of boiling dust to his left and ahead, about where the road would be. He rode more carefully now, his course erratic as he sought to keep himself out of sight in the rolling terrain, yet never so deep in any ravine that their dust was hidden from his watchful eyes. When the dust column was nearly abreast of him, he dismounted and crawled to the top of a low ridge to watch.

The Spur's posse was a cluster of hard-riding figures in the distance. Pruitt returned to his horse, calculating the time it would take them to reach the spot where Storrie lay, the time they would require to pick up his own trail and follow it. He thought: *An hour. And in an hour I'll have a fresher horse than any they're riding.*

When he rode into the Spur's big wire-fenced horse pasture, it was nearly four o'clock. He pushed a bunch of about twenty horses carefully into a far corner of the pasture, and his rope snaked out as the crowding bunch broke past him along the fence. His rope settled over the head of a big sorrel gelding, which quieted with resignation.

Pruitt dismounted, removed saddle and bridle from his tired gray, murmuring: "Fill your belly with Spur grass. They owe it to you."

He watched the gray lie down in the long grass and roll. Swiftly then he saddled the sorrel, swung up, and lined out toward the clay hills that lay smoky along the far horizon.

Savagely Felix Chavalas slammed the white picket gate behind him. He had just left Norell and could still feel the white-hot run of his temper over the tongue-whipping Norell had given him. Thirty minutes before, Norell and a dozen Spur riders had come pounding into town, sweat and dust caked on their faces and clothes, their horses frothy and beat. Norell had handled Felix with an unbridled harshness.

"Damn you, Felix, are you going to get him or not? I've chased him all afternoon. I picked him up, where he killed Storrie Taylor and tracked him into the Spur horse pasture where he stole a horse."

Felix had asked dryly: "You catch him?"

"No! Damn you, would I be here now if I'd caught him?"

Felix had shrugged. "How many men did you take?"

Norell had snarled irritably: "How the hell should I know? I didn't count 'em. Twenty or twenty-five."

"If you couldn't catch him with that many men, how do you expect me to get him without any?"

"You're the sheriff. Get a posse. Ride till you find him." Because Felix had so far been mild, Norell had let chagrin at his own failure control him. "Felix, Spur put you in the job you're in. The county's paid you a hundred a month for so many years I've lost count. You'd better earn that money now, or you'll find yourself out of a job."

Only then had Felix's face taken on the characteristic dangerous pallor. His voice had been low and brittle, the rattle of a diamondback. "Shut your damned mouth! There has never been an election but what I made my trip out to the Spur. Every time I told Spurlock his support was not buying me, that I'd do what I had to do no matter who got hurt. I'll still do it, Norell! You're the Spur foreman and nothing else. Don't be speaking for the Spur. Don't ever be telling me what I have to do unless you're ready to back it up."

Yet only part of Felix's angry resentment had been because of Norell's pressure. Most of it was caused by the fact that pressure also was being applied to him by his own daughter. She had told him bluntly not an hour past: "Bart Pruitt is no cold-blooded murderer, and you know it! That's why you're not pressing the search for him. But do you imagine Norell will bring him in alive? Your deliberate failure to catch Pruitt does not excuse you from responsibility for his death if the Spur catches him!"

On his way home Felix Chavalas had turned his thoughts to self-examination, even knowing that, when a lawman begins to doubt his own motives, he is finished. Felix had made a career of keeping the peace in Arapahoe, and it had not been easy. He had never allowed individuals or concern for individuals to enter into it at all, and he had kept the peace.

There had even been times when an individual had been sacrificed for the greater purpose of maintaining order, and now Felix was prepared to sacrifice Pruitt for the good of the many—the townspeople, the Spur riders, himself, even Norell. Felix had seldom allowed doubt to plague him before, but this time Mary was involved. He was in a vicious frame of mind as he crossed the vine-shrouded porch and reached for the door knob.

A voice and the prod of the gun came simultaneously, then Pruitt said: "Felix, use your head. If you turn or try for me, it'll only get you a lump on the head and as bad a headache as you gave me."

"What the hell do you want?" Temper goaded the sheriff to recklessness, and his muscles drew tight, but Pruitt's gun muzzle only prodded harder.

Pruitt's voice came, hard and savage: "Felix, because of Mary, I won't kill you unless I have to. You've run me like a wolf, and so has Norell. I didn't kill Spurlock, and I didn't kill Storrie, and you know it! I'll take only so much, Felix." He went on as Felix relaxed. "Storrie killed Spurlock because

Spurlock was playing around with his wife. Norell killed Storrie. That lets me out."

Felix laughed unpleasantly. "It would if I believed you."

Weariness touched Pruitt's voice. "I didn't expect you to. You can believe this, though." He handed an envelope over Chavalas's shoulder. "It's the money Storrie took . . . most of it anyway."

Felix fumbled open the envelope and felt the crisp bundle of banknotes. He said: "I'll return it to Gilbreath. But if you think you fool me any, you're mistaken. You were afraid of a shoot-out with Spurlock because he's too big a man to kill that way. He was getting to be a political power in the state, and because he'd have no chance against a gun-slick like you, the self-defense theory would be pretty thin. So you shot him in the back, figuring I'd give you credit for being above back-shooting. Now you're returning this money to make me think you didn't kill Storrie for it. You'd never have returned it if Norell hadn't happened to see you kill Storrie. It won't work, Pruitt. I'd have respected you if you'd come to Arapahoe with your gun smoking openly. You'll get away tonight, but I'll find you, or Norell will. You'd better hope I find you."

He heard Pruitt's soft sigh as his gun was lifted from holster. Never before in all his life had Felix Chavalas been disarmed. The thought of it now, piled atop his rage, his doubt, brought him around as swiftly as a striking sidewinder. His right hand came out in a short, powerful arc.

Pruitt's—"Why, you damned fool!"—soft and breathless was the last sound Felix heard as the long, heavy barrel of Pruitt's gun was laid against Felix's skull, and the world dissolved in blackness. . . .

Mary Chavalas blew out the lamps in the restaurant and

went into the street. Now she must face her own thoughts, her own despair. She had kept the restaurant open an hour longer than usual, not wanting to be alone, yet she had to close sometime just as sometime she had to face the certainty that Bart Pruitt would be caught and, if not killed outright, forced to pay the penalty the Spur demanded.

Mary was firmly convinced that Bart was incapable of committing the crimes of which he was accused. She had long ago quit wondering if love had blinded her eyes. Now, because she knew that once at home, scalding tears would flow, she deliberately looked for something to do, anything so she would not have to go home to that empty house, to the grief that could not be contained forever.

Remembering Sally Taylor, who had even more reason to grieve, she thought: *Why, I should have gone to see her before. At a time like this a woman needs another woman.* A few moments later she opened the Taylors' creaking front gate. A voice from the porch made its soft query: "Who is it?"

"Mary Chavalas."

Mary mounted the steps into the dim light that laid a square on the floor before the door. Sally Taylor rose from a swing.

Mary said: "I have come to tell you how sorry I am." Yet, even as she spoke, she was wondering at Sally's serene expression, at the calm in her voice.

"Won't you come in? It was good of you to come." Sally smiled.

Mary thought: *If Bart had been killed, I could never look as composed as she does.* She said: "If there is anything I can do . . . ," but stopped before her feeling of helplessness.

Again Sally smiled. "I need nothing."

It occurred to Mary that Sally Taylor's contentment must stem from some deep inner satisfaction, but hated herself for the thought. Yet before Sally's lack of grief, she could think of nothing to say.

Sally asked: "Will you have some lemonade? It's a hot night."

She went into the kitchen, and Mary suddenly wished she had not come. She sat stiffly upright on the shabby sofa, looking at the things Storrie Taylor had accumulated in his few years of living. Storrie had been an embezzler, and there must have been a reason somewhere for his desperate need for money. This comfortable, if shabby, house could not supply it to Mary, nor could Storrie's wife, so calm and serene and seemingly content.

Storrie Taylor's habits had been almost as regular as those of Roy Gilbreath, the banker. Storrie had not been a drinker or a gambler. In a town the size of Arapahoe, he could not possibly have carried on a love affair without the town's knowledge. Suddenly Mary knew that if Storrie Taylor had needed money badly enough to steal it, then since the house could not supply the reason, Sally could. The pieces began to fall into place. Sally's contentment could mean that she had cared little for Storrie, for his death apparently did not grieve her. Since the money Storrie had stolen was gone, Sally's satisfaction could not stem from her hope of obtaining the money. There was only one answer. Sally had another man.

Mary started guiltily as Sally returned, carrying a tray, a pitcher, and two glasses. She sipped her lemonade and made polite conversation that became more strained as the minutes wore away. Finally Mary rose. Her visit had been long enough to satisfy propriety.

She took Sally's hand, smiled, and hoped her thoughts did not show in her face. "If there is anything I can do, will you call on me?"

"Of course. Thank you, but there is nothing I need. Nothing at all."

It seemed to Mary that Sally was even more relieved than she at the termination of this visit. It had almost seemed that Sally was anxious for Mary to leave, as the clock hand had crept toward nine.

From the gate Mary called another—"Good bye."—and made her way thoughtfully toward Platte. Across the street she saw a broad, heavy man she recognized as Les Norell, foreman of the Spur. Anger stirred Mary, for, in a large degree, Bart Pruitt's troubles were this man's fault. Les Norell had killed Bart's father. He had attempted to drive Bart from the town, and now was vigorously behind the accusation and pursuit of Pruitt.

Vaguely troubled, she paused on the walk and watched Norell fade into the blackness of the street. Mary Chavalas knew of the women who drew men into the twisting, narrow alleys of shack town. Mary had a large tolerance for the weaknesses of humans, yet for Norell she could feel only disgust.

Shouting on Platte Street put an end to Mary's brooding. Hearing the voice of her father, she broke into a run. Her heart went cold as she caught his words: "Saddle up! I want ten men. I'll hunt Bart Pruitt down if it takes me the rest of my life! Spur wants him, does it? Well, by hell, I want him, too!"

XVIII

Mary Chavalas, hidden in the shadows, watched men run from the saloons. She saw a hostler bring Felix Chavalas's horse, saw her father mount and wait, a small, implacable figure atop the gleaming black. She knew at once that Felix had made his decision, that no longer would he hesitate. Something had happened to decide him, of that she was sure, and, whatever it was, Bart Pruitt had no chance now, for Felix had tracked down many an elusive fugitive in his years of being sheriff. He would anticipate each of Bart's ruses, and checkmate them. The result was inevitable. Bart would never be taken alive, and men would die. This Mary had foreseen in the restaurant that first day of his return to town.

Something rebelled in this girl, whose heritage it was to bow meekly to the will and wishes of the male. What Bart had sought to do had been good, as anything that benefits the many is good. Mary was convinced that his intentions had been good, as well. True, he had killed two men, and the fact that Norell had attempted to conceal the death of the first was in itself puzzling. Yet Mary knew that Bart had killed neither Spurlock nor Storrie Taylor. Bart Pruitt would defend himself, but he could never kill from ambush. Helplessly she watched Felix ride out of town with his posse at his heels, and noted that Les Norell was not among them. Revulsion touched her. He was lying in the arms of some woman down there in shack town.

She started violently as a hand touched her arm. The voice, with its gentleness, made her heart turn over with fear. "Watching the chase, Mary?"

"You fool! He's hunting *you!* How do you know he won't stop at the edge of town and sneak back? I know how he thinks, Bart."

He said—"Mary, stop it!"—and drew her close.

Flame blazed in Mary's veins. For an instant she was his, demanding and fierce. Then, just as fiercely, she jerked free. Her voice, although low, held unbridled savagery. "Go away! There is nothing but grief and heartbreak in you! If you kill Felix, I'll hate you. If Felix kills you, I'll hate him. If you stay here, there will be nothing but ruin for you and me, for Felix and for the town. Go away! If you want to send for me, I'll come."

Footsteps sounded on the boardwalk, and Pruitt faded into a doorway. A man said—" 'Evening, Mary."—and passed on.

Suddenly Mary's shoulders sagged. She had almost persuaded Bart to leave, but the interruption had spoiled it all. She knew that the instant he was beside her again. The realization of fate's implacability overcame her. Things were decided long before they happened—by the strength and the weakness, the willfulness and the stubbornness in a man. Words could not change them, nor could a woman.

Abruptly her thoughts broke off. She said excitedly, for truth had finally dawned: "Bart, it's Norell . . . and Sally Taylor! Oh, why didn't I see it before? I called on Sally tonight, feeling sorry for her, and I couldn't understand it when she showed no grief. She was anxious to get rid of me, too. When I left, I passed Norell going in that direction. He could have been going to shack town, but he could just as well have been going to see Sally." Her voice was anxious. "Couldn't he?"

Bart was silent, but she could sense the excitement in him. Then he said: "It's got to be! Norell's the only one who could have a stake in this besides me. If it *is* Norell and Sally, Storrie would have stood in the way . . . and maybe Norell wanted the Spur." Suddenly he shook his head. "It's just guessing. Norell's got a name for being loyal to the Spur."

Mary said, drawing on the ageless wisdom of her sex: "If money can't buy a man, sometimes a woman can. What if Sally's price was the Spur?"

Still Bart shook his head. "Why would Norell kill Storrie when he could just as easily have killed me?"

Mary said stubbornly: "They wanted to be rid of both Spurlock and Storrie. What would be easier than making Storrie believe Spurlock was the man, so Storrie would kill him and then run away from the law? Perhaps Norell saw Storrie kill Spurlock. Perhaps he *let* him get away, holding the murder over his head so he wouldn't return. Then he sees you bringing Storrie back. He would have to kill Storrie to stop his confession, and he would know you would be blamed for the killing."

Still Bart was not convinced. His voice was cold as he said: "Far-fetched. No woman can be as rotten as you believe Sally to be. I've never seen her, but surely she couldn't be like that."

His coldness chilled Mary, but desperation made her insistent. She gripped his arms, her fingers tight with panic. "Go up there! Wait until he comes out. Hear what they say to each other. Felix is always saying . . . 'Believe the worst and you'll never be disappointed.' Maybe Felix is too bitter, but he's seen more of crime and violence than you or I."

Bart's reluctance was plain, but he nodded grudgingly. "All right . . . all right." He moved away into the darkness.

Mary began to tremble, and finally to weep. Then, sobbing, she ran toward home, the neat frame cottage where soon either death or hate must dwell. Her theory had been the product of desperation, and it was no good. There was nothing left. . . .

For so big a man, Bart Pruitt could move softly. Like a shadow, when he reached Storrie Taylor's house, he took up a vantage point from which he could watch both front door and back. Lights gleamed from the shaded windows of the house, but there was no sound except for the muted night noises of the town, turned sleepy with the lateness of the hour.

To eavesdrop was as alien to Bart's nature as would have been the cold-blooded killings of which he was accused. Half a dozen times in the first half hour he determined to leave. But each time he settled back, for his stubborn nature would not quit a task once undertaken. Finally he heard the soft closing of the back door, heard low voices on the porch. Silently he made his way to within a yard of the vine-screened porch. He could distinguish some words now, could recognize voices—and Mary had been right. The voices were those of Norell and Sally Taylor!

Norell was saying: "They're hunting Pruitt. I'll be missed if I don't show up soon."

Sally said: "Be careful, darling. I've lost two lovers in the last week. I don't want to lose another." Her low, tantalizing laugh stopped abruptly in weak protest as Norell's heavy lips came down over hers.

Pruitt waited no longer. If Sally Taylor could laugh over the deaths of her husband and Spurlock, she was all Mary had thought her. Rage burned in Bart, rage at the sly machinations of these two that had caused so much suffering and death. The years had held little for Bart but bitterness and hate, most of this attributable in some way to Les Norell, and the good that Bart had sought to do had been viciously checkmated by Norell and Norell's scheming.

Moving swiftly away from the home, the need for personal retaliation against Norell became so consuming that little thought was left in Bart for anything else. Almost irresistible was the urge to call on Norell as he saw the man come down this street. Yet there was Mary, who also had a stake in this game. There was Felix, who would never believe such a far-fetched yarn from Pruitt alone.

Danger lurked in every instant of delay, for Pruitt was not fool enough to believe that Felix would spend the night in aimless search across the grass. Once the edge of his anger had worn away, Felix would return to Arapahoe. In some way, he must be made to know what Pruitt and Mary knew. Then there would be time for personal retaliation. In the meantime, every man abroad in the dark streets constituted a threat of death for Bart Pruitt.

Because with Spurlock dead there was no further need for concealment, Frank Killen rode openly into the Spur's big yard as the sun set. Unconcealed disgust was in his expression as he gazed up at the great three-storied stone house. Frank Killen hated the pretentiousness of great wealth and, despite his open expressions to the contrary, had no desire to ally himself with it. One thing only at Spur did Frank Killen want—Julia Spurlock—and he wanted her without the Spur, without the Spur's wealth. No one would believe him anyway, so he had never told anyone of his true feelings, not even Julia. It was inevitable when a poor man courted a rich girl that folks should say he was interested in her money. Frank Killen let them think so.

He had never lost confidence in his own ability. If he starved in Arapahoe, it was because of a lack of opportunity for his particular talents in a town so small. Now he meant to take Julia to the city—to Denver or San Francisco. What success he might have from now on would be due entirely to himself and dependent in no way upon how rich the Spur was.

Watching Julia as she came toward him down the steps, he was consumed with wonder and humility that she could care so deeply for him, a failure, a cripple. Her face held a softness for him tonight greater than ever before. He considered with brief, sharp insight the idea that perhaps she understood him better than he gave her credit for. Courted by every unattached male in the country, perhaps Julia sensed that this particular one was in no sense interested in her possessions but entirely in her.

Traces of grief showed in Julia's face, and Frank said: "It is bad for you to sit in the house and grieve. Come for a ride with me on the grass and forget for a little while."

Julia's eyes were grateful. "I didn't know a house could be so empty. He was only one man, yet he filled the house." Tears unshed put a shine to her eyes, but she smiled and called across the yard: "Shorty! Will you saddle Cigarette for me? I'm going for a ride."

Julia and Frank rode out as the clouds to westward flamed over the distant, jagged peaks. They rode in companionable silence, speaking but a word here, a sentence there, and, as they rode, the strain and grief went gradually out of the girl, leaving her calm and at peace. Hearing cattle bawling in the distance, they rode that way only from idle curiosity and also because a cow bawling usually meant a cow in trouble.

Both were utterly unprepared for what they saw as they topped a low ridge. Below, streaming out for a full half mile, straggled a long line of cattle, dim with failing light of day. Two men rode behind, and one on each flank.

Julia's voice was unbelieving. "It's incredible! No one steals Spur cattle this close to the home place!"

Killen said: "You could be mistaken. Perhaps they are your own riders."

"The Spur doesn't move cattle at night, Frank. Somebody has the idea that because Dad is gone, the Spur is helpless!" Anger was in her voice, tightened her face. "I'll show them how helpless the Spur is!"

Frank caught her rein. "Don't be a fool, Julia! Do you think a lone man and woman would mean anything to men who will risk what these men are risking?"

He caught the quick flash of contempt in her face. He gave

her his wry smile. "I'm not the type to break up a rustler gang single-handed, Julia. Let's say I've got too much sense to throw myself away on a bunch of morons when the odds are four to one. Besides, I haven't got a gun." She was silent, and he asked: "Disappointed in me?"

Apology was in her tone, mingling with impatience. "Of course not, Frank."

Suddenly whirling, she put spurs to her horse's side. Frank followed, fearing she might be foolish enough to ride down and question the outlaws below. But he quickly saw she was headed for home.

XIX

Just finished with his milking, Adolf Neese was carrying the bucket toward the house when he heard shots. Distant they were, a dim and unreal popping in the hot, still night. For an instant he froze, a hulking, bearded statue. Yet only his body was inactive. His brain was alive, savage. Realizing the implication of what he heard, he became a raging dynamo of action. The bucket went crashing across the yard, its white contents a brief, pale stain against the black ground.

Adolf Neese's four sons were out there, betrayed, fighting odds that could not help but be overwhelming! Neese's fingers, as he saddled, were swift and sure, showing nothing of the terror that rode him so mercilessly. But the spurs that sank into his horse's trembling ribs left no doubt in the animal that this was a night for running.

Toward the sound of the firing he rode, perhaps coming as close to prayer as ever he had in his long and lawless life. He heard, over the sharp popping of six-guns, the roar of Karl's Sharps, the distinctive crack of Otis's old Henry rifle. Then the Henry ceased firing, and pain at the cessation was almost physical in Adolf. He whispered with savagery: "The dirty bastard! He'll pay for Otis! He'll pay, damn him, he'll pay!"

The Sharps quit firing then, but Adolf would not believe that Karl was dead. "He's out of shells! Maybe he's using the Sharps for a club."

He tried to visualize Karl, huge and hulking, in a circle of Spur riders, swinging the heavy Sharps, breaking skulls like watermelons. But when the firing ceased entirely, he was forced to admit what his mind had so steadfastly refused. He had lost them all! Perhaps Adolf Neese was not so hard as he had thought. Perhaps that was why the tears suddenly flowed into his beard from his red and hate-filled eyes.

"Karl said he was laying a trap!" he shouted. "I wouldn't believe it! And now they're dead! Dead, damn him! Just like he'll be before the night's out!"

For half an hour he sat his horse not a quarter mile from the scene of the battle, raging, wanting to thunder into the midst of them so badly it was the effort of his life to control himself. He told himself fiercely: *I don't want them riders' hides! I want Norell's hide! He's to blame for this.*

Finally the Spur 'punchers rode off in a group, leaving the bodies of Neese's sons, but packing their own dead across their saddles. Neese picked his way slowly across the plain, dismounted, and knelt beside Karl. He struck a match so he could see Karl's face, could see the wounds that had downed his first-born.

A bullet had smashed Karl's shoulder, another his knee. One had entered his belly, and another his chest. None of these had silenced his terrible Sharps. It had taken the .45 slug that had torn through his throat to put him out of action. Tears ran unashamedly down Neese's cheeks as he rose and went to the next, Otis. Four bullets had ripped into Otis, the fourth finding his heart. The father's hand reached out with an unconscious gentleness, a gesture drawn from the dim past when the boys were children, and stroked Otis's hair. Otis had been the youngest.

Standing, he searched for Sam, who had always fought against his father's lawlessness, who had wanted an honest ranch, stocked with cattle not stolen. Sam had died fighting, perhaps reluctantly, but loyal all the same. Ross, the last, must have taken the first full brunt of the fighting. His body was a sieve, his shirt and the upper part of his jeans soaked in blood. Adolf Neese was a wolf, living off the flanks of the herd. But tonight, Adolf Neese would have the Spur's heart.

One more thing he did before he mounted to ride to town. Gently he lifted each of his sons in his arms, and laid them out together, for that was the way they had died. That was the way he would like to remember them—together.

Tonight the town of Arapahoe was a huge charge of blasting powder, with the fire lighted at the end of a short fuse. Bart Pruitt prowled the streets, a shadow, seeing much but unseen himself. He saw the messenger from the Spur come thundering in with news of the battle on the grass. He saw Felix Chavalas return at the head of his posse, saw the men disperse to the saloons. A light still gleamed from the front window of Chavalas's house where Mary waited.

Bart saw Slim Taney, shrunk to a living skeleton by the effects of his wound, ride in on a stolen Spur horse and knew Slim had taken advantage of the confusion at the ranch to escape. Bart thought Slim had been killed when the Spur had captured the windmill and, seeing him alive, gave him a start. Because he could not risk calling out, he took Slim's trail, well knowing that Slim could have but one purpose in town—to kill Norell.

Before the hotel Slim hesitated, then cautiously led the Spur-branded horse into the lot between the hotel and Riordan's saddle shop. Tie rails extended along this wall of the hotel to take care of the overflow of saddle horses on the nights when the Spur was paid.

Bart crossed swiftly over to the lot. Weeds rustled under his feet as he called out softly: "Slim! Slim, where you at?"

"Here."

Bart could finally distinguish the blob of black that was Taney's horse, the vague form at its head. He murmured: "I thought you were dead."

"I damn' near was. He shot me off the wagon seat from ambush."

"You hunting Norell, or still working for me?"

"Norell comes first."

"You can't have him."

"Think you can stop me?" Slim's voice was challenging.

"I know I can. Norell's got me framed for killing Spurlock and Storrie Taylor. If he's killed, the frame will stick."

A shout lifted downstreet, a shout that held surprise.

"Hey! Ain't that Neese?"

A shot banged out, its echoes reverberating from building to building as its noise zigzagged upstreet. Another shout went up, and galloping hoofs sounded muffled in the deep dust of Platte Street. The horse went past, its rider briefly showing in the dim light from the hotel.

Pruitt said to Taney dryly: "This is a poor place to be, my friend. In two minutes there'll be a raft of Spur riders coming through this lot after that rider!"

Already he could hear the confusion of voices, of milling horses, of running feet at the lower end of the street. Felix Chavalas's sharp, unmistakable voice shouted: "Norell, damn you, get back into the saloon, or get out of town! Too many men want your hide tonight!"

Slim said—"Aw, that was the tip-off."—and slid away in the darkness of the alley.

With complete suddenness, Bart knew what he had to do, and the ruthlessness, the cruelty of it bothered him not at all. He had been kicked around long enough in this country. He had stood all a man could stand. He would not stand for Slim Taney's settling a personal grudge at his expense. As Spur riders poured into the lot, he shouted to them excitedly: "He went down the alley toward Third! Circle around and cut him off!"

His very boldness prevented recognition of him. But by the time they had circled around, one of them might have remembered Bart's voice, and the hue and cry would be on. By that time, they would have Taney corralled. They would probably come up with a catch at the end of their chase, but would have caught a coyote instead of a wolf.

Bart set himself to catch a wolf of his own. When he reached Saloon Row and secreted himself in a long passage between two saloons, he found that his planning paralleled that of Felix Chavalas's, who'd had the sense to wait for the wolf at the bait—in his case, Norell.

Norell and Felix stood together across the street, talking in low and guarded tones. Once Felix's harsh voice was raised enough so that Bart heard: "Norell, you're a damned fool! What did you expect, when the Spur killed Neese's sons? You ought to be back at the spread instead of here, where I have to guard you."

Panic in Norell's voice put a grim smile on Bart Pruitt's wide mouth.

"I'll go now, Felix. I'll get my horse." With embarrassed self-consciousness the foreman stepped into the dust of the street and crossed directly toward where Pruitt was hidden.

Bart recalled that it was habit with Norell to tie his horse before Mary Chavalas's restaurant. It was probably there now. As Norell stepped up onto the walk, Pruitt came from his hiding place and fell into step ten yards behind the Spur's big foreman. When a couple of shots racketed at the alley mouth, Norell stepped off the walk, heading that way, but paused in mid-street, perhaps recalling his promise to Felix to get out of town. In the time his back was toward the walk, Bart slipped ahead of him and reached the restaurant a full twenty-five yards ahead of Norell.

He stood silently as disappointment coursed through him. Then he ducked around the corner to wait out Norell's next move. If Norell's horse had been here, it was gone now. He heard Norell's steps pause uncertainly, heard the foreman's soft-voiced curse. So Norell's horse *had* been tied here!

Norell turned back toward the livery barn. Smiling satisfaction overrode Bart's uneasiness as he followed. The dark, silent livery barn would be a good place for a talk, with the whole town on the street and the chase for potential killers running its howling course from one end of Arapahoe to the other.

Anticipation stirred in Bart. Already he was tasting the bitter pleasure that would be his as his fists landed solidly on Norell's heavy features. A little of this and he would confront Norell with his knowledge of the foreman's evil scheming. He would let Norell knock him down, and let Norell gloat. From what Norell was sure to say, boasting, Bart would know for sure that he and Mary Chavalas had been right.

Felix Chavalas had early learned that there was more honest law enforcement in the brain of a lawman than in all his brawn and gun speed. Because this night was so explosive, he stood still before the saloon where Norell had left him and let his brain have its way as it ought to anticipate the next move Adolf Neese would make. Failing at his open try for Norell, Neese, with animal cunning and patience, would try another way. Perhaps he would go to the Spur and wait, concealed in the darkness. Perhaps he would wait on the road and try an ambush.

Felix was finding both these answers unsatisfactory when he saw Norell, returning along Platte afoot. In spite of the tension that rode him, in spite of the raw edginess that made the man so unpredictable and dangerous, Felix smiled, wasting no time, but backing instead into the open and lighted doorway of the Idle Hour. Ignoring the few frightened townsmen who lounged in the place, he ran through the littered back room and into the alley.

At the alley mouth he paused, glancing up and down the street before he crossed. On the other side, he vaulted over the livery barn's pole corral fence, landing beside the water trough and sinking to his boot tops in the soft manure. The smell of ammonia was rank and stinging to his nostrils as it rose from his boots. A dozen horses stampeded away from him to halt snorting on the other side of the huge corral, and Felix cursed himself for overlooking them.

As he crossed the corral, a dozen calves eyed him nervously, their white faces disembodied blobs of light against the night. At the rear of the livery barn a plank canopy, perhaps twenty feet wide, supported by logs set in the ground, created shade for the horses in summer, and gave protection from storms in the winter. Now the canopy made a well of blackness where a man could wait unseen.

Felix lost himself in this blackness, then whispered: "Neese." He had expected no answer, and he got none. After a wait, he whispered again: "I'm not looking for you, man. Get out of the country before I have to start looking for you."

This time his answer was a laugh, low and vicious, and a faint whisper: "Damn you, Felix, you're too smart! The minute you knew his horse was gone from up the street you knew I'd laid a trap. Do you know what you're protecting? He came to my place and made a deal for me to run off Spur cattle while he kept the Spur riders off my neck. A fifty-fifty split." The whisper turned savage. "But he double-crossed me! He murdered my boys! Get out of here, Felix, and let me have him, or I'll kill you, too!"

Felix's pearl-handled Colt came silently and smoothly out of its well-worn holster. He heard the scuffle of feet, the fidgeting of horses in the stalls. Somewhere in that inky blackness Norell was unsuspiciously approaching. Pure instinct told Felix when Neese slipped into the stable, for he could see nothing at all. Discarding caution, he stepped boldly forward. His mouth had opened to shout a warning as he came through the door when flame and light spouted from the sputtering end of a match held by Norell. In the brief illumination before it died on the floor, Norell saw Neese, and Neese saw Norell. Felix saw Bart Pruitt dimly, farther back, immobile and somber-faced, with eyes only for Norell.

There was a sudden scramble as both the Spur foreman and Neese dived for the floor. A shot roared out—Neese's shot—and drew a sharp intake of breath from Norell. Felix knew then that in the moment of illumination Norell had seen only Neese. Norell spoke, his voice hoarse and panicked: "I was in town, Adolf . . . I swear it! I can prove where I was. Somebody else saw your boys with the cattle!"

Neese's only reply was—"Liar!"—flat and uncompromising.

Felix was thinking: *If Norell could plot to rustle Spur cattle, couldn't he also have engineered Spurlock's death?* But he waited, for this game was not yet played out. The time for interference had not yet come.

For a full five minutes the stable was silent, completely and ominously silent, as each man waited out his own particular adversary.

Bart Pruitt spoke finally. "I'm here too, Les, if you get away from Neese." He made a soft rustling sound as he changed his position.

Norell's shot in the direction of Pruitt's voice lighted the stable with its flash for the briefest instant. But it was long enough for Felix to see Bart dive into a stall, long enough for Neese to send another shot toward Norell. But Norell, with a fighting man's caution, had moved as he fired, and Neese's bullet thudded into one of the rough-hewn timbers that supported the roof.

XX

Carefully Felix calculated the panic that would be coursing through the Spur foreman. Norell was not lacking in courage, but he would have no liking for facing two men with the same purpose—his annihilation in darkness.

Taking his chances momentarily with Neese's bullets, Norell said: "Pruitt, listen! Help me with this bastard and I'll clear you with the sheriff. Storrie killed Spurlock because he thought Spurlock was playing around with his wife. I killed Storrie, but I had a right to do that . . . for Spurlock. Felix can't do a damned thing to me."

Pruitt murmured: "You were the one Storrie should have killed. No deals, Norell."

Felix could sense the movement of Adolf Neese as the big outlaw eased his way across the stable toward the sound of Norell's voice. Pruitt must have sensed it, also, for he called sharply: "If you kill him, Neese, you'll answer to me! I want to take him to Felix, so the sheriff can hear what he just said!"

Neese's chuckling rejoinder—"Never mind . . . never mind that."—gave his position away to Felix, and Felix moved to intercept him. He underestimated the distance between them, and, as their bodies collided, he felt the instant tightening of Neese's muscles and the man's recoil away from him. Now the muscular training that had been Felix's life, the instant co-ordination that had kept him alive all of these years, served him well. Like the lightning strike of a rattler's head, his hand came back and brought his heavy gun barrel in a sharp and slashing blow against Neese's ear. Neese groaned, and went to the floor, banging head and shoulders against a stall. Instantly Felix dropped, and Norell's shot whistled overhead, cutting the air clearly where his head would have been had he not dived for the manure-littered floor so promptly.

Norell croaked—"There's somebody else in here, Pruitt!"—and did the unexpected, the unpredictable thing that upset all of Felix's calculations. He rushed Felix, fully conscious of the odds against him and unnerved by their abrupt increase. His foot drove against Felix's chest, pushing all the wind from the sheriff, and, before Felix could rise, or turn, Norell was on him, beating and slashing savagely with his gun barrel. The first blow laid Felix's cheek open; the second tore loose one of his ears. The third came squarely across the middle of his head and brought a blinding flash, whirling lights, and complete oblivion.

Pruitt, who had recognized the sheriff's voice, heard the scuffle, the abrupt and ominous silence that followed. Then he heard a stealthy exit into the corral at the rear of the stable and knew instantly that Norell must be escaping, for nobody else in the stable would want to get away. Driven by urgency, he made his own slow and careful way toward the back door. He stumbled, nearly fell across a body on the floor, and whirled, gun ready.

Silence, heavy and complete, hung over the stable with its rank smell of horses, saddle leather, and manure, but from the corral came the loud suction of running steps in the mire beside the water trough. Pruitt thought he knew where Norell would go, so took a precious instant to strike a match and kneel beside the downed man. In its brief flare he saw both Felix's body and that of Neese—the rustler dead, unquestionably. He saw the blood on the sheriff's face, saw its pallor, but he was alive.

Relief and excitement ran their unchecked way through Bart. He murmured: "So you heard! That was what Neese meant!" Felix's breathing, scarcely audible, was slow and irregular. His face was the waxen color of death. Pruitt said decisively: "I can't leave you here. But on the street . . . well, come on."

He lifted Felix's slight body and strode toward the front door. He walked right into the inevitable crowd. Men, hearing the shots, had gathered to investigate, but their curiosity had been insufficient to draw them inside the darkened and bullet-riddled interior. One of them held a lantern at chest height and squinted at him through its yellow light.

Bart said: "It's Felix. Get the doc. Norell damned near beat his brains out." Because he knew what would come as soon as they recovered from their initial surprise, he laid Felix carefully down, and, when he straightened, his gun was fisted and cocked. "Don't any of you get ideas you can take me without a fight. Storrie killed Spurlock, and Norell killed Storrie. Felix heard Norell admit it."

He saw a man detach himself from the outer fringe of the crowd and run up Platte toward the doctor's house. He backed into the stable, stepped behind the door with his back to the wall, and waited the handful of seconds it took running feet to beat past him. Midway down the stable, the men stopped, and Bart heard their brief and ill-humored argument about the lantern, which had been left in the street with Felix. One man stumbled across Neese's body, and, while their thoughts were distracted from Pruitt, he slipped out the front door into the lighted street.

A lone townsman crouched beside Felix Chavalas, waiting for the arrival of the doctor. He glanced up at Pruitt, and his eyes widened with sudden fright. Pruitt said: "Keep your mouth shut and you won't get hurt."

Running up Platte to Second, he swung around the corner, and cut through the weeds, until he came into Prairie. The front door of Storrie Taylor's house was open, the interior of the parlor bathed with soft light.

Pruitt paused on the walk. He heard Norell's voice, raised and angry. "What the hell are you talking about, Sal? We've got to get out of here!"

Sally's laugh was low and bitter. "You've got to get out of here. I don't. I didn't kill Storrie. I didn't slug the sheriff. Pruitt isn't after me!"

"But, Sal, you said. . . ."

"You poor damned fool! Did you think it was you I wanted? It wasn't you at all. It was money! You haven't got any, and you're on the run. Get out of here. Get out!"

"Why, you little . . . !" Murderous, terrible rage sounded like a drum in Norell's savage voice.

"Les! No! Les, don't. . . ."

Pruitt bounded up the steps and into the parlor.

This had been a shabby affair. It was inevitable that it would have a shabby ending. Sally was on her back on the sofa, with Norell's strong fingers at her throat. Her face was suffused with blood, her eyes bulging with terror and from the fight she was making for air.

Pruitt said—"Norell!"—and hoped that just this once Norell's instinct would override his cunning, would make him fight. If he refused to fight, there would be nothing Pruitt could do, nothing Felix could do. Norell and this woman would go scotfree, for law on the frontier had not yet made any attempt to deal with conspiracy to murder.

Norell's head yanked around. His eyes were wide, savage, and wicked. With a smooth motion, he released his hold on Sally's throat, rolling sideward to his knees on the floor, half facing Pruitt. Bart knew now that the foreman would draw, but he did not know how fast this would be.

Pruitt saw Norell's gun clearing leather before he realized the man had reached for it, for Norell's movement toward his gun had been screened by his body. In a movement that was purely automatic, Pruitt's own hand plummeted toward the grip of his Colt.

Bart's racing thoughts told him: *You're late! You're too damned late!* The instinct of self-preservation screamed: *Hurry! Hurry!* Yet reason cautioned: *Speed will never beat him now.*

Norell was off balance. Even as his long gun barrel came level, his body wavered, and he flung out his left hand for support.

Pruitt's own gun came level, and strong was the temptation to loose his shot in mad haste. Yet he waited until the feel of the gun was right, until he was certain the muzzle was square upon Norell's broad chest. As he tightened down on the trigger, Norell's gun blasted, spewing an acrid and blinding cloud of smoke across the narrow room. An invisible fist smashed Pruitt's left side, turning him.

Again he waited, waited for his gun to center, but this was

harder now, knowing that Norell could loose the remaining three shots from his gun in as many seconds. Again Norell's gun bellowed, but his haste had taken its toll. The bullet missed.

Pruitt felt his own Colt buck against his palm. Norell went backwards as though given a rough and insistent push. Incredulity briefly touched his heavy features. Still falling, he got out: "Hell, I didn't think. . . ." On the floor, dying, he said bitterly: "For a damned slut."

Sally Taylor screamed, the terrible scream of a lost woman who at last sees the fruits of her scheming, the emptiness of her failure.

Uneasy and for once afraid, Bart looked at her. A man had no defense against a woman. She threw herself, unlovely and hard and harsh now across Norell's body, her fingers clawing for the gun he had dropped. Her voice was shrill with hysteria and madness. "You! You! Damn you, you spoiled it all!"

Bart Pruitt went out of the room at a run. He took the steps at one bound, losing himself in the shadows that cloaked the lawn, yet, even as he did, wildly triggered bullets from the doorway sought him, whining off into the night. Dizziness rolled in waves through his head.

Somewhere here in the street a man was counting. When he reached three, he stopped. Although the dizziness and the feeling of unreality persisted, Pruitt was certain it was the voice of Felix Chavalas, weak but with the old implacability and hardness to it.

Bart said: "Felix?"

Felix was beside him, torn ear dangling, his face a mass of crusted and dried blood. Felix asked: "How many times did Norell shoot?"

For some reason the question required considerable

thought on Bart's part. Finally he murmured weakly: "Twice."

"Then her gun's empty. I'll go on in."

He went up the walk with his slow and measured stride. When he reached the door, Bart heard Sally Taylor scream again, heard Felix's uncompromising order: "Get out of town. You have made enough trouble here."

Bart stood leaning against the picket fence for support. Things that had needed doing so desperately were done. But in his mind he stared bleakly at the future. Pain began its run through his side as feeling overcame the numbness. He realized he was soaked with blood.

He heard light steps running on the walk even over the noise of the gathering crowd. Faint was this sound, faint her soft cries as she reached him. But it was as though he had been waiting all of his life for this moment.

Mary Chavalas, with tears bright in her dark eyes, touched him, and felt his blood on her hand. In sheer terror she flung a hand to her mouth, muffling the scream that tore from her throat: "You're hurt!"

Because he was a man and because weakness did not become him, he used his remaining strength to take her in his arms. He said: "Not any more."

A home would rise on the grass because Bart Pruitt made it rise. There would be a woman, and there would be young Pruitts yelling in the yard. There was woman's softness in Mary, and things that could stir a man's blood every day of his life. Pruitt said—"Mary, the grass is waiting for us."—and lowered his lips to her tear-soaked face.